DEAD RIGHT

A Dan Shields Mystery
The detective who breaks all the rules

MARK L. DRESSLER

Published by Satincrest Press, USA
ISBN-13: 9780999062319

Previous novels by Mark L. Dressler
DEAD and GONE - published 2017
(A Dan Shields Mystery)

DEDICATION

This book is dedicated to those who came before me:
Benjamin and Annie
Max and Fannie
Isadore and Lebe
Jack and Miriam
And GP

Acknowledgments

Advisors: Ann Horan, Joellen Adae, Patricia Grigaitis.
Developmental Editor - Jill Fletcher.
Line/Copy Editor - Eileen Albrizio.

Cover designer - Jeanine Henning
Author photo - Jessica Smolinski
Formatting - Liz Delton

Special thanks to my support team: Suzy Sax, Martin Louis, Frederick Arnold, Robin Wagner, Audrey Bolz, Marshall Harris, Dick Meyer, Judy Englander, Harvey Beinstein, and Danny Sclare.

CHAPTER 1

By day's end, Detective Dan Shields would question his decision to return to Hartford's police force.

Approaching the modern headquarters rear entrance, he flashed back to the old Morgan Street jail's holding tank, and a surge of adrenaline rushed through him. Dan took a deep breath and entered the new facility, heading directly to the detention center.

When he got downstairs, he approached Sergeant Dom Denine, who was sitting at a desk outside the lock-up area. The gatekeeper stood to shake Dan's hand and said, "I heard you were coming back."

"Been a long year, but I needed the time off," Dan replied.

The calendar on the wall behind Denine read: Monday, October 3, 2015.

Dan eyed the locked metal door. "How's traffic?"

"Got a few," the sergeant replied. "Go take a peek."

Denine buzzed the curious detective into the confinement area. Dan's loafers landed harshly on the concrete floor as he marched down the center of the room, eight cages on each side. It was 7:20 a.m. and he recognized a guest who was lying on the bed in cell nine, so the detective stood by the iron bars and yelled, "Hampton, you awake?"

The lanky, long-haired car thief sat up. Yawning, he said, "Shields, long time no see."

"What'd you steal this time?" Dan asked.

1

Rubbing his crusted eyes, Hampton said, "Mercedes. I ran a light on Main. What an idiot."

Noticing what appeared to be a fresh mark on the detainee's neck, Dan said, "You get a new tat?"

Hampton approached the iron bars and wrapped his hands around them, an orange sweatshirt tied to his waist. "Yeah. It's a Harley. You ever ride one?"

"Not a biker," Dan replied. "You steal those too?"

Hampton smirked. "Not enough cash. Know what I mean?"

Dan looked into his harmless friend's eyes. "How long are you gonna keep stealing cars?"

In his high-pitched voice, Hampton replied, "Dunno. It's like a hobby, can't stop. In a few weeks I'm thirty. How about giving me a new ride for my birthday?"

Dan nodded. "Right. First off, I thought the last time I saw you, you said you were thirty-six, and that was over a year ago."

Hampton grinned. "Good memory. Man time flies."

"What's this, six, seven times?"

"Can't remember, second one in this new place. Know what? I'm a really good driver too. Never crashed one. Damned teenager's joyriding around are making a mockery of us pros. They steal 'em, and wreck 'em like they were toys." Hampton paused. "Didn't see the black and white when I ran that light."

Dan tapped on the bars. "They know the system, pal. They're not lucky enough to be in a hotel as nice as this."

"No shit, Dan. They kill someone and get a hand slap. I steal a car and here I am."

"Where you hanging out these days?"

"Doughnut shop on Mapleton. You wanna come hang sometime?"

"Go back to sleep," Dan said.

"Hey!" Hampton yelled as the detective started to walk away. "You a sergeant?"

Dan re-approached the cell and presented his ID to the car thief. The forty-six-year-old detective smiled. "Last time I looked, this said *Lieutenant.* Just like Columbo."

Hampton glanced at the photo. "You know, you sort of look like Columbo, same dark hair."

Dan snickered and rolled his brown eyes. "Ya think? I'm almost six feet, one -ninety. I'll admit we're both handsome, and our mothers were Italian. You sure you can tell a Ferrari from a Ford?"

Hampton smugly said, "I meant Clooney. You know, Ocean's Eleven. Sharp guy. You driving anything worth stealing?"

"Nothing that would interest you. Nice talkin'. See you around," Dan said as he walked away and headed upstairs.

Entering the brightly lit third floor squad room where half-walled cubicles provided the detectives' ergonomic workstations, he peered into his partner's cube and saw Scotty's jacket that was hanging on the back of a chair. Dan continued to the next workstation, brushed his hand along the name plate attached to the outside of the padded wall panel, and stepped inside.

Hanging his coat on a hook, an EpiPen tucked into a jacket pocket, Dan sat in his swivel faux-leather chair. On top of the white, L-shaped desktop was a twenty-two inch monitor, a laptop, printer, and a multi-functional phone. A two-drawer cabinet nestled in one corner, and storage bins above the desktop were filled with old case files. His in-box, and trash basket were empty. Turning to his rear, there was a chair and small table.

Dan got up and walked down a short corridor, passing two interrogation rooms and the bathrooms before entering Captain Harold Syms's office.

"Great to have you back," Syms said. "Have a seat next to your partner."

"Good to be back, I think," the detective said. "How's it going?"

Scotty, blond-haired and blue-eyed, was eight years younger and an inch taller than Dan. "Same as usual. Never know when that next dead body will show up," the junior detective said.

Dan spotted a familiar sight: a giant bottle of Advil on the captain's wooden desk. Glancing around the roughly twelve-by-twelve office, the detective noticed what appeared to be shrubs on the credenza behind Syms. "You growing weed now?"

Syms, fifty and shorter than his detectives had his curly afro replaced by baldness years ago. He turned and pointed to three bonsai trees. The raspy voiced captain said, "Not yet, but you might drive me to it someday. You never saw bonsais?"

"I have, didn't think you were the nurturing type."

Syms faced his detectives as he picked up the pill bottle.

"That full?" Dan quipped.

"I'm stocked up. You're back aren't you?"

Dan noticed the glasses resting on the captain's nose were different. "You got new rims?"

"Good eyes, Dick Tracy."

Dan said, "Either of you been downstairs?"

"The tank?" Syms asked.

"Yeah. I was just down there. Our old friend Hampton is a guest."

Scotty said, "He was here a couple of months ago."

"Well, he's still stealing cars. He considers it a hobby. I'm sure he'll be out later today. Probably won't be the last time we see him," Dan replied.

"That's what we need, a hobby. I can see us robbing banks," Scotty said.

Dan shook his head at Scotty. "Me and you, pal. Jesse and Frank James."

Syms nodded. "Nothing would pleasure me more than seeing your asses locked up downstairs."

Dan said to the captain, "So what's the chief up to these days?"

"Hardison? He's the same. Nothing seems to rattle his cage."

4

Syms eyed the wall clock that read 7:58 a.m. "I have to get up to Hardison's office. The chief hates it when I'm late."

Dan and Scotty headed to the squad room where they stood at the water cooler. A table next to it was where the damaged Keurig sat. Written on a chalkboard leaning against the wall was: *It's broke ... Forget about donuts too!*

"Who broke it?" Dan asked.

"Syms. Who else would write that on the board? If you want coffee, we have to go down to the caf."

The cafeteria reminded Dan of his high school lunchroom. He spotted Captain Dixon, who sat alone at a table with a half-eaten plate of food. Dan tapped the traffic division leader on the shoulder. "Hey, you sure you can eat all that?"

Dixon looked up. "Takes a lot of sustenance to run my unit you know. Good to see you. Scotty got you slumming already?"

"Not really. We're gonna grab coffee and head back upstairs," Dan said. "Just saw our buddy Hampton."

Dixon said, "At least he's innocuous. We have an epidemic of juvenile car thieves to deal with, and they're a bunch who think nothing of running down a pedestrian." Taking the last bite of toast, Dixon said, "Tell me something. How is it there are so many stupid people who leave their keys and fobs in unlocked cars? Probably won't be long before we have another wreck to clean up."

Chapter 2

Bells rang nine times from the church next to the Jeffers Street post office, as a silver Jaguar pulled out of the lot between the two buildings. The expensive new car headed south with Bob Marley's *Sun is Shining* blaring from the sound system.

The vehicle turned onto Frankland Avenue where shops had opened. Aromas from competing bakeries filled the air, luring in loyal patrons. Neighbors, some with dogs on leashes, walked the streets.

Traffic was unusually light. The Jaguar passed the only car in its path as the speedometer needle steadily climbed to 40, then 45, and quickly hit 55.

Two blocks ahead, at the intersection of Frankland Avenue and Braun Street, a twelve-year-old-boy wearing a black baseball cap and a Pittsburgh Steeler's sweatshirt, stood on the sidewalk. With a cell phone in his hand and headphones in his ears, he glanced at a text message from a friend and pushed the button on the light post. *Where you at?* As soon as the light turned red, he meandered into the crosswalk while the timer flashed … 10 seconds, 9, 8, and then 7.

With the Jaguar approaching 60 miles per hour, and the crosswalk timer now reading 6, Javier Ibanez was halfway across the street while texting back to his friend. Brakes screeched and a startled bystander yelled, "Watch out, run!"

That shout drew the attention of pedestrians and as the car got closer to the boy, the helpless onlookers watched in horror.

Javier felt the fast car approaching and looked to his left, his eyes opened wide and he froze in place. With fear on his face, the young boy was hurtled like a dart, twenty feet onto the sidewalk in front of the Rocking Chair Café, while the silver car sped away. The few vehicles that had been headed in the opposite direction abruptly stopped, narrowly avoiding a chain-reaction collision.

Crying and screaming, a witness dropped her bag of fresh pastry and rushed to the sprawled, bleeding, unconscious boy whose cap came to rest in the middle of the road. One sneaker landed several feet away, and his shattered cell phone ended up against the curb. Other horrified witnesses rushed to the victim's aid, but none could help the lifeless child. An elderly woman clutched the cross that was strung on a chain around her neck as she looked skyward as if praying for the boy's soul.

Several shop owners, upon hearing the commotion, rushed out to see what had happened. "That's my nephew, Javier," a shocked store owner yelled.

CHAPTER 3

It was 9:20 a.m. when Syms, who had returned from his meeting with Hardison, stood and shouted to Dan and Scotty, "You two, get down here!"

The detectives hurried to the captain's office. "Dixon just called me. Go to Frankland and Braun. Vehicular homicide, and the vehicle didn't stick around."

Dan and Scotty quickly departed the squad room.

When they got to Frankland, the street had been blocked off from traffic by uniformed police who kept the crowd of stunned pedestrians back. The detectives approached the covered body. "Nothing," a female paramedic said, as she shook her head. "He was dead by the time we got here."

"Got a name?" Dan asked.

"Javier Ibanez." The paramedic pointed to the inconsolable shop owner who was sitting next to the ambulance with a uniform by his side. "He's the boy's uncle," she said.

Dan looked at Scotty, knelt, and pulled back the blanket. To Dan, there was nothing worse than a dead child. He took a deep breath and turned to his partner. "Hits home, pal."

"I hear you."

Before covering the body again, Dan noticed a tattoo on the back of the boy's neck. "Take a look at this."

Scotty eyed the mark. "A stop sign with the word *Go*."

Dan took a snapshot of the neck artwork. He saw the traffic division captain who was talking to a bystander and said, "Let's see Dixon."

The detectives approached him. "What's the story?" Dan asked.

Dixon said, "Sergeant Ramirez got here first. We've talked to several witnesses. It's all the same. Happened fast and the car never stopped."

"Got an ID on the vehicle?"

"There's a difference of opinion, some say Jaguar and some say Mustang. The car was silver, but no one made out the plate. We'll see if the car shows up stolen."

"What about the driver? Passengers?"

"No one saw passengers. The only description of the driver was long dark hair."

"Male? Female?" Dan asked.

"Nobody could say for sure. The car was speeding and ran the light. Witnesses said the kid was in the crosswalk and appeared to be using his phone. He never heard warnings that were shouted. You can see from the skid marks how far he was thrown after impact," Dixon said. "One more thing. Reggae music was blasting from the vehicle."

"Where are the parents?" Dan asked.

"Haven't been able find them yet. According to the uncle, the family lives one street over on Shelton Place. We were there, but no one was home."

"What's the uncle's name?"

"Juan Estaban. He's tried to call the parents several times."

Dan heard screams and he turned to his left to see a man and woman racing toward the scene. The distraught man was nearly out of breath and his legs weakened, as he rushed to the boy's body. "My boy, that's my boy," he yelled.

A few seconds later, the shivering, hysterical mother yelled, "Javy!"

Gasping and breathing heavily, Eduardo Ibanez held his wife Ellina, who was on the verge of collapsing. Both paramedics rushed to the couple and escorted them toward an ambulance, while the detectives followed. Ellina's eyes fluttered, and with an EMT standing next to her, the woman fainted. The alert EMT caught Ellina and lifted the slender mother into the ambulance.

The grief-stricken father was shaking as Dixon placed his hands on the man's shoulders. Eduardo sat on the edge of the emergency vehicle. "I'm so sorry," the police officer said.

Dan said to the father, "Can we talk?"

Eduardo, who was no taller than five-seven, meekly uttered. "Tell me this didn't happen." Tears fell from the grieving father's eyes. "Such a good boy."

"I'm sure he was," Dan said. The detective paused. "Why wasn't he in school today?" he asked.

Eduardo took a deep breath, his voice weak as he said, "Teacher's conference. We were there. Someone called her."

Dan started to ask about the tattoo when Scotty nudged him. "We need to step back." He pointed to the female EMT. "She's telling us to go. They need to get Mrs. Ibanez to the hospital."

The detectives and Dixon stepped back as the other EMT guided Eduardo into the emergency vehicle along with Ellina before it took off for Woodland Hospital. Minutes later, the coroner's van arrived, and Javier was transported to the University Hospital morgue.

Dan asked Dixon, "Anyone come forward with a video?"

"Not yet. If we get lucky, one might show. Stop by in the morning. I'll have the incident report."

"Thanks," Dan said as he and Scotty walked back to the Accord.

Chapter 4

As Dan drove toward his four-bedroom, vinyl-sided colonial in Suffield, he had a hard time concentrating on the road. With two young children of his own, this vehicular homicide hit the veteran detective hard. He kept visualizing Javier Ibanez's bloodied body.

Dan's wife Phyllis, a child psychologist, practiced at a clinic in nearby Enfield. Mike, the oldest of their three children, was a full scholarship athlete at Arizona State University. He'd been drafted by the Red Sox last year, but passed up the baseball opportunity to continue his free education. The younger siblings Josh, twelve, and Kate, eleven, were typical middle-schoolers.

Sixteen months ago, Dan's eighty-two-year-old mother suffered a fatal heart attack. Since Nana was no longer around to watch the kids after school, Dan had convinced the more than willing, former owner of Connie's Place, Connie Castino to accept the task. The near-retirement-aged woman was a perfect choice. Her all-night diner which had been a sacred cop hangout, was razed along with the old Morgan Street jail in order to make room for the new headquarters.

Connie's Chevy Volt was parked in front of one garage, and Phyllis's red SUV was next to that vehicle, so the detective parked his Accord behind his wife's car.

Dan hung his coat in the foyer closet and placed his holster and weapon inside a custom-built lockable compartment. Looking into the mirror above a table next to the closet, he tried to hide his sadness.

He made his way to the kitchen, and placed his arms around Phyllis's waist. "You have a good day?" he asked.

"Fine," she said as she turned to her husband. "So, how'd it feel to be back?"

Dan took a deep breath and hesitated before answering. "Not exactly the way I'd planned it."

"What happened?" Phyllis asked.

Dan shook his head and sighed. "A hit-and-run. Car killed a twelve-year-old boy. Made me wonder why I went back."

Connie, who had been in the den working on a 1,000-piece picture puzzle, while listening to the news on TV, entered the kitchen. "Welcome home. How'd it go? I just a story about a kid who was killed on Frankland by a car that sped away."

"I was there," Dan said. "Scotty and I got called."

At that moment, Josh and Kate entered the room and Dan hugged his kids.

Kate, with a flyer in her hand, showed it to her father. Dan smiled at his little girl and said, "Girl Scout cookies. Put me down for four boxes of mints."

"My class is taking a field trip to Mark Twain's house next week," Josh said.

"Didn't you recently read Huck Finn?"

"Yup."

"That should be fun."

Connie picked up her purse. "I have to go, cards tonight."

"I'm going upstairs to change," Dan said. "How long until we eat?"

Phyllis removed her chef's apron and replied, "About ten."

Dan returned, dressed in a pair of jeans and his Giant's sweatshirt. He sat between Kate seated to his left, and Josh who was on his right. Phyllis served dinner, but the troubled detective pushed his plate aside. "I'm not hungry," he said. He got up, but he knew his wife could tell that something was wrong.

The detective sat in his den chair and watched TV. After the kids had gone to bed, Phyllis entered the room. Dan held the remote in his hand, clicking it with no real purpose, and looked at his wife. "Never been shaken like I was today," he said. "Seeing that boy, all I saw was Josh."

Phyllis took the remote, clutched his hands, and they both sat on the couch. "I couldn't imagine. I can see you're not okay?" she said.

Dan kissed her cheek and then stared into her eyes, realizing his children were safe, asleep in their beds. "Sometimes living in the suburbs makes you lose sight of reality. That kid had no chance."

"Talk to me," she said. "Reality? Like there's no crime here? This could have happened anywhere, even here."

"True. It could have, but this one bothers me more than any other homicide I've ever seen."

Dan kept talking and an hour later after listening to him, Phyllis looked into his eyes and said, "You know you can't bring the boy back, but you can do your job and find the driver of the vehicle."

Dan sighed. Sounding more relieved, he said, "You know, you're right. The best thing I can do is find the murderer."

CHAPTER 5

Dan walked into the squad room, his head was clear, and he was focused on tracking down Javier Ibanez's killer. Reaching into a pocket of his blue sport coat as he headed for his cube, Dan removed recent school photos of Josh and Kate, as well as pictures of Mike and Phyllis, and leaned them up against the back wall of his desktop.

Scotty tapped on Dan's padded wall. "Hey, you okay? When you left here yesterday, you looked pale as a ghost."

"Guess it hit me harder than it hit you. I'm fine, let's hit the caf."

Dan opened the cafeteria door as Dixon was on his way out with two hot cups in his hands. "Low on caffeine?" Dan asked.

"One's for Charlie Ramirez. He's finishing up the incident report. I'll get it to you as soon as it's done, probably within the hour."

As soon as the detectives got back upstairs, Syms called out, "Boys."

Dan and Scotty headed to the captain's office where Syms bowed his head. "What happened? Any word on the car or driver?"

"Nothing yet," Dan said. "As of now, we can't be sure if the car was a Jag or Mustang."

"Who told the parents?"

Dan clasped his hands. "They'd been at a parent-teacher conference, and a witness called the school." Dan shook his head.

"If there had been school yesterday, that kid would still be alive. Both parents were in shock. They were taken to Woodland. We need to talk to them about Javier." Pulling his hands apart, Dan said, "There's a tattoo on the kid's neck that could be a gang mark. I want to know if he was in any kind of trouble."

"Are you saying this might not have been an accident?" Syms replied.

Dan grimaced. "I'm not saying it was or wasn't. One thing's for sure. Javier Ibanez isn't coming back."

The detectives went back to the squad room. It wasn't long before the phone in Dan's cube rang. "Dan," Dixon said. "We have a report of a stolen vehicle. A silver Jaguar that belongs to a lawyer named Angelo Biaggio. Claims the car was taken sometime yesterday from the yard in back of his office."

"You think it could be the hit-and-run vehicle?"

"Maybe. You need to check it out. He's got an office at Greenback Square. Come on down. I'll give you what I've got on him. Ramirez just gave me the incident report too."

"I'll be right down."

Scotty stood. "What's up?"

"A lawyer named Angelo Biaggio just reported his Jaguar stolen. I'm going down to see Dixon."

After Dan browsed the incident report, he turned his attention to the stolen car report and nodded. "Let's see if I have this straight. The owner of a brand new Jaguar, a lawyer, doesn't report the car stolen until the next day. You find that a little odd?"

"I find that a lot odd."

"The accident occurred a little after nine, right? If it was stolen from the lawyer's office, what time did he park it, and where was he?"

Dixon interjected, "If it's the same car. Can't jump to that conclusion, but it's worth checking."

Dan shrugged. "No we can't, but it doesn't explain how he got home last night without his car. He didn't report it missing until this morning."

Dixon sat back. "Good point. He has some explaining to do."

Dan got up and took the two reports with him.

Once he got back upstairs, Dan tapped Scotty on the shoulder. "Got the reports, but something's very odd. This lawyer, Biaggio didn't report his Jag stolen until today. It might or might not be the car that killed Javier, but it's strange. We're talking about a new Jag, not an old Chevy or Ford, and it was supposedly stolen yesterday. Let's go pay the lawyer a visit."

While on their way to Biaggio's office, Scotty said, "You still keep a spare EpiPen in the glovebox?"

"Oh yeah. I'm never riding with you again. Phyllis makes sure I don't leave home without one in my jacket."

"So you're still blaming me for your stupidity?"

Referring to an incident that had occurred when, while at a subject's house, Dan had taken a bite of banana bread containing nuts. "No. You did call nine-eleven."

It was easy to spot the lawyer's office. An oval white sign with blue letters was anchored in the ground by metal posts and it read: *Attorneys Biaggio and Sturgis.*

Parking was always an issue on this street. A sign was posted at the attorney's driveway noting parking in back was reserved for clients and employees. Dan thought about driving down the narrow passageway, but he spotted an open space across the street from the office.

Four steps led up to a porch where Dan opened the office door. Hanging on the cream-colored walls were several framed paintings, all with a common seascape theme. Three healthy looking potted plants were in the room, one between each set of matching cushy armed chairs, six in all. An assortment of magazines, neatly arranged, was on a square table beneath a wall mounted TV.

The detectives moved to the glass partitioned window straight ahead. A receptionist slid the windows apart. "Can I help you?" asked the attractive young staffer whose hair was rolled in a bun.

Dan noticed a name plate that read *Rozalie*. He presented his badge to her. "We'd like to see Mr. Biaggio?"

She replied, "He's in court today. Full schedule of arraignments. Can Mr. Sturgis help you?"

Soft music was playing in the background. Dan easily recognized Sinatra's voice. "Maybe. Maybe you can too," he said. "Are you aware Mr. Biaggio's car was stolen yesterday?"

She nodded. "He told us this morning. He said it was taken from the back lot. I've never seen him so upset. He was in his office for a while and then he left for court."

"Do you remember seeing the car yesterday?"

"No, but I don't drive. I take the bus so I wouldn't have been in the back where he parks the car."

"Do you know what time Mr. Biaggio got here yesterday morning?"

"I was here at eight, and he was in his office."

"Was he here all day?"

"Yes, until his son picked him up around five-thirty. They went to a basketball game."

Dan handed the young lady his card. "Please give this to Mr. Biaggio. Mind if I have one of his cards?" She handed the detective the lawyer's card and Dan asked, "Did you say Mr. Sturgis is here?"

"He is, but he's with a client. Did you want to wait for him?"

"We will. What time do you expect Mr. Biaggio back here?"

"Hard to say. It varies from day to day."

"Thank you," Dan said as the detectives took seats in the waiting area. Scotty picked up *Sports Illustrated* and thumbed through it. "That reminds me," he said. "How's Mike doing?"

"He's doing okay. They've already played six games and won five. He's batting third and he said he was eight for twenty-one with one homer."

The door to the outer office opened, and an elderly couple walked out. A tall man dressed in a blue suit escorted the couple to the front door. "Mr. Sturgis. These two gentlemen would like to see you," Rozalie said.

Dan and Scotty introduced themselves and the three men walked to the attorney's office, passing an open room where two young males had their heads buried into thick books. By the bindings, Dan could tell the books were legal reference volumes. Sturgis ushered the detectives into his office and they sat at a round table. Dan noticed what appeared to be a mahogany wooden desk. He also eyed several diplomas on the walls. "Mr. Sturgis," Dan said. "You know Mr. Biaggio's Jaguar was stolen yesterday."

The attorney, whose receding hairline had only a patch of brown strands remaining, adjusted his wire-rimmed glasses and said, "Yes."

"According to the report, it was taken from the parking area out back," Dan said. "Were you in this office yesterday?"

Sturgis replied, "No, I flew in last night from Houston."

"Do you know if anyone heard or saw anything unusual?"

"No one said they did."

Dan paused. "What about the two attorney's in the other office?"

Sturgis mildly laughed. "They're paralegals."

"Mind if we ask them?"

Sturgis got up and stepped out of his office, returning a few seconds later with his staffers. Both employees stated they hadn't heard or seen anything suspicious and the attorney excused them.

Dan asked Sturgis. "What exactly did Mr. Biaggio tell you?"

"He'd been dropped off this morning and when he went out back, the Jaguar was gone. He rushed in here and I told him it wasn't there when I got here. He stormed into his office and after he called to report it, he flew out of here with his briefcase and headed to court."

"Have you heard about the accident yesterday, where a twelve-year-old boy was killed in a hit-and-run?" Dan asked.

"I heard it this morning on the radio."

"Witnesses described the car as a silver Jaguar."

Sturgis bowed his head. "Oh my God."

"We're not saying it was Mr. Biaggio's car, but it is a possibility." Dan paused. "I gave my card to your receptionist and asked her to have Mr. Biaggio call me."

Sturgis held his hand to his head. "I have two boys and I'm sorry about the young kid."

"We all are," Dan said. "We understand your partner has a full morning of arraignments."

"That's not unusual."

"How's your schedule?"

"Light. I'll be off the rest of the week."

The detectives stood and shook Sturgis's hand. "I'll see you out," the attorney said.

Dan asked. "Mind if we go out the back door? We want to take a look at the parking area."

Sturgis turned toward the rear door and let the detectives into the yard.

"Small lot, Dan said. "Room for six, eight cars max."

Scotty pointed to two spaces that abutted the back of the house. The spots were reserved for the attorneys vehicles. A red Tesla was parked in the place marked for Sturgis. "Obviously, the Jaguar was in this spot with Biaggio's name."

Dan noticed a fence that enclosed the area, and leaning against the fence was a bicycle. "What do you think? Belong to a paralegal?" Dan asked.

"Only one way to find out," Scotty replied.

Dan took out his cell phone and snapped a few pictures of the yard and one of the bike. "Odd too. There don't appear to be any cameras out here."

Sturgis was standing at the door and let the detectives back inside. "Got a question for you," Dan said as he pointed to the fence. "Who owns that bike?"

Peering out, Sturgis said, "Never noticed it."

"Does it belong to an employee?" Dan asked.

After confirming no one had ridden a bike to the office, Sturgis was stumped and he said, "It doesn't belong to any of us."

"We'll have to ask Mr. Biaggio about it," Dan said. "Maybe he knows. Oh, one more thing. We noticed there don't appear to be cameras in the lot."

"We've discussed it. I guess now we'll do it," Sturgis said.

The detectives headed back to the Accord and Scotty said, "We don't know if the hit-and-run vehicle was a Jag. Some witnesses think it was a Mustang."

Dan said, "My gut tells me it was a Jaguar, Biaggio's car. Another thing. Don't you think it strange Biaggio kept his court schedule for arraignments? I mean Sturgis could have subbed. Seems to me, most people whose cars are stolen want to talk to the police, and if he was so angry, how the hell did he simply run off to court? Is he attempting to avoid us? Was his Jaguar really stolen?"

As Dan drove past the courthouse, he thought about the legal system, one where money talked and criminals walked. With no fewer than three bail-bond businesses within shouting distance, *get out of jail money* flowed like the Connecticut River.

The hardened detective had a bad feeling about Biaggio. Was he one more bottom-of-the-barrel lawyer who thought he could manipulate the truth and get away with murder?

Chapter 6

Dan had taken a photo of Javier Ibanez's tattoo. The detective took a look at it and stood at Scotty's desk. "Hey. Take another look at this tat. I should have shown it to Dixon at the scene, but I didn't. Maybe he can identify it. Let's take a walk down to his office."

Dixon was nowhere in sight. Dan said, "We have the Ibanez's address. I think it's time we pay them a visit."

Shelton Place was a short street that ran between Frankland and Mapleton. Passing the scene where Javier had been killed made Dan cringe. He stopped his car at a red light and said, "You'd never know anything happened there."

He heard a horn and looked at the now green light. "Okay, I hear ya," he muttered as the Accord moved forward and turned onto Shelton Place.

Two and three-family houses were on both sides of the street and Dan parked at number sixty-eight. Scotty rang the first-floor bell. Eduardo opened the door with his Chihuahua by his side. The friendly dog shimmied and Eduardo said, "Taco won't bite. He's a lapper."

Ellina entered the room where several photos of Javier were present. The smell of incense filled the home and the spicy aroma reminded Dan of his college days when the fragrance was used to hide marijuana odors in dorm rooms, but today it was burning to help ease the Ibanez's pain. Ellina opened the curtains to let light into the apartment's small living room where Dan and Scotty sat on the three-cushioned couch. "We're all sorry. We know it's rough," Dan said.

"He was our only child, a good boy," a teary-eyed Ellina said. She and her husband sat on chairs opposite the detectives as the small dog hopped onto Eduardo's lap.

"Can I ask you something?" Dan said. "We noticed a tattoo on Javier's neck. Do you have any idea what that tattoo might mean? Was he in a gang or any type of trouble?"

"No," Eduardo said. "Javier got that tattoo a few days ago. He wanted it for his birthday. He would have been thirteen in two weeks."

"Where was he headed when he was hit by the car?"

"A friend's house."

"Did Javier have many friends?"

"He did."

"Do you remember if any of them have the same kind of tattoo?"

"Yes, they all do. That's why Javier wanted it."

Dan stopped because he didn't want to shed a dark shadow on the Ibanez's, but the detective had gotten enough to believe Javier may have been in a gang, or was about to join one. That information didn't translate into the boy getting killed by the Jaguar, but it did mean Javier might not have been the innocent kid his parents thought he was.

The detectives stood. "Thanks for your time. We're doing everything we can to find the driver," Dan said as he and Scotty headed for the door.

As soon as they got back to headquarters, Dan and Scotty went to Dixon's office. "Hi guys. What's up?" the traffic captain said.

Dan took out his cell phone and showed Dixon the boy's tattoo. "I meant to show you this earlier. Do you recognize the tat? That's Javier Ibanez's neck."

Dixon said, "I sure do. That's the mark of the juveniles who've been stealing cars. Damned kids ride around on their bikes and ditch them when they spot a target."

"Probably steal the bikes too," Scotty said.

Dixon nodded. "That's what we've heard. The mayor is putting a task force together with school supers and parent groups to address the issues and see what makes these kids tick. Meantime, we're stepping up patrols."

Dan said, "So Javier Ibanez was part of the car theft gang."

"I'd say so," Dixon replied.

"His parents said he'd just gotten the tattoo for his upcoming thirteenth birthday. They said all his friends had the same tat."

"Whoa. That changes things," Dixon said. "It's more likely he hadn't joined the gang yet. The thirteenth birthday would have been the day he'd have been initiated into the gang. He would have had to steal a car."

"Really." Dan said. "According to the parents, Javier was a good kid. Never been in trouble."

Dixon shook his head. "You ever do things at that age your parents weren't aware of?"

Dan knew Dixon was right. "Good point, but I don't see the need to burst the Ibanez's bubble and discuss this with them. They lost their only son and I think they should hold onto the good-boy image. "Thanks. Have a good day," Dan said as he and Scotty headed upstairs.

CHAPTER 7

D an didn't like when people refused to return his calls. He waited for Biaggio to call him, but the detective's phone had remained silent too long. *Did Rozalie give him my message? Is he trying to avoid me? If so, why?* Dan paced the squad room floor.

"What's buggin' you?" Scotty asked.

"Biaggio. He should have called me by now, unless Rozalie forgot to tell him."

"That's possible, so give him another try."

Dan's desk phone rang. "Maybe it's him." Picking up the receiver, Dan heard Dixon. "We got the Jaguar," he said.

"Where'd you find it?"

"It was abandoned at the Gordan Lane Magnet school."

"Who found it?"

"A teacher reported the car parked in her space."

"Is the Jag still there?"

"Yeah."

"Great. Don't have it towed. I want to look at it right where it is. Anyone told Biaggio yet?"

"Not yet. I already sent the lab guys down there."

"Let me break the news to him. Any damage on the car?"

"You tell me after you see it."

Dan rapped on Scotty's cube. "That was Dixon. They found the Jag in a school lot. Let's go take a look."

When they arrived, Dan spotted the lab guys who were at the silver Jag that was parked in a space marked *Teachers Only.* The detectives approached the car. "Aki. How's it looking?" Dan asked.

The young forensics specialist said, "Interesting."

"Interesting?"

"It appears the inside of the car is clean as a whistle. Someone wiped it down."

Dan thought for a second. "Who the hell wipes down a stolen vehicle and abandons it?"

"How about someone who knows they killed a kid?" Aki replied.

Dan and Scotty walked around the vehicle. "Looks like the left front struck the kid. Bumper is out of whack, chipped, and the headlight is cracked," Dan said. He turned back to Aki. "So are you shitting me? There's no fingerprints, hair follicles for DNA, nothing?

"We got fibers from the impact point and we can match those to the clothes the kid was wearing. That should nail down this vehicle as the murder weapon. We're gonna wrap it up. I'll send you a report as soon as we've got results."

"Wait," Dan said. "Did you guys check the glovebox and console?"

"Nothing out of the ordinary. Registration and stuff in the glovebox belong to Angelo Biaggio. A bunch of music CD's are in the console."

Dan said, "I want to take a quick look."

The detective remembered witnesses had heard Reggae music coming from inside the car as it sped away.

Opening the center console with Scotty looking on, Dan poked through a half dozen jewel cases. "Strange," he said. All the music is contemporary. Bennett, Sinatra, Nat King Cole, and one Marley. That jewel case is empty."

"Check the CD the player," Scotty said.

"Nice. How do we get the disc out?" Dan replied. "I know in my car, it won't eject unless the car is on."

"You don't have a Jag. Try the button on top."

Dan hit it and the disk ejected. "Go ask Aki for a baggie and gloves. I don't want to get my prints on this. If I'm right, the driver's prints are on it."

Scotty obtained the needed items and handed them to Dan who slipped the rubber gloves on his hands, removed the CD, placed it and the jewel case into the bag, and handed it to Aki. "How about logging this and checking for prints. I have a hunch this belongs to the car thief," Dan said.

CHAPTER 8

Dan hadn't brought it to his partner's attention yet, but there was something missing from the squad room. Scotty's muffins were nowhere to be seen, and Dan had wondered about the lack of fresh-baked goodies. He saw his empty-handed partner walking toward him. "You forget something?" Dan asked.

"What do you mean?" Scotty replied.

"Muffins, Mister Crocker."

"Oh no, don't look for the return of the muffin man. That ain't happening. Gave that up when Sally took over the kitchen."

"Okay, but in case you forgot, orange-cranberry is my favorite."

"Right, I gotta take a leak, so think about something else while I'm gone."

Dan thought about Biaggio, and the detective's innate dislike for lawyers rose another notch. *They're all a bunch of thieves.*

Scotty returned and Dan said, "Don't sit. Let's go see Biaggio. Can't wait to hear what he has to say about his found Jaguar."

The detectives again entered Biaggio's office. Dan noticed a white-haired woman who was seated in the waiting area. She was wearing a long green-patterned dress and a red scarf. Sitting next to her was a teenaged boy clad in patched jeans, a blue buttoned-down shirt, and he wore a brace around his neck.

The detectives approached Rozalie, who slid the window open. "Did you give Mr. Biaggio my message?" Dan asked.

"I told him you wanted to talk to him."

"Is he here now?"

"He is, but he has several appointments, and he's with a client."

"Mind if we wait?" Dan asked.

"Go ahead. It could be a while."

The detectives sat and waited. Dan turned and eyed the boy whose neck was in a brace. "What happened?"

The woman, whose front tooth was missing, said, "My grandson was in the backseat of his mother's car when it was rear-ended. He has to wear that thing for two more weeks. Didn't know he was hurt so bad, but Mr. Biaggio said whiplash doesn't show up right away. He sent us to a chiropractor."

The waiting room door opened and Biaggio appeared. A well-dressed man was with him and the lawyer said, "I'll call you later. We have a strong case." Biaggio watched his client exit the office and turned his attention to his waiting clients. "Please come in Mrs. Freitas. You too Leandro."

Dan stood and said to the woman, "Would you excuse us for a few minutes?" We'd like to talk with Mr. Biaggio."

"Who are you?" the short, stocky lawyer asked.

Dan showed his badge. "You didn't call me, so we figured we'd come by again. Let's talk. It shouldn't take long."

Biaggio said to his clients "Please wait here."

Dan and Scotty followed close behind the fifty-three-year-old Biaggio as they entered the lawyer's office. Biaggio sat behind his desk in a high-back leather chair while the detectives sat opposite him in padded-cushioned chairs. Dan noticed the dark furniture, including a matching credenza and file cabinet. The attorney's walls were lined with the usual academic degrees, bar association certificates, and licenses. In one corner was an ebony and ivory chess set sitting on a round glass-top table. Dan noticed old photos of a sailor, one with Biaggio and an island woman. "Navy man, I see."

Biaggio turned and smiled. "Those were eight great years. What a way to see the world, and our generous government helped pay for law school. Those days are long gone." He grinned. "And those girls loved uniforms."

Dan also saw a more recent framed photo on the wall above the credenza. Assuming the picture of two boys appearing to be teenagers, and the woman with blonde hair were Biaggio's wife and kids, Dan said, "Nice looking family."

Peering over his glasses Biaggio replied, "Thanks. So what can I do for you? You find my car?"

Dan sat forward. "Yes sir, and we suspect the vehicle may have been involved in a hit-and-run that killed a boy on Frankland Avenue."

Dan studied Biaggio's demeanor as the unflinching attorney said, "You think the thief who stole my car hit that kid?"

"We don't know for sure yet. Your Jaguar was taken to impound and it will be checked."

"Any damage?"

Dan was coy. "We haven't had a chance to check it out yet."

"Damn. That car is brand new, barely broken in. Where was it found?"

Dan, as if not hearing that question, quickly replied, "As we understand it. You didn't notice the car was missing until the next morning. Why is that?"

Biaggio rocked back in his chair. "What are you insinuating? My son picked me up here and we went to a basketball game. He drove us home in his car and my wife dropped me off here in the morning. That's when I noticed the Jaguar missing."

Dan said, "Just curious. Did you see the bicycle that was up against the fence?"

Biaggio shrugged. "What are you talking about? My car was gone. What's some bike got to do with it?"

"That's what we want to know."

"What are you talking about? There's no bike out back."

"Mind if we take a quick look?" Dan asked.

"Look all you want, but there's no bike."

The detectives peeked into the yard. The bike was gone.

Back inside the lawyer's office, Biaggio sat smugly. "Is it there?"

Dan replied, "No it isn't." He took out his cell phone and showed Biaggio the snapshot of the bike. "That's it. So you never saw it?"

"No." The lawyer leaned forward. "Wait a minute. What about that gang of teen car thieves? I heard they ride bikes too. That's it. One of them left their bike here, swiped my car, and came back for the bike last night."

Dan nodded. "I guess it's possible, but it would have been easy to catch the thieves if you had cameras outside."

"So now that's a crime?"

Dan peered into Biaggio's eyes. "Your secretary said you were quite upset, angry when you noticed your car was missing."

"Damn right? Wouldn't you be?"

Dan leaned in toward Biaggio. "You bet I'd be mad, I probably wouldn't have been able to concentrate on my job as well as you did."

"I had a full slate. I had to be in court."

"Have you ever missed a court date, been sick, had Mr. Sturgis fill in, or called for a postponement?"

Raising his voice, Biaggio said, "You're out of line, detective. I'd back off if I were you." The attorney sneered at Dan. "Are we done now?"

"For now. I'm sure we'll be talking again," Dan said. "Thanks for your time."

Biaggio escorted the detectives out.

Upon getting into his Accord, Dan said, "He's a lying bastard. He was more concerned about the damn car than he was about Javier. Never once mentioned the kid. He also didn't really seem to care where the car was found. He asked me, but I never answered. It's almost like he knew the answer. Not like a sharp attorney to let that fact slip. And did you see how fast he went on the defensive?"

Scotty nodded. "Comes across as pretty arrogant."

"Yeah, and I'm not buying the teenage car thief ring. He knows there's one running around town. But his Jaguar would have been crashed or simply abandoned, not wiped clean and dropped in a school lot … And pulling that Houdini act with the bike was a pretty slick stunt."

Chapter 9

Dan approached the front door of his home, eager for some down time with his wife and family. When Phyllis opened it, his jaw dropped. "Oh my God," he said with a huge grin.

"Like it?" she asked.

"I love it. What possessed you?"

She threw her arms around his waist. "You always said how you loved Sally's hair."

Dan shut the door while still in her grasp. "I never imagined you with red hair. It's gorgeous. We're not alone are we?"

"No. Try your luck later."

Dan hung his coat and stowed his weapon in the closet before they walked to the kitchen where Connie greeted him. "Think I'd look as sexy in red hair?" she quipped.

"You couldn't be any more gorgeous than you already are," Dan said as his nose detected a familiar aroma.

"I recognize that smile," Connie said as she glanced at Dan and opened the oven door.

"You kidding? I'd know your chicken pot pie anywhere. Haven't had that since the diner closed."

"Good nose, detective. Another five minutes and we should be all set. Go round up the kids."

"Yes boss. You sound like my mother."

Phyllis laughed. "Do as she says dear."

"All right, but I'm going up to change."

Dan hurried and returned dressed in a blue sweat suit. Dinner was served, only to be interrupted by the phone. Phyllis answered. "It's Mike. Hi, how are you? How's school? We're eating dinner," she said

For a few seconds everything was calm and then Phyllis uttered "What? How did that happen?"

Dan perked up. "What happened?"

Phyllis handed the phone to Dan. "What happened?"

"I dislocated my shoulder. I'm out for at least six weeks," Mike said.

"How'd you do that?" Dan asked.

"I slid headfirst stretching a double into a triple. I jammed my shoulder on the bag. Lucky it's not my throwing arm."

Dan sighed. "So were you safe or out?"

Mike laughed. "Thanks for your concern. I was safe, went three for four. I'm wearing a sling."

"School okay?"

"Yeah, tell mom I'm three-point-six." Mike paused. "I'm running low on cash. How about sending some?"

"How much do you need?"

"How much you got?"

"I'll see what I can spare. You should see mom. She's a redhead."

"You serious? Send a pic."

"Wanna talk to Kate and Josh?"

"Yeah. I miss those brats?"

"Hold on. Kate, Josh. Mike wants to say 'hi.'"

The two younger siblings were excited to talk to their older brother and each spent a couple of minutes chatting with him. Josh spoke last and handed the phone back to his mother. Phyllis said to Mike, "You do what the doctor says and take care of yourself. We love you." She placed the phone back on its stand.

Josh said, "He's sending us Arizona State sweatshirts."

Dan then knew why Mike had asked for money, and he knew who was really buying the sweats.

The family finished dinner and Connie went home. After the kids had gone to bed, Dan was watching TV in the den when Phyllis entered the room. She took the remote from his hand and casually stroked her red hair. "Come with me," she whispered in his ear.

Chapter 10

Dan walked toward the headquarters rear door. Fellow detective Randy Landry was standing by the entrance with a cigarette in his hand, a cloud of smoke wafted around him, and he coughed. "You need to give up those nasty things," Dan said.

Taking another puff, Landry said, "I did, but those nicotine patches don't work. I guess if a bullet doesn't get me, lung cancer will."

"Some death wish!"

Landry took one last puff and tossed the butt to the ground, crushing the half-smoked cigarette with his shoe. "You been to Blues? I think the name is a reference to the uniforms."

Not yet. I hear it's pretty good, but nothing will replace Connie's," Dan said.

"Come on. I'll wait here," Landry said. "You go get Scotty. I saw him go in. I think Luke is at the dentist."

The three block walk took little time. A red and white sign in Blue's' window read: *Special of the day – 2 eggs, 2 pancakes, bacon, hash browns, toast and coffee - $7.99*

"Didn't this used to be a book store?" Dan asked.

"Yeah, it was Huntingdon's," Landry said. "And I remember that neon sign from the jewelry store down the street. Peace Of Mind Guaranteed."

Dome-shaped lights hung from the ceiling, and blue walls closely matched the police uniform colors, as did the tablecloths.

Missing were a counter and swiveling stools that had been fixtures at Connie's Place.

Blues was about one-third occupied with a mixture of business people and uniforms. A sign read: *Seat Yourself,* so the three detectives walked past tables in the center of the dining area and squeezed into one of two dozen booths.

Landry ordered the special. Dan and Scotty opted for coffee and English muffins.

Dan lifted his cup and said to Landry, "You know anything about Angelo Biaggio?"

Landry sipped his coffee and then said, "Heard he's an ambulance chaser. Luke has a neighbor who was rear-ended about a year ago. Biaggio was quick to get hold of the guy even though he wasn't hurt. The sleazy lawyer sued the other driver's insurance company and they settled for ten grand."

Dan took the last bite of his muffin, swallowed, and said, "I need to speak with Luke when we get back." Dan quickly finished his coffee. "You done?" he said to Scotty.

"Will be in a second."

Dan picked up the check, and he tossed a ten-dollar bill at Landry. "Here, finish your breakfast. We need to get back."

Landry quickly chugged his coffee. "Wait up."

Back at the station, Luke Hanson was at his desk. "Just the guy I'm looking for," Dan said.

Luke swiveled his chair around. "You guys were at Blues. Right?"

Dan smiled. "Your partner took us. We left him downstairs to have a smoke."

"Idiot says he tried to quit, but that was a hell of a short effort," Luke said. "Crap, I'm still numb from Novocain."

Dan said, "We need to discuss something."

Landry entered the squad room and leaned into Luke's cube. "Missed a good breakfast, kid."

Luke stood and Dan looked up at the six-four comrade. Pointing at Landry, Dan said, "He told us about a neighbor of yours who Angelo Biaggio talked into suing an insurance company."

"It was an auto accident," Luke said. "Ed Burgess. He was rear-ended about a year ago and Biaggio contacted him the next day convincing Ed that he might have been injured. The lawyer told him whiplash doesn't always show up right away."

"But, he wasn't really hurt. Right?"

"Damn right he wasn't. He wore a neck brace for a few weeks after Biaggio had sent him to a chiropractor."

Dan flashed immediately to Biaggio's office and the woman with her grandson who was wearing a neck brace.

"Tell me more."

"As I remember, Ed said Biaggio contacted him a day after the banged-up car had been taken to the repair shop. I think Biaggio has someone there to supply him with names of people involved in car accidents."

"That's pretty slick," Dan said."

"You onto this guy?"

"Maybe. We think his car was the one that struck and killed Javier Ibanez. We saw the vehicle yesterday, before it was towed to the impound lot. Thanks Luke." Dan turned to Scotty. "Let's go see our favorite captain."

⋏

The detectives approached the captain's office where Syms had the phone to his ear and wore a frantic look on his face. "Jesus Christ!" he shouted. "Just what we need."

Dan and Scotty listened to the intense conversation as Syms pointed to them. "Sit the fuck down." The captain said as he slammed his fist on his desk. He ended the call and turned to his detectives. "What a fucking mess. Hardison is down on Viner. Officer Wallace shot an unarmed black kid who was fleeing a convenience store, and there's a near riot down there." Every red light on Syms's phone was lit, and he picked up line two. Without saying a word, the captain heard Mayor Mary Fernandez's voice. "Where's Chief Hardison? He won't answer his phone."

"Just talked to him. He's on his way back here."

"Tell him to call me."

Dan stood and asked, "What the hell happened?"

Syms hung up. "A couple of hours ago, a teenager robbed a convenience store. Wallace arrived and spotted the suspect who was running down the street. All I know is we've got a white cop shooting and killing an unarmed black man, and it's chaos down there."

Syms pounded his fist on the desk again, sending splashes of coffee onto the desktop. "We got a near riot going on. Hardison said the news people are there."

Syms picked up his remote and clicked the local TV channel. Scrolling across the bottom of the screen in big red letters was *BREAKING NEWS: HARTFORD WHITE COP GUNS DOWN BLACK MAN.*

Dan, Scotty and Syms sat; all eyes were fixed on the screen and staring at Hardison who had a microphone shoved at him as he attempted to avoid a reporter. Cameras scanned the crowd of angry protesters. Three males, all appearing to be in their mid-teens, waved fists at the camera.

"God damn it!" Syms shouted. "He said he was on his way back here." The captain hopped up from his chair. "I gotta get down there."

Dan grabbed his angered boss. "Hold it. Where the hell do you think you're going? They don't need you down there. They need the riot squad."

"Shit!" Syms shouted, "Where the hell are they?"

A TV camera caught Chief Hardison getting into a squad car as a mob rushed toward the black and white. Dan, Scotty, and Syms helplessly looked on as the camera disappeared. "They could set the car on fire," the nervous captain said.

Another camera zeroed in on three armored vehicles that had arrived. Angry neighborhood residents began to back away as officers clad in full battle gear got out aiming to settle the crowd. One blast of tear gas filled the area with white smoke. A second similar grenade hit the ground in the midst of a protesters spewing four letter words and throwing stones. The armed riot squad's message had been sent and the street began to clear. Syms, Scotty, and Dan sat back wondering if Hardison would safely return to headquarters. The captain's phone rang. He answered it and heard the chief's voice. "Where are you?" Syms asked

"On my way back. That was close, but we got out when the big guns arrived."

"Had us worried, sir."

The call ended and Syms looked at his detectives. "He's okay."

Chapter 11

Hartford was now bloodied by an incident involving an apparently unarmed black man who was killed by a white cop. This city hadn't seen civil unrest since 1968, when riots occurred all over the country.

Hours later, after being blasted with streams of cold water and smoke grenades by the riot squad and National Guard, only a handful of protesters remained in the streets.

As soon as Dan arrived at his desk, he placed his jacket on the back of his chair and headed for the men's room. While standing at a urinal, he saw the lavatory door open. Syms entered and faced the porcelain wall unit next to his detective. "Hardison got any details on the shooting?" Dan asked.

"Wait until I tell you what he's learned. Follow me back."

Both urinals flushed and after the men washed their hands, they walked to the captain's office. "Close the door," Syms said. He sat and spun around in his chair. "Casey Wallace is a problem. This isn't his first incident with an African-American man."

Dan sat. "What's that mean?"

"According to Dixon, Wallace is twenty-eight and was hired three years ago. It seems about ten months ago he approached a black suspect who had been sitting in a car in a parking lot. That guy ended up in the hospital."

"What happened?"

"Wallace claimed the man appeared to have sold drugs to someone in another vehicle that had driven away. Wallace questioned the suspect and it turned out the guy had a warrant and upon searching the vehicle, a loaded thirty-eight was found, along with several bags of cocaine. He had just cause to arrest the man, but by the time back-up got there, the suspect was on the ground bleeding from the face and handcuffed despite a broken arm."

"What are you saying? It was an unprovoked beating?"

Syms shook his head and eyed Dan. "Wallace stated the detained man resisted and a tussle ensued with him finally wrestling the suspect to the ground. Several punches were thrown, but we don't know for sure what happened. Wallace's body cam wasn't working, and guess what? It wasn't working this time either." Syms leaned forward. "The other odd thing is, according to the second officer who arrived before the ambulance came, the suspect had facial bruises and a broken arm, but Wallace appeared to be unmarked. If there was a fight, then why was Wallace not showing any signs of a struggle?"

Dan shut his eyes for a moment. "Does Dixon think there were racial implications?"

"He suspects that's the case, but he can't prove it. Dixon had to let the incident go, but if it comes to light, it will surely add fuel to the neighborhood fire."

"What happened to the suspect?" Dan asked.

"What do you think? He was released from the hospital, booked and got bailed again after paying the fine for missing his previous court appearance. Never showed for this court appearance either and he's gone."

"What about the kid Wallace shot?"

"Hardison can't string Wallace up by his balls yet. He needs proof, indisputable proof Wallace shot in self-defense. The body cam not working again is all too coincidental."

Syms opened his pill container, removed two tablets and washed them down with water from the bottle on his desk. He said, "Ready for this? That kid was no kid. His name was Vandor

Jerricks, twenty-one with a list of priors, and a probable gang member."

Scotty entered the captain's office. "What's the latest?" he asked.

The captain continued as Scotty took a seat. "I was telling Dan a few things. Wallace responded to a robbery at a convenience store on Viner. When he arrived, he saw a black man fleeing the store. The suspect had on a dark jacket and a red bandana, and he had a brown paper bag in his hand. Wallace began foot pursuit, yelling several times for the suspect to stop. Jerricks momentarily stopped before rounding the corner. Wallace followed and the suspect turned around. Wallace saw him reaching into the bag and the officer fired a shot, says he feared the robber was about to pull a gun from the bag." Syms paused again. "Wallace was sure the jacket belonged to the Knights."

"What about the store clerk? What did he say?" Dan asked.

"That's where it gets cloudy. The owner's name is Sterling Moses, sixty-nine, and he says he was held up at gunpoint. He described Jerricks to a tee, including the bandana, and he said the robber pointed a gun at him demanding money. Moses opened the register and shoved about a hundred bucks into a bag and the robber left."

"How was Wallace there so soon?"

"Oh yeah, the register was rigged with a hot button. Wallace was only a block away, so he got there fast."

"Is there a video from the store?" Scotty asked.

"Dixon has one. Unfortunately it's out of focus," Syms replied. "You can make out the robber, and even though Moses said he was held up at gunpoint, you can't really see a gun. You can see the robber pointing to the register and a hand in his pocket, but no gun was found on Jerricks."

"Where is Wallace?"

"He was here until late last night with Hardison. Dixon brought the video up and they watched it. Then the chief sent Wallace home."

"Is he suspended?" Dan asked.

"Not yet. There'll be an inquiry. He's officially on leave. His weapon is in evidence. He lives alone, no wife or kids, but he said he'll be staying with a friend. Wallace deserves a fair hearing, and Hardison has to back Dixon."

CHAPTER 12

Scotty was reading the Hartford Courant sports pages at his desk when his partner approached him. "I like the Giant's chances of going to the Super Bowl," Dan said.

"You would, but the Patriots are going for sure."

"Maybe, but who beat them in the big game twice already?"

"That's pretty low, my friend. As I recall the Red Sox won the World Series a couple of years ago. How long has it been since the Yankees have won it?"

"Now we're playing dirty, pal," Dan said as he retreated to his cube. He turned to his computer and saw an email from Aki. The detective had part of the information he needed: confirmation Biaggio's Jaguar was the murder weapon, but who was the driver? Dan rapped on Scotty's cube. "Wanna take a ride to the lab to pick up the CD? Aki got prints. No positives, but the shreds on the bumper match Javier Ibanez's clothes."

▲

The forensic lab and medical examiner's offices were located at the University Hospital Campus in Farmington. All crime-related autopsies were performed at that facility. Dan and Scotty had been to the two-story building before. The forensics lab occupied the second floor, while the first floor and basement were home to the medical examiner and morgue.

Skipping the elevator, the detectives walked up one flight and entered the forensics lab's outer office where black and white photos of bizarre evidence were hanging on the walls. Dan spotted a picture of a cue ball. "What the hell do you think happened with that one?" he said to Scotty.

Aki came out to greet the detectives. Wearing his white lab coat, the technician said, "Your disc is right here." He reached under the counter and placed the plastic bag, containing the disc and jewel case, next to a computer. "Sign it out and it's all yours."

"Right," Dan said. "Wish we could say this is evidence."

"Sorry, but at least we can prove the lawyer's car was the vehicle that killed Javier Ibanez."

"You can be damn sure we're gonna nail the driver," Dan said. He pointed to the cue ball. "What's the story with that?"

"Happened in a bar in Bridgeport a few years ago. Some guy lost a match and shoved the ball down his opponent's throat. Choked the guy to death."

"Jesus, must have had some big mouth?" Scotty said.

Dan nudged him. "Keep up that Patriot's crap and see what can happen?"

Scotty picked up the plastic bag. "Thanks, Aki." The detective pointed to a photo of a screwdriver. "I don't want to know what happened with that."

"See you," Dan said as he and his partner exited the lab.

On the way back to headquarters, Dan drove past Landon Place. "Remember when you met Sally? Man, you were smitten right from the start."

"Damn right. As soon as we walked into the model office, and Sally was standing there, I was speechless. Her long red hair."

"You couldn't take your eyes off her. You never heard a word I said to her. I think you had a hard-on from the get-go."

"Jesus, she was the prettiest woman I'd ever seen."

"Beats me how she fell for your ass."

Scotty smiled. "See this face? And I happen to be quite charming."

"Take another look in the mirror."

"At least I'm not aging like you old man."

"You think Sally will return to work?"

"Probably not until Bri starts school, and that'll be a few years down the road. Eli will be a teenager then."

"You thinking about more kids?"

"We've discussed it. She'd like another, but I'm not so sure. I still have a few issues with my ex, and Eli still goes to her every other weekend. Sally handles it very well."

"You could do what I did. Snip it in the bud."

Scotty laughed. "Vasectomy? Damn, I remember you walked like a duck for a week after yours. Funniest thing I ever saw, you claiming to have a possible hernia."

"Okay, but you should know it doesn't impact your drive or satisfaction."

"We'll roll the dice."

Dan grinned. "You won't believe this, but Phyllis surprised me the other day. She had her hair dyed red. I love it, real sexy."

"So what are you saying? The vasectomy reaping a few more dividends lately?"

"Damn straight," Dan said with a huge smile.

Scotty's cell rang and when the conversation ended Dan said, "Did you sell the old fifty-seven Chevy?"

"Yeah. It was time. The Camaro and Sally's Beemer weren't cutting it with the two kids, so we traded the BMW and got an SUV. I may end up trading the Camaro too."

CHAPTER 13

There was a chill in the air this morning, but it was uncomfortably warm inside police headquarters. When Dan arrived, he rapped on the Syms's door and opened it. He saw the worried look on the captain's face. "You look like a squirrel who lost his nuts," Dan said.

"Me? The chief's blood pressure is through the roof. The board is dragging its' feet and the more time that goes by only prolongs the restlessness."

Syms sat back and clasped his hands behind his head. "The riot squad and guard are still hanging around. Things could be worse. No one's been seriously injured yet."

Dan switched gears. "Listen," he said as Scotty entered the office.

Syms pointed to the chair next to Dan. "Have a seat. Your partner was about to tell me a story."

Dan continued, "The CD Aki checked had untraceable prints, but I have a sneaking suspicion about the driver. And get this. Biaggio got the car out of impound. He's as dirty as a pig in mud."

Scotty snickered, "Aren't all attorneys?"

"Right," Syms said.

Dan shook his head. "We need to have another chat with Mr. Biaggio."

Syms stood. "Go. I have to get up to see Hardison."

Dan thought about making another unannounced appearance at Biaggio's office, but he didn't want simply to surprise the attorney, so he took the card from his wallet. Turning to Scotty he said, "Let's see if he can squeeze us in. I'm calling his office."

Rozalie answered. "Attorney's Biaggio and Sturgis," she said.

"Hi, this is detective Shields. Does Mr. Biaggio have time today to meet with me and my partner?" he asked.

"Let me check." She put Dan on hold and while Sinatra was softly singing in Dan's ear, she went into Biaggio's office. A minute later Rozalie returned to her station, picked up the phone and said, "Mr. Shields, he's got a court case in an hour," She paused. "And he's booked after lunch." She paused again. "I'm afraid he's not available today."

Her hesitance piqued Dan's interest. He was sure Biaggio had told her to tell him a lie. The quick-thinking detective said, "Tell me something? Does he break for lunch?"

"Yes. He goes to Cefalu almost every day."

"Thanks," Dan said. He was sure if he and Scotty happened to eat lunch at Cefalu, they'd run into the elusive lawyer. Turning to his partner, Dan said, "We're going to drop in on Mr. Biaggio at Cefalu. Rozalie said he eats there all the time, and I've always wanted to try the place."

Cefalu was a fine Italian restaurant. Its' name derived from the small namesake Sicilian town situated an hour from Palermo. The eatery, located a couple of blocks from the courthouse and intersecting with Lawyer's Row, was a place where Dan knew not only lawyers hung out, but so did local politicians as well as influential businessmen.

It was 12:20 p.m. when Dan and Scotty arrived at the restaurant. Dan pulled into the nearly full lot and parked his humble Accord in a space between a Cadillac and a Lexus. The corner brick building had a green and red awning over the front entrance. Similar coverings were above three windows facing the street. A young man in a dark suit toting a briefcase held the restaurant's door open for the two detectives. "Thanks," Dan said.

The aroma of savory Italian food was mouth-watering. Hand-painted murals of Sicilian scenery, towns such as Palermo, Trapani, and Marsala covered the walls. To the detective's left was a long bar with half the stools being occupied by men dressed in suits. Attorneys, and politicians, every one of them, Dan thought.

A host wearing a red silky shirt with Cefalu's Italian villa logo embroidered on the pocket took the diners to a table, handing the detectives menus as they sat. Dan glanced around the busy restaurant. Next to them were two females who appeared to be in their mid- thirties, and both dressed in dark pantsuits. "Probably lawyers or corporate execs," he said to Scotty.

Scotty scanned the bar, "Isn't that Thompson Brown?"

Dan took a look. "Yup, and if he runs for Governor, we're all in big trouble. He's as corrupt as they come. Wonder who he's waiting for?" Dan spotted three men who were seated at a table in the rear of the restaurant. "Biaggio," he whispered to Scotty without pointing. "Don't turn around. He's in the corner with two other guys."

The waiter returned to fill the water glasses. Dan said to him. "I see a friend of mine, Angelo Biaggio seated at a table in back. How about moving us to the empty table next to him."

"Sorry, that one is reserved."

"That's okay. We're going to say hello to Angelo."

The detectives slowly approached Biaggio's table. The lawyer held a glass of red wine in his hand and stared at the intruders.

"Mr. Biaggio. It's nice to see you again," Dan said. "Your secretary told us you had a full schedule today."

Wearing a gray silk Armani suit with a pocket hanky and blue striped tie, the surprised attorney put his glass down and pointed his fork at the detectives. "Just who the hell do you think you are? We're having lunch. Now get out of here."

Biaggio's friends stopped eating. The big guy on his left with slicked back hair and a large mole on his forehead stood. "You heard the man," the goon said.

Seated silently in the other chair, was an unsmiling man whose nose was abruptly flat at the tip.

Dan remained calm. "Yes sir, we'll be leaving in a minute." He eyed Biaggio. "Why don't you come with us back to your office?"

Biaggio stared hard at the detective and raised his voice. "I told you to get out of here."

Dan pulled up a chair from the reserved table and sat next to Biaggio as the attorney's cohorts stopped eating again. "We can discuss this here with your friends then," the daring detective said.

The big man stood again and shook his finger at Dan. "Vincenzo. Sit down," Biaggio ordered as he put his wine glass down and pointed at Dan. "Just what the hell is so important, Mr. Detective?"

Dan pointed back at him. "You want to know what we know, you'll take the time to talk to us. Like I said, here is fine, but you may want to take it back to the privacy of your office."

The attorney got up and threw his napkin on the table. "God damn it, let's go."

Dan, Scotty, and Biaggio, who toted a leather briefcase, headed out of the restaurant. The waiter looked at the men and Dan said, "Something came up. We have to go."

The trio exited the restaurant and walked back to Biaggio's office. Not a word was said the entire way.

The detectives and a clearly ruffled Biaggio headed into the attorney's office. He slammed the door shut behind the detectives, and placed his briefcase beside his chair. The flustered lawyer sat in his high-back leather chair. Staring at the detectives he said, "Now we're on my turf. Start talking."

Dan, still standing, leaned forward placing his hands on the desk. "There are a few loose ends we're curious about. For one, how is it you were able to get the Jag out of impound?"

Biaggio rocked his chair. "It's my car. What's it matter to you?"

"It's just a little unusual a car that's considered evidence in a hit-and-run gets released before the investigation ends."

"I have friends."

"So we see," Dan said. "And so did Javier Ibanez."

Biaggio leaned forward. "And you think it was my car?"

Dan stared at him. "Come on. We know it was your car. The fibers collected from the fender matched the boy's clothes," He paused. "And don't play stupid, we know you know it."

"So what are you getting at smart-ass detective? Go find a car thief." Biaggio sat back. "What about a bicycle thief? Go check out those kids."

Dan looked Biaggio in the eye. "Get off it. You know they didn't steal your precious Jaguar. Those kids crash and trash the cars they steal."

Biaggio stared at the abrasive detective.

Dan said. "By the way, didn't you say your son picked you up and you went to a basketball game?"

"Yes. Why?"

"Mind telling me what game?"

"We went to the Hawks game. University of Hartford. My son Rocco is going there next year, and for your information they beat Stony Brook seventy to sixty-one."

Dan glanced at the framed photo of Biaggio's sons. "What school do your boys go to?"

"Conrad. Bryce is a freshman."

"Handsome boys. What kind of car does Rocco have?"

"Why is that important? It's a four-year-old SUV."

"So why didn't you take the Jag to the game?"

"I didn't want the new car jammed into that small parking lot."

"You got the Jag out back?"

"It's in the shop. My wife dropped me off here."

"Is your wife a lawyer too?"

"She's in real estate. Works for Keney and Goodwin."

Dan said, "Can I ask you one more thing? How would you explain the fact there were no prints inside the car?"

"Whoa! Wait a second," Biaggio said as he stood while removing his glasses. Staring menacingly at Dan, he said, "That sounds like an accusation. I'd take it down a notch if I were you."

"Sorry," Dan said. "We'll be on our way."

The detectives moved toward the door, and Dan turned back to face Biaggio. "By the way … Judging by the CD's in your car, it looks like you enjoy soft music. Sinatra, Tony Bennett, Nat King Cole."

"No one better," Biaggio said.

"I like those guys too, but sometimes for a change of pace I listen to Reggae. You like Reggae?" Dan asked.

"Not really," Biaggio replied while pointing to the door. "I think you're headed in the right direction. And I'm not forgetting the lunch intrusion."

The detectives exited the building and walked back to Cefalu where the Accord had been parked. "Wonder if he's coming back to finish his meal?" Dan said.

Chapter 14

A FedEx truck sped past Dan's Accord as he drove down his cul-de-sac. As soon as he entered his house, he spotted a large unopened box on the floor in the foyer and heard Phyllis shout, "It just came. It's from Mike."

Dan saw the excitement on Josh and Kate's faces as he carried the box into the kitchen, and placed the carton on the floor. "I saw the delivery truck speeding out of here. I'd have pulled him over if I could have. Want to hand me a knife dear?"

Phyllis removed a steak knife from a drawer and handed it to her husband.

Slicing the cardboard box open, he pulled back the flaps and removed a layer of bubble wrap. Dan held a pink Arizona State sweatshirt with the words *Sun Devils* written on it. He handed it to Kate. "I think this is yours." Dan then pulled out a maroon and gold sweatshirt with the same logo and tossed it to Josh "Here you go, buddy."

The other pink one was Phyllis's, and the large maroon and gold sweatshirt was Dan's. "Mike's a good kid, the proud father said." Noticing a white envelope inside the box, Dan opened the letter.

Hope you like the sweats. Heard it's getting cold up there.
Love you all.
Mike

P.S. Dad- I hope you don't mind if I used your credit card. My shoulder is coming along fine. Will call soon. Oh yeah, Mom-love the hair.

The credit card comment was no surprise to Dan. After all, he'd remembered Josh's remark about Mike sending sweatshirts.

Phyllis shook her head at her husband. "You sent him a credit card and a photo?"

Dan shrugged. "Got me."

There was something else on the bottom of the parcel. Dan grabbed a box containing a Grand Canyon puzzle. "What a great kid. This is for Connie."

"She'll love it. Let me put it in the den and surprise her tomorrow," Phyllis said.

When Phyllis returned, Dan said, "How about going out for pizza?"

"Can I wear my sweatshirt?" Josh asked.

"Sure," Phyllis said.

"Me too," Kate said.

Dan turned to Josh who was all smiles with his new sweatshirt on. "Hey, did you go to the Mark Twain house today?"

Josh smiled. "We did, and they showed us the whole house. It's old and lots of winding stairs. There was a lady dressed like a maid and she said she worked for Mark Twain. He smoked big cigars, and he had three dogs named *I Know, You Know,* and *Don't Know.* He was weird."

"Did you get anything?"

"I got a bookmark and we saw an old printing machine he invented."

"I'm not sure he invented it," Dan said. "I think he invested in it and lost a lot of money. Sounds like you had a good time."

"Yeah. Can we get pizza now?"

"Sure," Dan said as he turned to Kate. "You have a good day too?"

"Yeah. I want pepperoni."

"Okay, let's go."

Phyllis nudged Dan. "You want to put the knife back and take the box to the garage?"

The detective had his orders, so he smiled at his loving wife. "Will do. I'll meet you guys in the car."

CHAPTER 15

D an exited his car in the police headquarters parking lot, and looked up to the threatening gray clouds, unaware of the storm brewing inside the building. As the detective headed to his cube, he peered down to Syms's office and saw the captain pacing. As Dan got closer, he heard muttered, undetectable words coming from the captain's mouth. "What's going on now?" Dan asked.

"Trouble, more trouble," the captain said. "A phone video of Wallace gunning down Vandor Jerricks has surfaced. It appears to support the claim the victim had no weapon. It was run on TV about a half-hour ago. Mayor Fernandez is livid and Hardison is on the hot seat. They're scared shitless the video is going to spark a riot. The mayor needs to get the frickin' board off their lazy asses."

"What's Hardison going to do?" Dan asked.

Syms slammed his desk. "All he can do is speak to the community and hope to maintain civil rest. And get this for a kick in the ass. Wallace got a lawyer, a black one at that." Syms peered at Dan. "You wanna guess?"

Dan thought for a few seconds and then shook his head knowing it could only be one defense attorney, a guy who had a reputation for getting criminals off with hand slaps. The last time Dan had battled Hancock Sasser was when the slick lawyer got bail for a drug dealer named Julio Vegas. "Do I have to say it? Hancock Sasser. Really? Why the hell would he defend a white cop?"

"You know Sasser. This case will put him in the national spotlight, win or lose."

Dan saw Hardison approaching Syms's office. "Here comes the chief," the detective said.

Syms stood. "Get out of here."

Dan started toward the squad room. "Morning chief," he said.

Hardison kept walking as if he hadn't heard the detective.

When Dan entered the squad room, he saw Scotty, who said, "Chief blew past me like his pants were on fire."

"Pants? It's the city that might be on fire, Dan said, "Keep your jacket on. Let's get out of here. "I have a couple of things to tell you."

"Hold it. It's raining. Want to go to the caf?"

"Let's go," Dan said as he spotted a manila envelope on Scotty's desk. "What's in there?"

"It's the title to the Chevy. I need to sign it over to the buyer. He's supposed to call me today."

The cafeteria was filled with uniforms. "How about heading back to my desk," Dan said. "This place is too noisy to talk."

Back upstairs the detectives sat at Dan's table and he said, "The media got hold of a video that appears to crucify Wallace. Hardison, and the mayor are scared shitless, and unbelievably Wallace has a lawyer, a pretty slick defense attorney. Get this. He hired Hancock Sasser."

"What? Why the hell would Sasser get involved with an already racially charged case?"

"I think, he thinks he's Johnny Cochran, and will become famous."

"Famous? He'll get run out of town."

"Maybe not," Dan said. "That sly bastard has no ethics. He'll make sure his client gets thrown in jail, and then he'll say justice was served."

Scotty's cell vibrated and he answered the call. A few seconds later, he said to Dan, "I gotta go. The buyer wants to pick up the car, and I need to meet him at the bank to complete the transaction."

"Go ahead. I'll hold down the fort, pal."

Scotty picked up the envelope containing the title and headed out, while Dan remained at the table and thought about the convenience store video. Having viewed it once, there was something about the fuzzy video and the convenience store owner's story that bothered the detective. He headed to the captain's office. Hardison was gone and Dan said, "I need to talk with Moses Sterling. You know as well as I do sometimes witness stories change, and we need to know if there was a gun." Without missing a beat he said, "Scotty had to run down to the bank. I'm gonna take a ride to the convenience store."

Syms stood. "You can't go down there now. It's pretty hostile territory."

Dan gritted his teeth. "Someone has to, and I'm better off going alone than bringing a posse."

"I can't let you go right now."

Dan squinted at Syms. "I'm going."

The daring detective had a propensity for walking into unfriendly territory. The last time was when he conned Scotty into accompanying him to a pawn shop called Lucky's. That day, nearly two years ago, made even Dan sweat as he retreated from the shop, somehow avoiding being attacked by the store guard's Rottweiler.

Dan got within a block of the convenience store, but the road was closed off to traffic, and a heavy presence of police filled the area. With light rain falling, he opened his umbrella and stopped at the barricade to speak with one of the uniforms. Stating he had to speak with the Moses Sterling, an officer walked with Dan to the store.

There were bars on the windows and door. The rectangular tin sign above the door read: *Sonny's Snacks*

The brazen detective stepped inside where he saw an interior crammed with several rows of merchandise, everything from snacks to necessities. A milk-soft drink cooler was along the back wall, and gum and candy were beneath the cash register counter.

Three customers were inside, two women at the register ready to check out and one man wandering the aisles. Feeling a little out of place, Dan drew leery looks from the regular patrons. He folded his damp umbrella and waited until only he and Moses were inside, Dan approached the shop owner and showed his ID to the man. "Can I ask you a few questions about the robbery?"

Moses sat on a stool behind the counter. To his back were racks of cigarettes. Beside the register were rolls of lottery tickets. "I already talked to the police and they have my video."

"Thank you for that," Dan said. "You're aware the video is quite blurry."

"I bought the darn camera used."

"Tell me what you remember about that day?"

"I was right here when he walked in, came right up to the counter, shoved a gun in my face, and told me to hand him cash."

Remembering the out of focus video never really showed a gun, Dan asked, "Do you remember what kind of gun? Was it long, short?"

Moses thought for a second. The man raised the eyebrows on his wrinkled face. "It was in his pocket."

"Did you actually see the weapon?"

The store owner scratched his head. "Now that you mention it. I don't remember seeing the pistol. He said he had one, and it looked like he did. It all happened so fast."

"Did he have that brown bag when he came in here?"

"No. I took it from under the counter and put money from the register in it."

"Did you ever see him in here before?"

"I get lots of kids, but I think he'd been in here a few times. When I heard his name was Jerricks, I kinda remembered a kid they called Jay. I'm sure it was him."

"Anyone else in here that day who might have been suspicious?"

"Like I said. Kids are always in and out of here."

"How many times have you been robbed?"

"This makes twice. The other one happened a few years ago."

The door swung open as an older woman holding a canvas shopping bag entered the shop. She closed her umbrella and propped it against the counter. The store owner stood. "How are you today, Bessie?" he said as she inched herself forward. "A little wet, but I'm doin' okay. Rain's just about stopped. You can sit, I don't need any help."

Dan asked the store owner. "Do the Knights bother you much?"

"I saw the jacket on that kid, but you know something?" Moses said as he scratched his nearly bald head. "They pretty much stay away from here."

"Pretty much?" Dan replied. "What do you mean?"

"Nothing. They don't bother me."

"You wouldn't lie to me would you? You sure they never give you any trouble?" Dan paused. "Are you paying them to leave you alone?"

"They don't bother me. That's it."

The shop owner stood as Bessie came to check out with her bag of items. Moses scanned them, and placed the food back into the tote. She opened her purse, took out five dollars and handed the money to him. "Have a nice day, Bessie," he said as she took her umbrella and purchases.

"Thank you, Moses," she replied as she exited the store.

Dan watched the woman leave, and then said, "I noticed she gave you a five, but she owed more than ten."

Moses shook his finger at Dan. "You're a sharp young fellow, but that's all she had, and I'd have given the stuff to her for two if that's all she had."

Dan smiled at the man. "Thanks for your help."

As he exited the shop thinking about what Moses had said about the gangs, Dan was sure store owners were paying the thugs business insurance, so why would Jerricks rob the store?

One other thing bothered Dan. If the brown bag had contained money, what happened to the cash?

The rain had stopped and the detective walked back to his car alongside the uniform who had waited outside the store. "It might be calm down here now, but I sense a real storm coming," the patrolman said. "This little rain might just have delayed a flood."

Dan looked down the nearly deserted street. "Kind of an eerie feeling," he replied as he shoved his umbrella inside his car and got in.

CHAPTER 16

A few hours after Dan left the tense neighborhood, a crowd of protesters invaded the streets.

The National Guard and riot teams had again unleashed barrages of tear gas grenades, and streams of water from high-powered hoses. A few cars, including a black and white, had been set on fire. Several looters, and rock throwers were arrested, but thankfully, there was no gunfire. As dawn arrived, the unrest had eased.

Clouds of smoke lingered miles from the area, and the neighborhood streets were strewn with debris. One sign stuck firmly into the ground had a sketch of a white police officer, blood pouring from his chest. In red letters, the troubling marker read: *Devil's blood.*

▲

It was 6:45 a.m. when Dan exited his vehicle in the police lot. Dixon, heading for a squad car raced past the detective. "Where you headed?" Dan yelled.

Dixon stopped and turned to him. "They burned a fucking cruiser last night. I'm going down to check out the damage. It's calm right now. This shit better end."

"I can smell smoke down here. Glad I left when I did," Dan said.

"Left?" Dixon said.

Dan replied, "I talked to Moses Sterling yesterday afternoon. Something isn't right with his story."

"You went down there? You nuts?"

"Maybe. I have to see Syms. Talk to you later?"

A few minutes later, Dan entered the captain's office. "Make it quick. Hardison is coming down here."

"Okay. Moses Sterling. He never really saw a gun. He said Jerricks pointed a weapon at him, but the old man never actually saw it."

Dan started to fill the captain in on the details when Hardison burst into the room and slammed his large fist on the desk. "Christ. Never seen anything like this. The whole fucking city could go up in flames. Rocks and stones are one thing, fire is another, but if it turns to gunfire, those streets will resemble a shooting range. Dixon stormed out of here a few minutes ago and guess what? He told me he can't find Wallace."

"I just saw Dixon," Dan said. "He didn't tell me about Wallace. Anyone contacted Sasser?"

"Good idea," Hardison said.

"I'll take care of that," Syms said.

Hardison breathed hard. "There is one person down there who might be able to help out. I talked with Pastor Jonathan. He's a good man. I know him, and I'm going to see him. He's a voice of reason in that neighborhood. If anyone can stop the chaos, he can." Hardison hastily turned and left the office.

Syms stood. "Time to pay Sasser a visit."

Wait," Dan said. "I'm coming with you."

Syms held his hands out. "Hold it. Sasser will have a bird if he sees you."

"Then let him tweet his ass off. We're coming." Dan looked at the wall clock. "Don't you think it's a bit early? Cool off. I'll call him a little later."

Syms pointed to the door. "That's my job. Just go back to your desk."

Returning to his desk, Dan saw Scotty approaching. "You finally unload the Chevy?"

"Got the cash and already deposited it." Scotty sat at his desk and Dan said, "Listen. I went to the convenience store and spoke with Moses Sterling."

"You did what?"

Dan filled his partner in on the conversation. "A couple of other things you need to know. Wallace is missing. The captain and I are gonna pay Mr. Sasser a visit."

Shortly after nine a.m., Syms rushed to Dan's cube. "Let's go. Sasser is waiting for us."

Hancock Sasser was known to have accepted cocaine for pay, and to have at least one judge in his back pocket. The attorney had gotten several gang members off with hand slaps, and with his connections, he'd managed to get the most violent thugs little jail time. Sasser didn't like Lawyer's Row, so he occupied an office in a small strip plaza on Blue Ridge Avenue.

Nearing the plaza, Dan saw Sasser's sign above the end unit, and said, "That used to be the old Northside Merchant Credit Union."

"Remember it well," Syms replied as he parked his Ford in a *Customers Only* spot. A black Lincoln was in the next space.

They walked to the front entrance where Dan opened the outside door. He and Syms entered a small lobby. A round table, with a few magazines and comic books spread on it, two chairs and an artificial tree that was opposite a bathroom door was all there was. Sasser's office door was ajar. Syms rapped on it and entered before the lawyer could say anything.

Sasser was sitting with his feet resting atop his desk and he had a newspaper spread open in his hands. "What's up?" the attorney asked as he folded the paper and tossed it into a trash bucket.

Dan stepped into the room. "You didn't tell me he was coming," Sasser said to Syms.

"Nice to see you too Hancock," Dan said.

"Have a seat. Like my digs?"

"Well, it's neat," Dan said. "Also pretty empty. Where are your diplomas? All I see is a fedora on the credenza."

"I like it clean and simple. Besides, law degrees are over-rated."

Dan rolled his eyes. "Are you saying you never got one?"

Sasser adjusted the red handkerchief in the pocket of his blue pin-striped Calvin Klein suit. "What do you think I am, an imposter? Damn right I got one. Howard University Law School, and just for the record, I passed the bar on my first try." He pointed to his left and on the wall was his license to practice law. "And it's current too."

Sasser, in his late thirties, slim and dapper, with slicked down hair, was always glib as well.

Syms asked. "Where's your client? Tell us he hasn't skipped town."

Light from the window to Sasser's back cast a glare on his computer screen. "Let me pull the shade. Is that your car next to mine?"

Syms said. "If that Lincoln is yours, then yes."

Sasser yanked the blind down and returned to his desk. "Got a text from him a little while ago. He spent the last two nights with a female friend, didn't tell anyone. He's not going anywhere."

Dan stared at the attorney. "So why the hell are you defending a white cop?"

Sasser sat back and laughed. "What? He's white?"

"Funny," Dan said.

"I'm a respectable attorney, an equal opportunity lawyer. What's wrong with me taking him on?"

"Come on," Dan said. "You've spent your career protecting gang bangers, irritating cops, and freeing criminals."

Sasser again smiled. "Take a good look around. What don't you see?"

"Beats me. This place is pretty empty," Dan replied.

"Exactly. Where the hell do you think I've been for the past nine months? And don't you get smart and say maternity leave."

Dan thought for a second. "Federal protection?"

"Right, Eliot Ness. I'm clean. Haven't done coke in nine months. I was in a clinic in Providence. I'm straight as an arrow, and I'm done with the gang bangers. I think Wallace has a case."

"What makes you say that?" Syms asked.

Sasser fired a verbal shot at the lawmen. "Because whoever is investigating the shooting is incompetent. They haven't done shit yet."

"What are you saying?" An irritated Syms barked.

"Have you seen any witness reports? Anyone bother to talk to the store owner or anyone else?"

Dan pointed his finger at Sasser. "Hold it right there. I talked to Moses Sterling yesterday. He never actually saw a gun."

Sasser unmoved by Dan's finger said, "You got statements from anyone else?"

"Just Wallace," Syms said.

"That's my point. No one's bothered to sift through the neighborhood." Sasser turned to the computer on his desk. "Come around here. I have something interesting to show you."

The lawmen gathered around Sasser as he brought up a video he'd obtained from a witness. Dan got a whiff of cologne that nearly overpowered him. "What the hell did you spray on yourself?"

"It's new, eighty-five bucks for a small bottle. Want a shot?"

"No thanks. It's very nice."

Sasser started the video. "This is the one the press has been playing."

"No shit," Syms said. "It doesn't bode too well for Wallace."

"Right. Take a look at this one that was taken from another angle."

Dan and Syms stared intently at the video.

"See anything?" Sasser asked.

"Holy mother," Dan said. "Damn right. From that angle it looks like Jerricks was moving his hand into the paper bag, but from this angle, his hand clearly isn't in the bag. It's reaching into his pocket."

"And what's in the pocket?"

"Holy shit," Dan said. "Looks like the handle of a gun."

Syms jerked back. "But no gun was found. What the hell? What happened to it?"

Sasser turned to Syms and Dan. "Bingo. Take a look at this other video."

Dan and Syms couldn't believe their eyes as they both saw a young male who was wearing a dark hoodie. The boy was running over to Jerricks fallen body and he lifted the gun out of the pocket, grabbed the brown bag, and fled the scene. It was clear Jerricks indeed had a gun and he was reaching for the weapon. "Where the hell was Wallace when this was happening?" Dan asked.

Sasser said, "As he tells it, right after he shot Jerricks, he went back to his vehicle and called for back-up. He never saw the kid, and everything happened fast. By the time Wallace got back out of his car, a crowd of crazy neighbors were already screaming at him. He waited for help. It's too bad his cameras weren't operating."

"We need these videos," Syms said.

"You sure do, but they don't belong to me."

"So how the hell did you get them?" Syms asked.

"Sources. I have sources."

Dan put his hand on Sasser's shoulder. "Stop the crap. I know you know who gave these to you, so spit it out or we'll subpoena you."

"And what will that do? Okay, relax. Move your damn hand. No need to get hostile."

Sasser opened his desk drawer and pulled out two cell phones. "Here. I had to pay for these. Two hundred each."

"Who do they belong to?" Dan asked.

"Nosy bastard aren't you? I can't tell you. They don't want their names bandied about."

Syms said, "Stop the games, or we will subpoena the phones and you'll have to identify the witnesses. You do realize we can do that, so we'll get them one way or another."

"No need for the legal action. If you guys pony up, I think I can get the video takers to come here and make sworn statements that these are their phones, and they shot the videos."

Dan, still standing by Sasser said, "Hold it. I didn't like one thing you said."

Sasser snickered. "You mean pony up?"

"Not that. You said you *think* you can get them here. I don't want think, I want *will*. You got that?"

Sasser put the phones back in his drawer. "That's what I meant. Will."

Dan smiled at him. "And what exactly did you mean by pony up?"

"I was thinking my Lincoln is already a year old, and I need a new one. It's an image thing, you know. I have to look prosperous around here."

Dan rolled a hand inside his jacket, revealing his sidearm. "Okay Hancock, how about us making nice again?" The attorney eased back in his chair, and Dan added, "So what about the kid in the hoodie? Any line on him?"

"I got a holler out."

"If somebody ID's him, you better clue us in. You need my card?" Dan pulled one out of his jacket and placed it on Sasser's desk. He stuffed another one into Sasser's pocket, squeezing it in with the red handkerchief. "This is in case you lose the other one."

"Hey. You got anything yet on the hit-and-run?" Sasser asked.

"We're working on it. Why?" Dan replied. "You know Biaggio?"

"I know he's an ambulance chaser."

"We know that too. Talk to me about those scams."

"Scams? I object to your supposition!"

"Come on. You know they're insurance company rip-offs, talking uninjured people into suing insurance companies for easy payouts," Dan said.

"Whoa! You're giving personal injury lawyers a bad name."

"We're only interested in one right now. Biaggio. We know doctors are involved, and we know one way Biaggio is getting his clients. He has a rat at an auto repair shop. So tell us what you know about these scams."

Sasser clasped his hands together. "Fellows, I don't know how they do it. I'm not that kind of guy."

Dan couldn't keep a straight face, and he laughed. "You know, I'm beginning to like you. Now cut the bullshit!"

Sasser grinned. "Okay, I may have done a little chasing while I was in my last trimester at law school. You know those loans are steep and paying them off can take half your life." Sasser sat back. "I did some running for a small law firm. I hung out in hospitals and outside courtrooms to hustle clients. The attorney I ran for had a scanner. Actually, he had three of us running for him. It's easy money. Once you nab a client, they're directed to specific doctors who are all paid off by the lawyers. Insurance companies settle fast. They all have dollar amounts that they won't fight. Say ten grand. Costs them more to defend the lawsuit than to pay out the cash."

"They teach you that in law school?"

Sasser laughed. "Yeah. Fraud one-oh-one."

"Thanks for the *off the record* lesson," Dan said.

"You know, I'm beginning to like you guys," Sasser said.

"See you around, pal," Dan said as he and Syms turned to exit Sasser's office.

CHAPTER 17

Phyllis was ready to leave for her office, but she'd noticed the expiration date on Dan's EpiPen had elapsed, so she left him a note.

Dan came downstairs and saw the reminder. He picked it off the counter and read it. *You need to get new EpiPens. The expiration date was three days ago. Stop and get fresh ones. Today!*

He knew there couldn't be any excuses, so he grabbed the pen on the counter and the not so subtle *warning* his adoring wife had left him.

With two EpiPens in his hand, he entered the drugstore and approached the pharmacy counter. "Hi, Sarah. My wife noticed the expiration date on these was a few days ago."

He handed the pens to the young pharmacist. "She's right. We got a batch in yesterday. Let me get you new ones."

She reached under the counter, took a two-pack of pens and handed it to Dan. "What's the expiration date?" he asked.

"These are good for eighteen months."

Dan took out his wallet, pulled out a credit card, swiped it and Sarah handed him a receipt. "I'm curious. What would have happened if I had attempted to use my expired pens?" he asked.

Sarah said, "Good question. Epinephrine slowly loses potency, so there's a chance if you had needed it, the pen may or may not have done its job."

"Thanks Sarah," he said as he turned to exit the drugstore. Upon getting into his car, he opened the sealed pack, placed a new pen in his glovebox and put the other one inside his coat pocket.

When Dan entered the squad room, he saw Scotty who was staring at a photo of the '57 Chevy. "Miss it already?"

"Kind of, but hey, it had to go."

"Just like my muffins," Dan said with a wry grin.

"Remind me to get you a can of nuts."

Dan laughed and pulled out his new EpiPen."I'm ready. Brand new." Placing the medical device back into his jacket pocket he said, "What's happening here this morning?"

"Syms is up with Hardison. Landry and Luke are in the caf."

Dan placed his jacket on the hook in his cube and thought about his visit with Sasser. He had to admit the lawyer seemed to be telling the truth about kicking the cocaine habit as his eyes were clear and he stayed on point. Dan and Sasser had gone down the road a few times, and the detective had to wonder why the slick attorney had let him off the hook last time.

It was only a little over a year ago when Sasser had threatened to file charges against Dan for planting evidence inside a truck owned by one of Sasser's clients, a charge the detective knew would stick, but for some reason, Sasser never did follow through. Maybe it was because Dan dropped the charges against the suspect.

Dan and Syms had heard an earful and the detective still couldn't wrap his head around the attorney's claim that he'd turned his practice away from gangs and street thugs, and was now on the right side of the law.

Dan returned to Scotty's cube and sat beside him. "Syms and I had quite a visit with Sasser. The guy is some piece of work."

After telling his partner about the chat, Dan said, "Time to check in with you know who."

The captain had returned from Hardison's office a few minutes earlier, and Syms pointed to the two chairs opposite his desk as the detectives marched in. "Park it," he ordered.

"You tell Hardison about our visit with Sasser?" Dan asked.

"I did, but the chief is focused on the board. He and the mayor met with them and they're finally getting their shit together." Syms rocked back in his chair. "Hardison talked with Pastor Jonathan as well, and he thinks the well-respected church leader can help keep the community calm. They think of him as a Martin Luther King kind of person. He's good with the kids. From what I hear he's kept several out of trouble."

"Speaking of calm," Dan said. "There is something strange about what has and hasn't happened. If Jerricks was a member of the Knights, why has the gang been so silent?"

Syms sat back. "Interesting."

It was a question possibly only the head of the gang unit could answer. "We're gonna go see what Garcia has to tell us," Dan said.

Dan and Scotty entered Garcia's office where the captain was standing at a water cooler, pouring himself a cup.

Captain Hector Garcia's face had been scarred from a knife incident when he was eighteen. Garcia had been a gang member and his own hoodlum brothers raped his sister. That was the moment he knew he had to get out and he had to fight the gang leader. Twenty-three years later, to this day, Garcia's only regret was leaving the bastard with broken ribs, and a head gash.

"Hey," Dan said. "Got a few minutes?"

Garcia chugged the water and dropped the paper cup into a basket. "Have a seat guys," he said as he returned to the chair behind his desk.

"Got a question for you," Dan said. "Where are the Knights? If Jerricks were a member, then why would he have robbed the store? I know Moses Sterling and all the other shop owners are paying insurance."

"You're right." Garcia said. "My guys have been sniffing out some answers. Seems like Jerricks wasn't exactly in good standing with the gang. He was sort of a renegade, did what he wanted to do."

Dan said, "They deal with that stuff pretty harshly, don't they?"

"Normally his ass would have been found in a dumpster by now, but he had one thing the gang wanted. He had a source for weapons, but my guys tell me the gang had plans to execute him."

Dan put his hands up to his face. "So Wallace did them a favor?"

Garcia rubbed his chin. "I suppose you could say that."

"Thanks," Dan said as he and Scotty stood. "Let us know if you hear anything."

What Dan and Scotty had learned about Jerricks and the Knights was startling. They had to tell Syms and Hardison. Returning to the squad room, Dan peered down the corridor to Syms's empty office. "Seen the captain?" Dan said to Landry.

"He's up with the chief."

"Let's go," Dan said to Scotty.

Hardison's office was exceptionally neat, every paper on his desk was stacked in a specific order. The large office had a forty-two inch TV mounted on the wall. A long credenza underneath the TV displayed pictures of Hardison's deceased wife, his two sons, and three grandkids.

Dan and Scotty knocked on the chief's open door. "This looks like trouble, as if we haven't got enough already," Hardison said.

"Got some interesting news," Dan said.

Hardison made room at the round table where he and Syms had been chatting. "Have a seat, you two."

Dan said, "Talked with Garcia. He told us Jerricks was an outlier. The Knights had bad plans for him. Wallace may have done the gang a favor."

Hardison peered out his window. "What?"

"Garcia thinks that's why the gang's been silent so far."

"Heard you talked to that store owner. I also heard about your visit with Sasser," the chief said.

Dan smirked. "He's a barrel of laughs that guy, smart though, I'll give him that."

"What about Biaggio? Anything new?"

Shrugging, Dan said, "He's trouble. He also has a couple of goons who protect him."

"Be careful," the chief said.

Dan knew what Hardison meant. *Don't you dare go rogue again.* "Yes sir," the detective replied.

CHAPTER 18

Dan remembered seeing a photo of Biaggio's family and something registered with the detective. He tapped Scotty's desk. "How's this hit you? Biaggio's son Rocco has long dark hair. He could have been driving the Jaguar." Dan paused. "Wouldn't be the first time a lawyer's kid got into a mess, and daddy got him out of it. Biaggio could be protecting his son."

"True," Scotty replied.

Putting his hands on his partner's shoulders, Dan said, "I want to get a CD from the kid's SUV and match the prints to the Marley one in our possession. That might put Rocco Biaggio behind the wheel, and it may make the lawyer sweat up a storm."

"Even if we do get a match, it would only be circumstantial evidence, might not prove anything," Scotty said.

"Right, but it's worth a try. If the prints on the discs match, then Biaggio will have to explain how the Marley CD ended up inside the Jag."

"You wanna run this by Syms?"

"I don't want to, but better he hears about it now rather than later. Stay here, let me handle him."

"Oh no. I want to see this show."

Dan's gut feelings didn't always prove right. The one time he was dead wrong had nearly cost him his life. The scar on his chest was a reminder of the days he'd spent in Woodland Hospital, after a .22 caliber bullet had been surgically removed. That standoff with Biggie Littlefield didn't have to occur, but the detective's resistance to call for back-up had put him in grave danger. Only after the gunshot had felled Dan, did he regret abandoning protocol.

Scotty was silent and Dan smiled while approaching the captain.

"What are you gloating about?" Syms asked. "I can tell this conversation is going to require Advil."

"Take it easy. I need to run something by you. It's Biaggio and one of his kids."

Syms sat back and twirled the pill bottle in his hand. "Go ahead."

The captain listened to Dan's plan. Syms cringed, sat forward, glared at him, and raised his voice. "Bullshit! Don't you pull any of your crap!" The captain paused. "Great. Now it's breaking and entering."

"Not if the door is open," Dan smugly replied.

"What are you going to do, follow the car around?"

"Not really. It should be in the high school lot."

Syms opened the plastic bottle and removed two tablets. "No way. You get your evidence some other legit way. Get out, and take your silent partner with you."

The detectives headed back to the squad room. "Not cool, Dan," Scotty said.

Dan rubbed his chin. "We have to see someone."

"Who's that?"

"Hampton."

"Oh no."

"Oh yes. You got a better idea? Hampton considers it a hobby. I'm sure we'll find him at the doughnut shop, but first I need to get the license number of Rocco Biaggio's car."

Dan went to his computer, tapped into the Motor Vehicles data base, learned the SUV was registered to Angelo Biaggio, and wrote down the plate number. He tapped Scotty on the shoulder. "Got the tag number, let's go see Hampton."

Hampton, by his count, had stolen more than forty vehicles, and had been paid by the local chop shop enough to eke out a living. He'd stolen a few Jags and other high-ticket rides for money, but his own joyrides were of his choosing, not his employers.

As soon as the detectives entered the doughnut shop, Dan spotted Hampton, who was sitting with a friend at a table in the corner. The aroma of coffee, and baked goods hit Dan's nose. Three customers were in the order line. "Grab me a cup. I can use a second," Dan said to his partner. "I'm gonna talk to Hampton."

"How about a muffin?" Scotty asked.

"Funny, pal."

The car thief stood as Dan approached. "Jesus, be Jesus, what the heck are you doing here? You ain't got a warrant have you?"

Dan waved his hands at Hampton. "Sit down. I came to chat."

Hampton introduced his friend Rollin, who sported a gray beard, red bandana, tattoos on his arms and neck, and gold earrings. His Harley jacket labeled him as a redneck and he never cracked a smile. "Nice to meet you," Dan said. "Mind if I borrow your buddy for a few minutes?"

Hampton got up and followed Dan to a nearby table. Scotty joined them, placing two hot cups on the table. "Want another coffee?" Dan asked Hampton.

"No. I know you didn't come down here to buy me coffee."

"Right. You know Scotty?"

"Hey Scotty. What's he up to?"

"Good to see you. Been a while. I don't get down to the tank as often as my partner."

Dan blew on his drink and took a healthy chug. "Got a deal for you," he said to Hampton.

"What am I stealing?" Hampton's eyes opened wide and he grinned. "Oh, man I hope it's a Ferrari?"

Dan smiled. "No it's an SUV."

"A what? I don't steal crap like that."

"Let me back up. I don't want you to steal the car. I only want you to break into it and take a few music discs."

"Say what?"

"You heard me."

"So what's the deal?"

Dan took out a pad and pen and wrote down the description of the vehicle, license number and likely location, Conrad High School. "Here, this is all you need to know. I'll give you ten bucks for each CD and a bonus if you find a Bob Marley one."

"Ten? You think I work for cheese? What if I get caught?"

"What are you? A frickin' lawyer now?" Dan asked.

"Hell no. They steal more than me."

Always quick on his feet, Dan immediately thought about Sasser and the lawyer's comment about needing a new Lincoln. "What do you think a year-old Lincoln will bring you at the chop shop?"

"Might be prime. You know they don't all get chopped. Some go straight to a boat and end up overseas somewhere. Might be a grand, fifteen-hundred."

Dan chugged the rest of his coffee. "So if you do me this favor, I can get you an easy Lincoln to cash in on. I'll tell you where it will be, and I'll even keep the owner busy while you drive it away."

Hampton grinned at Dan. "So whose car is it?"

"Someone who did me dirty once."

"Must have been some mud bath."

"One more thing. Be sure to wear gloves when you grab those discs. You call me when you have them and we'll pick them up here. What's your cell?"

Hampton took out his phone and Dan wrote the number on the back of his own business card. "How soon?" Hampton asked.

"Tomorrow morning. Get the discs and then we'll set up the Lincoln. I'll call you first thing."

"No need. It'll be done by nine. I'm an early riser."

"I appreciate that, but I'll check in with you anyway. Okay?"

"Have it your way."

With a barely touched cup in front of him, Dan got up. "I'm gonna dump this," he said.

"Mine's empty. Let me have yours. I'll trash them."

As the detectives were leaving, Hampton said, "Wait Dan. How about an advance? Me and Rollin are goin' to OTB to bet on the horses."

Dan stopped, pulled out his wallet and handed Hampton a twenty. "That's for you." The detective pointed to Rollin. "He's on his own. Tomorrow. You forget and I'll be here with a posse to drag you down to the tank."

"I got it. Never welshed on a deal. My word is solid."

Back in Dan's car, Scotty said, "Syms was right. You're going rogue again."

"Wrong. We're going rogue. Enjoy the trip, pal."

Chapter 19

Dan had to make sure the car thief was ready to do the job. At seven-forty a.m., from his desk, he called Hampton. "Hey, you up?" he asked.

"What time is it? I'm up now."

"I thought you said you were an early riser. It's nearly quarter to eight."

"I am, but me and Rollin got a little buzzed at OTB last night."

Dan sighed. "You win or did you spend my money on booze?"

"Hell. I won three big ones. Had to celebrate."

"Damn it. You sober?"

"Yup. Not too sure about Rollin. Reminds me, he has to pick me up."

"Jesus Christ. Get moving and if Rollin is still in the bag, call me, and I'll pick you up."

Dan heard a laugh. "Forgot, he's here on the couch. I'll be there in an hour."

"You remember where?"

Dan heard a yawn. "Conrad," Hampton replied. "Don't have a bird, boss."

"Call me as soon as the job is done."

"You sound like my old boss."

"Really? You had a boss? You had a real job?"

"You're gonna make me late if you keep talking. See you later."

Scotty entered the squad room with a Tupperware container in his hand. "This should shut you up for a while," he said to his partner. Placing it on Dan's desk, Scotty removed the top. "Orange-cranberry."

"Do I get all six?"

"Only one, but you better choose the right one because five have nuts."

Dan laughed. "Asshole," he said as he plucked a muffin from the container. "I just called Hampton to make sure he's on the job. He should be on his way soon."

Hampton was indeed a man of his word and he'd gotten into the SUV. Ninety minutes later, Dan's cell vibrated. Answering it, he said, "Hampton, you got the discs?"

"Sure do."

"You wear gloves?"

"Still have them on."

"Good. How many discs did you take?"

"Don't know?"

"What do you mean you don't know? Do you have them or don't you?"

"They're in the console."

Dan heard brakes screeching.

"Hold on. I ran a stop sign."

"Stop sign? Where the hell are you?"

"On my way back to the doughnut shop. Rollin dropped me. He has my car."

Dan didn't like the sound of that remark "Hampton, you didn't … Did you?"

"I had to see how one of these shit-boxes ride. Let me tell you, I'm not too impressed. Wouldn't let my kid drive one."

Dan shouted into the phone. "Great! You get that car back to the school right now, and have your buddy pick you up. All I asked is one simple thing. Hampton, get those discs and be at the doughnut shop in an hour. You have a kid?"

"Okay, okay. Calm down. This thing needs shocks. No, I don't have a kid, but if I did, he wouldn't have one of these things."

Taking a deep breath, Dan relaxed his voice. "You didn't bust the ignition did you?"

He heard Hampton laugh. "Old tech, my man. These new cars all have push button. I have a power amplifier. Easy as pie. I can get you one of these things for ten bucks."

"Call me as soon as you get to the doughnut shop." Dan ended the call, and turned to his partner. "You won't believe what Hampton did?"

Scotty rolled his eyes. "I have a pretty good idea."

Landry had entered the room as Dan was talking to Hampton, and asked. "What was that all about?"

"Nothing." Dan said. "Scotty's got muffins. Dig in." *Should have known. Should have known Hampton wouldn't just break into a car. Should have known he'd steal it.* Dan finished his muffin and waited. An hour passed and his cell rang again. "Hampton. You put that car back? Are you where you're supposed to be?"

"Yup. Rollin came and got me."

"Got the discs?"

"In a bag. Come get them. And bring cash."

Dan turned to Scotty. "Let's go. He's got the goods."

The detectives entered the doughnut shop. Dan walked over to Hampton and Rollin who were seated at their usual table. "Hi Rollin," Dan said. "We need to have another chat with your friend."

Hampton sipped his coffee and looked at Dan, "It's okay, boss, he knows the deal."

"Where's the bag?" Dan asked.

Hampton reached to his left and handed it to Dan who looked inside, but without gloves, didn't remove any discs. "How many?"

"I counted fifteen. You said ten apiece."

"Any Marleys?"

Hampton furrowed his brows. "Beats me."

Dan opened his wallet and shoved a twenty on the table. "You'll get the rest after you steal the Lincoln. Kind of like collateral."

"So when do I get the Lincoln?" Hampton asked.

"Tomorrow. I'll get you the details. Give me your number again. And what exactly did you do before you took up stealing cars as a career?"

"Sold Harley's. Me, and Rollin worked for a shop until we quit."

Dan rolled his eyes. "Quit. You quit, like just left, or like was asked to leave?"

Hampton looked at Rollin. "You remember?"

Rollin threw his hands up and shrugged. "Memory isn't that good."

"Okay you clowns, I get it," Dan said as he turned to Hampton. "About the Lincoln. I'll call you with the details."

Hampton nodded. "Can't wait."

With the bag containing the discs in his hand, Dan said to Scotty, "Let's get these over to the lab."

As they headed to Farmington, Scotty said, "You really gonna have Hampton steal Sasser's Lincoln?"

"Bet your ass. Sasser is going to learn not to yank my chain. He said he wants a new Lincoln, and he's gonna get one."

When the detectives arrived at the lab and went upstairs, Dan spotted Aki who was standing at the counter. "How's it going?" Dan asked as he placed the bag in front of the forensics specialist.

"Great. What's in here?" Aki asked.

Dan opened the bag. "I need to have these jewel cases and music discs checked for prints. I think they will match those on the Marley CD that we'd had you examine before."

Aki put on latex gloves and removed the discs from the bag, placing them on the counter.

Dan saw the top disc. "Taylor Swift. Let's see the pile."

Aki spread the discs out. The pile included Justin Timberlake, Bieber, another Swift, Alabama, Sugarland, and other like kinds of music. "Damn! Nothing remotely like Reggae," Dan said.

"Still want me to check?" Aki asked.

"Yeah," Dan replied. Never know."

Aki restacked the discs. "You log these downtown?"

"What do you think? It's faster if I bring them here."

"Okay. I'll log them and send you a report."

"How soon?"

"Probably have it to you in a day or two."

"Thanks," Dan said. "You married yet?"

Aki grinned. "Soon. I gave Mayu a ring and she's planning a big wedding."

"Going to invite us?" Dan asked.

"You want to pay your way to Kyoto? That's where her family lives."

"Maybe we'll pass. Congratulations. Where's your folks?"

"They're here, but the rest of my relatives are in Osaka, about an hour from Kyoto. You'd love Japan."

Dan smiled. "Send me an invite."

"Will do. You realize you'll have to send a gift."

"On second thought," Dan said. "I'd keep the wedding to family."

Aki laughed, picked up the bag and headed inside the lab.

Returning to headquarters, Dan and Scotty approached the captain's office. "Hey," Dan said as he rapped on Syms's door.

"Since when are you so polite?" Syms asked. "What did you guys do? I can see you're intent on raising my stress level. So what's on your minds?"

"Biaggio," Dan said. "We ran some evidence down to the lab for a prints check."

"What evidence?"

"A few CD cases that belong to Biaggio's kid."

Syms toyed with his Advil as he sat back and closed his eyes. "You did obtain those items legally, right?"

Dan replied, "Of course. Actually we didn't take them. They were given to us by an anonymous snitch."

Syms opened his eyes and focused on Scotty. "Oh no, not me," Scotty said. "Dan is right. The items were given to us."

Syms rubbed his forehead. "Okay. So let's say the prints match the ones inside the Jag. What does that prove? You can't say for sure Biaggio's kid was driving."

"True," Dan said. "But if we build a big enough fire, Biaggio's likely to get burned."

Syms stood. "Okay, but you better be careful not to light too many matches or you clowns might get singed too."

Chapter 20

Dan saw a message on his computer. Opening an email from Aki, he read it. Disappointed to see Rocco Biaggio's prints didn't match those on the discs taken from the Jaguar, he said, "Damn it." Those words were loud enough for Scotty to hear.

"Now what?" Scotty asked.

"Dan stood at his partner's desk. "Rocco's prints don't match the ones in the Jag."

Scotty shook his head. "You don't suppose the Jag really was stolen?"

"I know it wasn't stolen."

Hardison stomped his way past the detectives and headed to Syms's office. Seconds later, Dan and Scotty both heard Hardison's loud voice resonating down the corridor. "What the hell is that all about?" Dan uttered. "I gotta find out. You coming?"

"Not me. We'll find out soon enough."

As he walked toward the captain's office, Dan saw Hardison's hands waving like a windmill, profanity echoing down the hall.

Dan entered the office as four-letter words spewed like a volcano from the chief's mouth. The detective noticed every light on the captain's desk phone lit. He also saw fire in both Hardison's and Syms's eyes. "What the hell is it now?" Dan asked.

Hardison pointed to the TV. "Look what that fucking lawyer did. I'll string him up by his balls."

Dan watched. "Are you serious? Sasser leaked those to the press?"

"Leaked?" Syms yelled. "I suppose that sleaze ball lawyer thinks he's doing us a favor by releasing those to the press, but I think he just shit on us. Makes us look like a bunch of incompetents."

"I spoke with Fernandez and she's off the wall too. I'm not answering any phone calls." Hardison started to exit Syms's office. "I need to see Pastor Jonathan," the chief said as he reached the door.

"I'm gonna wring Sasser's neck," Syms said as he stood and donned his jacket.

"Hold it," Dan said. "I have plans to see him later. Let's go then."

"Hell. Later that idiot will be downstairs in handcuffs."

Dan held his hands up. "Hold on. Wait. I have to make a phone call, and then we can go see Sasser. You look like you might shoot him."

"Might? I'm thinking about it. Make it quick," the captain said.

Dan went back to his partner. "What the hell was that about? Hardison stormed past me like a hurricane," Scotty said.

"Our good friend Hancock Sasser released those videos, and they're all over the news. Syms wants to go down and shoot him."

"So where's Hardison off to?"

"He's off to see Pastor Jonathan again."

Dan held his cell phone and called Hampton. The car thief answered on the first ring. "Hampton," Dan said. "You ready to grab a Lincoln?"

"I'm set."

"I'll call you right back. I need to make sure the car will be there. Hang loose for a few."

Dan then called Sasser. "What's up Dan?" the attorney asked.

"Up? You know damn well what's up. The jig is up. Syms and I are on our way to your office."

"Not good. I have an appointment."

"Cancel it. We're coming down and you better be there."

"I can't just cancel an important appointment."

"Who's it with?"

"Lighten up my man. I need a trim."

"You have a fucking hair appointment? Cancel it or Syms will give you a haircut with a machete."

"Okay, okay, come on down."

"That's more like it, buddy."

Dan called Hampton back. "We're on. The Lincoln will be there. Scotty will pick you up at the doughnut shop."

Scotty tugged Dan's arm. "Here comes Syms."

"Now," the captain said. "Let's go filet a fish."

Dan whispered to Scotty. "Go pick up Hampton at the doughnut shop and drive him to Sasser's." Dan joined the captain as they headed to the parking lot. "Let's take my car," the detective said.

The ten minute drive to Sasser's must have seemed like an hour to Syms as the captain anxiously tapped his feet all the way. Dan parked his Accord next to Sasser's Lincoln, and he and Syms marched to the front door and tore into Sasser's office where the lawyer was sitting in his familiar position with his feet on his desk.

Syms lunged at him, and Dan held the captain back. "You bastard," the captain yelled. What the hell are you doing?"

Never one to sweat, Sasser pulled his legs down and raised his hands. "Relax, have a seat. Let me explain something to you."

"Oh this ought to be some explanation," Syms said. "Hardison is with Pastor Jonathan right now."

"Good. I spoke with Jonathan earlier."

Dan pointed his finger at Sasser. "You were supposed to get me those videos. What happened?"

"That's what I'm going to tell you." Sasser pulled two pieces of paper from his drawer along with the cell phones. "Here, these are yours. I got signed affidavits from Ames Tatum, and Jerome Smith. They're willing to testify if need be."

"So why didn't you call me?" Dan asked.

"I knew you would try to stop me."

"Nice guess," Syms yelled. "So you went to the TV asses anyway."

Keeping an eye on the window in back of Sasser, Dan spotted Hampton and Scotty. Dan stood and pulled his Smith and Wesson from his holster.

Sasser jumped up. "What the fuck? Put that thing back."

Dan placed the weapon back where it belonged. His eyes stared right into Sasser's. "Is the press paying you?"

Sasser leaned into Dan and their faces were a few inches apart. Anger in his voice, the attorney barked, "Are you crazy? Jesus no. Think about it. Once the TV stations play the videos a few times, and word spreads that Jerricks did have a gun and could well have shot at Wallace, then it might change that tune. Know what I mean?"

Dan eased off. "Maybe I do, but don't you pill anymore shit."

Sasser sat and calmly said, "It's not shit. I got a name, the kid with the hoodie who stole the gun. Devon McCray. He's a street kid, fifteen, and from what I hear, he's a juvie with one robbery charge, but you won't find it. Those juvie records are sealed. I think I can get the weapon Jerricks was carrying."

Dan glanced out the window again and he saw Sasser's Lincoln enter the street. "So where's Wallace?" the detective said as he sat.

Sasser replied. "I got him in a safe place, and I think he'll be cleared in a few days unless the board, and some of your stiff-ass legal eagles stall until they cause a real riot."

Syms replied. "You got that part right. Our internal system is piss-poor slow. Maybe they'll get the message and finally do something."

"What about the gun and that kid Devon? You going to get him to come in? We'll have to charge him you know," Dan said.

"Okay. I'll get him to come in."

Dan knew the Lincoln was gone so he extended his hand to Sasser. "Thanks. We'll be in touch, buddy."

Syms rose from his chair. "Dan's right. We'll be in touch."

Dan and Syms stepped into the hallway and the captain pointed to the bathroom. "I gotta take a leak."

"Go ahead," Dan said. "I'll pull my car around and pick you up in front."

CHAPTER 21

Scotty carried a soft brown attaché into the squad room and placed the case on Dan's table. "Open it. I think you'll find this interesting."

Dan unzipped the case and pulled out a computer. "You get a new laptop?"

"Kind of. This belongs to Sasser. I grabbed it from the front seat of his Lincoln before Hampton stole the car."

"Did he have any trouble getting into it?"

"Fricking guy is a magician. That device he has is amazing. By the way, you owe me fifty bucks. I made a deal with Hampton and you don't owe him more for the discs."

Dan grinned, opened his wallet and handed his partner the cash. "The guy's a pisser isn't he?" Dan placed the computer back inside the case. "We have to get this back to Sasser."

"And how the hell are we going to do that?" Scotty asked. "What are we going to do? Drop it back on his desk, or have some homeless person you know bring it to him?"

"I don't know. I mean he could have important stuff on here. I don't feel bad about taking his car, but the computer is a different story."

"I don't know what might have been in the trunk," Scotty said.

The resourceful Dan thought for a second. "Got an idea. We're gonna see an old friend."

Scotty shrugged. "You sure have a lot of old friends. Which one is it this time?""

"Dewey."

"Pawn Shop Dewey? Think he'll take it?"

"He'll take it."

"So you're gonna pawn it?"

"Sort of. I'm gonna give it to him and have him call Sasser to let the attorney know the computer had been pawned."

Scotty grinned. "Sounds good to me."

Dan saw Dixon leaving Syms's office, and he stopped the traffic division captain. "What's going on now?" Dan asked.

"You want to hear something funny?" Dixon replied. "Hancock Sasser's Lincoln was stolen sometime yesterday."

Dan stealthily put the laptop down, sliding it inside Scotty's cube. "Really? I was in Sasser's office yesterday with Syms."

"I know."

"Obviously Sasser is pissed. Hope he has good insurance. Anything valuable in the car?"

"His laptop. There were a bunch of Tee's in the trunk that were for a kid's basketball team he was sponsoring."

Syms appeared. "In my office, gentlemen."

Dan and Scotty followed the captain who shut the door behind the detectives. He eyed Dan and then turned to Scotty. "You're a detective, right?"

Scotty's face went blank. "If you say so."

"Let me ask you something? Don't you find it a little strange two law enforcement officers like Dan and me were inside Hancock Sasser's office, and magically the attorney's car was stolen? It was there when we visited him." Syms pivoted to Dan. "Don't you tell me you had something to do with it, cause if you did, I don't want to hear it." The momentary silence in the room was deafening. Syms eyed Dan once again. "So did you?"

Dan threw his hands up. "No, I'm shocked you think I would break the law. Maybe that gang of teen car thieves stole it."

"Put those hands down! Don't play with me. You know Sasser said he could use a new Lincoln. Is this your way of having his insurance company pay for a new one?"

Dan dropped his hands to his side. He knew his next line was a lie. "Wow, I never would have thought of that, but it's brilliant. I still think it was those kids."

Syms picked up his pill bottle and washed down two tablets, then he pointed to the door. "Get out."

The detectives exited. "Come on, let's get down to Dewey's," Dan said.

"He knows."

"No shit, but I think Syms likes the move. Grab your jacket."

When they arrived at the pawn shop, Dan noticed a hulking guard by the front door. A ring of pawn balls hung next to Dewey's gold and silver sign above the entrance. There were iron bars on the windows and the blinking red sign in the window flashed *OPEN.*

Dan and Dewey had a long history. Despite the proprietor's propensity for taking in stolen goods, the detective had always turned his head away from the hot items spread throughout the shop. However, Dan's ignoring Dewey's wrongdoings didn't translate into a clean arrest record for the shop owner. He'd been closed down on a couple of occasions, but restocking was never a problem.

When the detectives entered the busy store, Dan was toting the computer case and he spotted Dewey who was standing behind the counter straight ahead. Dan saw the usual assortment of electronics, jewelry, and other goods. He knew most of the items had been pawned by thieves.

Employees were tending to customers and Dewey, who had just handed a patron a pawn ticket, smiled as his visitors approached him. Dewey's cap covered his nearly bald head, and earrings dangled from both of the skinny man's ears. He extended his multi-ringed hand to Dan. "Long time no see, you need another gun?"

"No. By the way. I noticed the guard. Nice touch."

"Keeps the kids out."

"You remember Scotty?" Dan asked.

Scotty shook Dewey's hand. "How's the chemo going?"

"Still in remission. I may make it to my fiftieth," Dewey said as he leaned over the counter and looked into Dan's eyes. "So, what little favor do you want this time? Never told me what happened to the Pico."

The last time Dan had been to the shop, he'd purchased that gun, an undocumented sale of an untraceable weapon. "Can't tell you Dewey. Let's just say it was put to good use." Dan paused. "And just how old are you?"

"Forty-two. Don't look a day over sixty, right? So now you want to tell me what you did with the Pico?"

"Can't," Dan said. "I'd have to shoot you if I told you." Dan hid the truth he'd planted the weapon in a vehicle in order to get a felon to rat on friends. "So how's business?"

"Can't complain." Dewey replied as he eyed the case. "What's that?"

Dan placed it on the counter where Dewey opened it and pulled out the laptop. "It's a gift from me to you," Dan said.

Dewey shook his head. "Right. Tell me a story. Who does it really belong to?"

Dan leaned over the counter. "I need a favor."

"Isn't that what you always want?"

"This one's special. You know Hancock Sasser?"

Dewey laughed. "You shitting me. This is his?" Dewey inspected the computer and saw a sticker on the back that had Sasser's name.

"Keep it down. It seems his car was stolen yesterday and this was in it."

"So you got the car and I get the computer?"

Dan said, "Come closer and listen. We don't know shit and you don't know shit either. All I want you to do is take the computer and call Sasser to tell him it's here."

"What do I say? Some dude pawned your computer?"

"Perfect. That's exactly what I want you to say."

Dewey placed the laptop back into its case. "I have to tag it. You owe me."

Dan turned and made a three-sixty around the store with his eyes. "I just paid you back. I bet if Scotty and I checked close enough we could find, let's say, a lot of funny stuff in here. Right?"

Dewey grinned. "You're okay for a cop. See you around."

Dan smiled at Dewey. "That's my man. Thanks."

CHAPTER 22

The videos Sasser had given to the press temporarily eased tension in the neighborhood. However, the bombshell that reared its ugly head this day was the release of Wallace's police record: one showing he'd made a traffic stop, beaten a black man, and broken the guy's arm. That news sparked a new outrage.

Hardison was once again in Syms's office, and Dan saw the chief's arms flailing away. It was clear to the detective something had riled the chief. As Dan neared the captain's office, he again heard four-letter words coming from Hardison's mouth. "It's about to blow," Hardison yelled.

"What now?" Dan asked.

Hardison replied, "The mayor is through the roof, and we've got a storm brewing. Some shit-ass reporter dug up the story about Wallace's incident with that black suspect. God damn it," the chief snapped. "Freaking press." Hardison put his hands on the desk. "I spoke with Pastor Jonathan again and he's concerned he may not be able to be the voice of reason much longer. The Guard is on stand-by, and the riot squad is on alert too. The mayor wants to have a press conference tomorrow morning at ten sharp." Hardison eyed Syms. "You get the auditorium set up."

"What about Wallace?" Dan asked.

"Sasser needs to bring him in."

Hardison stomped out of the captain's office as Scotty entered it. "Nice mess," Syms said. "Mayor Fernandez says the army will

96

be ready if need be. We have our own guys to worry about. I can't believe this shit." Syms opened his pill bottle and swallowed a couple of tablets. "I need to call Sasser. He needs to be here with Wallace and the video takers."

"I'll call him and make sure he does what we tell him to do," Dan said.

"If he balks," Syms said. "Tell him Hardison will beat the sleazy attorney's ass with a battering ram. I gotta go get the auditorium set up."

Syms exited his office with the detectives following him. The captain headed to the auditorium while Dan and Scotty settled in at Dan's cube. "I'm calling Sasser," Dan said. The attorney's phone rang, but there was no answer and Dan didn't bother to leave a message. "I'm calling his cell. He better answer this one."

On the second ring, Sasser answered. "Hey, my friend," he said. "Before you get your ass fired up, it wasn't me who leaked the story."

"We know. It was a reporter. Listen. Hardison is setting up a press conference tomorrow morning here at ten. You need to be here with your client and the two witnesses who shot those videos. And bring the kid who stole the gun. Hardison is gonna get the Pastor here."

"Hey, it's not easy without my car."

"You need a ride? We'll have a cruiser pick you up."

"A black and white! Hell no. I ain't riding in one like a criminal."

"What do you want, an Uber?"

"Horse crap. I want a damn stretch limo."

"Here's the bottom line. You be here by nine o'clock with your friends, or Hardison will come after you with an axe. Got that?"

"Cool down, cowboy. I'm getting a ride to the rental place. See you in the morning."

Dan hung up and turned to his partner. "He'll be here."

CHAPTER 23

Girl Scout cookies were on the kitchen island and Dan's face lit up when he spotted a green and white box of thin mints. He also noticed the smile on Kate's face. "Thanks sweetheart," the adoring father said.

"There are three more in there," the little girl said, pointing to the cabinet to the left of the refrigerator.

Josh said, "Mom won't let us open them."

"Right," Phyllis said as she looked at her children. "After dinner you can each have two cookies."

"How many can I have?" Dan asked.

"Two, big boy."

"Connie go home early?"

"It's her cards night."

"We went to the dentist today," Phyllis said. "We have to talk later."

Dan didn't like the sound of that comment. "Talk?"

Josh said, "I'm getting braces."

Dan rolled his eyes, then looked straight at his wife.

Phyllis shied away. "Time for dinner," she said.

After dinner, Dan sat in his lounger and watched TV. He knew bad news was coming. Phyllis waited until the kids had gone to bed, before she entered the den. Dan said. "So what's the deal with the braces?"

She showed him a pamphlet from the dentist's office. "Dr. Zerling says Josh has an overbite and the doctor recommended an orthodontist."

"Really? Braces cost a fortune."

Phyllis paused. "Kate has an overbite too."

"Double great," Dan said. "Every kid has an overbite. I had an overbite, and I never had braces. My teeth are fine."

"Kate's can wait. Josh should have them now."

"I don't buy that crap," Dan said as he got up. "I'm going to get my cookies now."

"Hold it," she said. "You're being selfish."

Dan raised his voice a notch. "Selfish? I think the dentists are being selfish. It's all about money. What a scam. Why didn't Mike have braces? I'm sure he has an overbite, but our old dentist never recommended them for him."

"Calm down. We haven't even seen the orthodontist yet. And our old dentist retired."

"How much did Zerling say they cost?"

"He said about three thousand."

Dan felt his blood pressure rising. "Each?"

"Yes," Phyllis said as she quietly left the room.

"Where are you going?" Dan said. "We're not done talking."

"Upstairs."

Dan threw his hands in the air. "I can see I'm not going to win this argument. Wait a minute," he said. "Come back here, please."

Phyllis turned back and faced Dan. "You'll consider it?" she said.

He put his arms around her. "I guess so."

She kissed him. "I'm going up to read."

"I'll be up in a while. Maybe you can take a break between chapters."

Phyllis smiled. "Better make it soon, or the library might be closed."

Chapter 24

Another night of violence in the troubled neighborhood had occurred. The National Guard and a reinforced riot squad quelled the upheaval. While the north corner of the city was on the brink of exploding, Mayor Fernandez waited patiently with Pastor Jonathan and Hardison in the chief's office. Syms and Dixon, both wearing their dress uniforms, entered the office. Hardison, similarly decked out in his dress blues, stood with his back to the door while looking out onto Bushwell Park. Turning to Syms, he said, "This better go well, or we'll all be fighting to keep this city from total destruction."

⬥

It was nearing nine a.m. Dan and Scotty were stationed in the back parking lot. "Sasser better show soon," Dan said. He took a few steps and saw a car entering the lot. The sedan parked next to Syms's Ford.

"That's him," Scotty said.

Sasser, Wallace, and three other people got out of the attorney's rented vehicle. They were Jerome Smith, Ames Tatum, and Devon McCray.

"Hey," Dan said to Sasser as the detective eyed the Cadillac. "Didn't they have any Lincolns?"

Sasser cracked a smile. "I took what they had, not a bad ride. I see the pastor is here. That's his car next to the black Accord."

"Introduce the crowd," Dan said.

The attorney made the introductions and then opened the vehicle's trunk. He retrieved his briefcase and laptop. Turning to Wallace, he said. "How about taking our witnesses up to Hardison's office?"

"I'll take everyone up," Scotty said.

Sasser stood next to Dan. "You wanna hear something weird? See my laptop?"

Dan glanced at the computer and said nothing.

"Strange. It was on the seat of my Lincoln. Somehow the laptop ended up at Dewey's. Some guy pawned it. Dewey saw my name on the back and he called me. How's that for shit luck?"

Dan shrugged. "Pretty good."

Sasser grinned while staring at Dan. "Dewey claims one of his associates paid eighty bucks for it. Imagine that? Dewey let me have it back for only a hundred."

Dan replied, "Hey, it's a little chilly out here. Let's take it in."

◢

Sasser and Dan entered Hardison's crowded office. The chief stood and asked Syms to escort Pastor Jonathan, the witnesses, the juvenile McCray, and the mayor to the auditorium. "Dan and Scotty. You head down there too," Hardison said.

The chief eyed the clock and he pointed to Wallace. "I want Dixon to take you down to his office until the conference is over.

"Good idea," Dixon said. "I'll get Ramirez to keep him company and then I'll come to the auditorium."

Sasser said to Hardison. "We have a few minutes. I want to show you something." Once the chief's office was cleared, Sasser reached inside his jacket and handed Hardison the weapon that had belonged to Vandor Jerricks, "Here's the gun Devon McCray took from him. Devon needs a little tutoring, not some juvie detention center. I've talked with Pastor Jonathan. He's going to help the kid."

Hardison said, "We haven't charged him with anything yet." The chief paused and looked into Sasser's eyes. "I need to tell the press something. Wallace is still your client isn't he?"

"Yes."

Hardison took a deep breath. "You know, he's been on administrative leave, but I don't think he's expecting to hear what I will be telling the media." The chief paused. "Dixon and I have reviewed the officer's traffic stop record. Not good. It's not simply the suspect he'd beaten a few months ago, Wallace is a profiler. The mayor and I spoke with the board last night and they concur … He needs to go. He's been fired, but he doesn't know it yet. Let's get downstairs."

▲

Inside the auditorium, Mayor Fernandez, and Syms were seated on the stage. Syms pointed to Dan and Scotty. "Sit in the front row. I expect a crowd soon."

Hardison and Sasser entered the room and headed for the stage. Dan stopped the sharply dressed attorney, who was clad in a silky gray suit, paisley tie, and red handkerchief in his jacket pocket. "Hey," the detective said. "Where's Wallace?"

"The chief didn't want him down here. He's in Dixon's office with Ramirez. Hope the cameras get my good side," the lawyer replied, as he stepped onto the stage and sat beside Hardison.

Pastor Jonathan was seated in the front row next to Scotty, while Dixon, the witnesses, and McCray took seats behind the detectives.

The auditorium clock read 9:52 a.m. Media personnel had filled the room. Dan counted six cameras and more than two dozen reporters. He recognized several of them and wondered which one had leaked the Wallace story.

A few minutes later, Mayor Fernandez approached the podium, where she stood on a platform and adjusted the mic. "Good morning. May I have your attention? I need silence."

TV cameras began rolling. "We're going to begin the conference. Let me bring Chief Earl Hardison to the podium."

Hardison stood facing the crowd. With his burly voice, he didn't need the mic, but he used it anyway as cameras focused on him. "Thank you," he said. "I'm appreciative of the lawful citizens of this great city who have been patient and peacefully staying away from the protests. The recent violence was not the acts of our good people, but the acts of young people bent on causing trouble. Hopefully, today we will put everyone at ease and allow this city to get back to the wonderful place it is."

Hardison poured water from a pitcher near the podium and drank half the glassful. "I now want to address the deadly shooting of Vandor Jerricks." The chief paused, I'm grateful to the three witnesses." He pointed to them. "They have come forward and proven officer Wallace acted as any other officer would have done in his situation." Hardison took another drink and then said, "As we have all seen very clearly, Vandor Jerricks did have a weapon and he was clearly reaching for it after he'd been ordered to halt. Officer Casey Wallace has been cleared of wrongdoing in the Vandor Jerricks case." The chief turned and pointed to Sasser. "I'm also thankful for Attorney Hancock Sasser who scoured the streets for this evidence."

Sasser stood, waved his hands, and nodded a thank you.

Hardison surveyed the room and paused. "I must now address another matter relating to Officer Casey Wallace. As you all know by now, there was an incident several months back involving Wallace and an African-American suspect. That case has been re-investigated by me, Captain Dixon, and the police board. We have determined Officer Wallace's conduct was inappropriate. An internal review of the officer's record has revealed a disturbing trend that has given us reason to request his badge. The board has agreed, and as of this minute, Casey Wallace is no longer employed by the Hartford Police Department."

Cameras panned the room and reporters were ready to ask questions. Fernandez and Hardison stood at the podium together and the chief spoke. "We thank you all for coming this morning and I'm asking you to clear the room. We will not be taking or answering any questions. Thank you again for being here."

The crowd began to slowly clear the room when a reporter shouted. "Where is Wallace now?"

Hardison ignored the query. "Keep the line moving," he ordered. The chief approached the pastor and Sasser. "Pastor Jonathan," Hardison said. "Thank you for coming and volunteering to tutor Devon. I have a small favor to ask. Would you mind taking the witnesses and Devon home. Mr. Sasser and I have some unfinished business."

Pastor Jonathan shook Hardison's hand. "I will get them home."

"Thank you," Hardison said as Mayor Fernandez exited the building, and the rest of the crowd, including the detectives, headed back to work.

▲

Sasser joined Hardison, Dixon, Ramirez, and Wallace in Dixon's office. The chief stood, looked straight at Wallace, and said, "Listen. I didn't want you out there because there is something you have not heard yet. Dixon, I, the mayor, and the board have reviewed your entire record and we are all in agreement. As of now, you are no longer a Hartford police officer."

Wallace protested. "Wait a minute. I was cleared of the shooting."

Hardison stared him down. "But you administered an unprovoked beating on a suspect."

"He attacked me. He's a known felon who had a warrant."

"The felon, and warrant parts are correct, but you can't look me in the eye and tell me he attacked you. You know there was no fight, except for you forcing him down, striking him, breaking his arm and cuffing him. Not a scratch on you, so let's not play games now."

Wallace looked at Dixon. "I'm not playing games."

"You're a profiler." Hardison said. "You have an interesting record. Ninety-five percent of your tickets and arrests have been African-American and Hispanic people. And it's kind of strange there have been only two incidents of body-cam failures in the entire department, not to mention one car-cam that wasn't working. Yours every time."

A red-faced Wallace said, "This is a lynching, and you know it."

Hardison cut Wallace off before the former employee could say another word. Raising his voice, the chief said. "You got lucky Jerricks had a gun, but you would have shot him anyway, wouldn't you have? You don't have to say it. You can turn in your badge. We already have your weapon, and you don't want us to press charges on the unprovoked beating."

Wallace glared at Sasser. "He's right," the attorney said. "You could be arrested for the attack, so I'd advise you to do as the chief says and leave peacefully."

Wallace got up, tossed his badge at Hardison's feet, walked toward the door and said to Sasser. "Don't bother offering me a ride. I'll take the bus back to my place."

Sasser shook Hardison's hand. "That was a great speech, sir."

Hardison had a wry grin on his face. "Did you just call me sir? Now I know I'm in deep trouble, and which sermon were you referring to? "

Sasser laughed. "Both, sir."

Chapter 25

Javier Ibanez's killer haunted Dan. The detective pounded his desk with his fist, turned to Scotty, and said. "I'm gonna break Biaggio, one way or another."

Scotty shook his head. "Take it easy. You know you sometimes take things too personal. How about hitting Blues?"

When they entered the diner, Dan saw Landry and Luke who were seated in a corner booth. Scotty slid in beside Luke as Dan squeezed next Landry. "Looks to me like you two are always on break," Dan said.

"Working break," Landry quipped.

Dan turned to the waitress who stood at the booth. "Coffee," he said.

"Same here," Scotty echoed.

Dan looked at Luke. "Tell me something. Your neighbor who was coerced by Biaggio. What was his name?"

Luke swallowed the last bite of his omelet. "Burgess."

"How well do you know the guy?" Dan asked.

"Why? What are you getting at?"

"I'm getting at scumbag attorneys who bilk the system. You think Burgess would come forward and admit collusion with Biaggio?"

"You serious? Burgess could go to jail," Luke said. "That's a big door you're wanting to knock down."

"I know, but if we open a few doors, even a little, maybe Biaggio will begin to breathe heavy." Dan blew on his hot coffee and drank some. "I think if we can get Burgess and someone else, perhaps two or three clients who went along with Biaggio's ambulance chasing scams, we can bring his ass down." Dan eyed his partner. "We need to find all the lawsuits Biaggio has filed over the past two to three years and start knocking on those doors."

"But these people won't talk," Scotty said. "They broke the law and pocketed easy cash."

"I think it's worth a try. We'd have to go to a DA or a judge and have them guarantee immunity to those testifiers," Dan replied. Turning to Luke, he said, "You think you can get Burgess to talk?"

"Jesus, that's asking a lot. I don't know. Look, our wives are friends. They're in a book club and they shop together, but me and Ed aren't too tight. I could ask my wife to talk with his. This is a little touchy."

Dan saw the uncomfortable look on Luke's face. "Listen, I don't want to get your wife involved. You talk to the guy right?"

"Yeah, but what am I supposed to do? ... Rap on his door and jump right into it?"

"What's he do? Where's he work?"

"Ed's an engineer at P and W."

Landry interrupted. "Luke. How about approaching him and telling him there's an investigation involving Biaggio and you want to talk about the lawyer. Ease into it. Maybe he'll open up."

Luke sighed. "You know, I feel like Custer right now. The only difference is, he was killed when he was ambushed. Okay, I'll talk to Burgess."

The four detectives rose and Dan picked up the tab. "We telling Syms?" Luke asked.

"Absolutely," Dan said. "When it's over."

When they got back to headquarters, Landry stayed outside to have a smoke. Luke, who had been roped into a chore, made his way to his desk while Dan and Scotty sat at Dan's desk. Dan tossed around the idea Biaggio's wife could have been the Jaguar driver, and said, "You remember who Biaggio said she works for?"

"Keney and Goodwin. One of their agents showed Sally and me a few places before we bought our condo. Look them up."

"I think we should meet her. For all we know, she might have long dark hair. She was blonde in the picture in Biaggio's office, but that doesn't mean she's still blonde." Dan turned to his laptop and keyed in the real estate company's name. "Got it." Scrolling the list of twenty-six agents who worked for the company, he came to the name Cassandra Biaggio, and clicked on it. Up popped her picture. "Blonde," he said. "Looks to me like this photo was taken about the same time as the one in Biaggio's office."

"Take a peek at her listings," Scotty said. "Why don't we set up an appointment to view a house?"

"I like that thinking, pal. I'll print a few."

Dan did so and placed the photos on his desk. "Nice houses. Which one you want to see? The five-hundred-grand colonial, the one-point-two-million estate, or the pricey condo?"

"I'd love to see the estate, but we'd both have to buy new suits and cars. Let's shoot for the colonial."

Dan picked up the receiver from his desk phone and then put it back. "I just realized. I can't use this phone, or my cell, nor can we use yours. I don't want there to be any chance that she knows our names." Dan stood and a few seconds later he tapped on Luke's cube. "I need a favor."

Luke looked up. "Another?"

"I want you to call a real estate agent and set up an appointment to see a house." Dan handed Luke the photo. "This one."

"Hell of a place. You moving?"

"This is Cassandra Biaggio's listing. I want to meet her here without her husband's knowledge. I also don't want her to know who we are, so I need you to make the call. Use your name. She'll see it on the caller ID."

Luke took out his cell, made the call, and a few minutes later, he smiled at Dan. "All set. She'll meet you there at noon."

"Thanks. You did specify the colonial, right?"

"Right."

At eleven-fifteen, the detectives headed to Dan's Accord. "Wait a second," Scotty said. "We should lose our holsters."

"Good idea," Dan said as he popped his trunk and they placed their weapons inside. The detectives got into the vehicle and Dan entered the address into the GPS screen. "This should be interesting," he said as they headed to Avon.

It was ten before noon and Dan's car was parked in front of the targeted residence. The house reminded him of his own, but this one was much larger. It appeared to have a sizable yard, and three car garage. A blue and white Keney and Goodwin sign was planted in the ground.

Dan saw a lock-box on the front door. "Hey," he said. "You know we're going to have to play the partner card."

"We are partners," Scotty said as he nearly caught himself in mid-sentence. "Oh no … Not that partner card."

"Oh yes, that one."

"Can't we just be brothers?"

"Sure, pal. We look a lot alike don't we?"

A few minutes later, a blue Mercedes pulled into the driveway. Cassandra stepped out of the vehicle. Toting a purse and soft maroon attaché, she walked toward the house. The detectives approached her and introduced themselves. "I'm Luke Hanson," Dan said.

Somewhat caught off guard, Scotty said, "I'm Larry Bird."

"Nice to meet you both. I'm Cassandra Biaggio. Shall we go inside?" She opened the lock-box and they proceeded into the house.

Cassandra had short dark hair. She appeared to be about Phyllis's height and size, Dan thought.

"Come in," she politely said. "This is a lovely house, well maintained and the neighborhood is very quiet."

The detectives followed her through every room, the patio out back, the garage, and finished basement. Throughout the tour, the detectives made complimentary remarks and when they returned to the chef-quality kitchen, she asked, "What do you think?"

Dan looked at Scotty, and said, "Beautiful. A great place, maybe a bit too big for us. The dogs would love the yard though."

"How many dogs do you have?" she asked.

Dan quickly replied, "Two Boxers named Ali and Frazier." He eyed Scotty. "What do you think?"

"I think we should sleep on it. Great house."

Wanting to close a sale, she pressed harder. "I know the owner is anxious to sell, and would be willing to come down a bit from the four-ninety asking. You can always make an offer, but I wouldn't wait too long on this one. I know it won't stay on the market long."

Dan turned to her. "I'm sure you're right, but we just started looking and we need to think about it. Can I have your card?"

Cassandra reached into her purse and handed one to Dan.

"Can I have one as well?" Scotty asked.

She handed him a card.

"Thanks for showing this terrific house to us," Dan said. "We'll let you know."

"It was my pleasure. If you decide to pass on this one, I have others I can show you, so don't hesitate to call."

"Thank you," Dan said as they all headed out the front door.

Cassandra got into her vehicle and the detectives got into Dan's car. Thinking ahead, Dan had a baggie in his glove box. "Open the box," he said to Scotty. "Grab the baggie and put the cards in it. Let's get to the lab. Did you notice the short dark hair?"

"Sure did. Think she may have had it cut recently?"

Dan said, "Maybe so, pal." He laughed. "So, Larry Bird. I guess she doesn't follow basketball."

Scotty chuckled. "Boxing either."

They arrived at the lab with Dan holding the baggie. Aki was there to greet them. "You guys back again?"

Dan smiled. "We love it here. Maybe we'll have to move our office down here."

"What's it this time?"

Dan handed Aki the baggie. "These business cards belong to Cassandra Biaggio. We're hoping prints on them match the ones on the CD that was in the Jag."

"Wish me luck."

"Wedding still on?" Dan asked.

Aki grinned. "You kidding? Mayu's family is huge. We're up to four-hundred guests from all over Japan. If I back out now, they'll come after me with Samurais."

"Nothing like a little pressure," Dan said. "Let me know as soon as you get the print results."

"Sure thing, but we're a little backed up right now. Could be a few days."

"Okay," Dan said as he and Scotty turned to exit the lab.

A light rain began to fall and when they got back to the headquarters parking lot, Scotty got out and headed for his car. "Time for home. See you in the morning," he said.

"Bright and early," Dan said.

Neither detective had any idea how soon morning would come.

Chapter 26

Late-night calls were a sure sign of trouble, so when Dan's home phone rang at 11:53 p.m., he knew it wasn't good news.

This hadn't been the first time he'd been rudely awakened by Syms, but this time he was shaken by the call. Sitting at the edge of his bed with the phone to his ear, he yelled, "What! Where? I'll be there as soon as I can."

"What is it?" Phyllis said as she sat up.

With the receiver still in his hand, he flipped on the end-table light. "It's bad." He slammed the receiver back on its stand. "I gotta go. I'll be late, maybe very late," he uttered.

"What do you mean bad? How bad?"

Breaking into a cold sweat, the detective knew he'd already said too much to his wife; he knew she'd worry about his late-night adventure. "A shooting, two victims. I gotta go."

"Want coffee?" Phyllis asked.

"Sure," he replied as he hurriedly hit the bathroom.

Dan didn't waste time, not bothering to shower or shave, he brushed his teeth, washed his ashen face, and sprayed deodorant under his arms before getting dressed. He ran downstairs where Phyllis, clad in her pink robe, closed the lid on his thermos and handed her husband the hot instant coffee. "Thanks, hon." He kissed her on the cheek. "See you later."

Traffic wasn't an issue, but keeping his mind on the road was. His head spun, his blood boiled, and his thoughts stirred up images of his own brush with death several years ago. The gunshot he'd survived sent chills through his angry bones.

While chugging coffee and driving in a misty rain, he pushed the gas pedal to the floor. It was almost as if his car couldn't go fast enough as he sped to the crime scene. His heart beat heavily as he approached the corner of Clarkson and Eastland at 12:32 a.m. With flashing blue and red lights blinding him as he parked his Accord, Dan took another swig of coffee from his less than half-full thermos. Wearing a gray raincoat and a black all-weather Cambridge cap, he exited his vehicle.

Streetlights shed some light as a crowd of shocked neighbors, some with open umbrellas, stood watching as police swarmed the area around Pastor Jonathan's church.

A wisp of cool misty air blew from Dan's mouth. "Jesus Christ," he said to one of the uniforms who was standing a few feet from the bullet-riddled white Lexus. Dan saw bright lights inside the church, and he spotted the coroner's vehicle that was parked by a hydrant.

With droplets falling from his cap, Dan looked inside the Lexus. First responders had already opened the driver's door. Shattered glass was outside as well as inside the vehicle. Blood was spattered everywhere. Dan turned to Sergeant Ramirez and asked, "What's his status?"

"I don't know. When I got here he wasn't moving, but he was breathing. First set of paramedics rushed him to Woodland."

"How many shots?" Dan asked.

"At least two, maybe three. Scared the shit out of me. I thought he was dead. Pastor Jonathan is dead. His body is still inside the church."

Dan leaned into the car again and he saw Chief Hardison's hat on the passenger side floorboard of the vehicle. "God damn it. Who the fuck did this? And what the hell was Hardison doing here at this time?"

Scotty got out of his car and approached Dan. "Syms told me. Is he here?"

"Said he's on his way. Take a look. Hardison is alive, shot twice. He's at Woodland. Pastor Jonathan is dead."

Scotty peeked into the Lexus. "Jesus Christ!"

Dan pulled his partner back. "Come on, let's get inside the church."

At that moment, Captain Syms appeared, his eyes crusty. "These flashing lights can blind a moose," he said. "Dixon's got officers at the hospital. He says Hardison is in surgery. Doctors didn't promise anything."

Dan turned to Ramirez. "Any witnesses?"

Eying the crowd, Ramirez ordered the rest of the uniforms to disperse the bystanders, and then said to Dan, "Not that we've been able to tell, but you know the code around here. No one rats."

"I think we'll be here a while," Dan said.

"Been inside the church?" Syms asked.

Dan replied, "That's where we're going now."

Inside God's building were wooden pews, about twenty rows on each side of the center aisle. Dan stopped and looked at the crucifix on the back wall. "I need to get to church more often," he uttered to himself.

Syms and his detectives approached Pastor Jonathan's draped body. "Let's get a look," Dan said to the medical examiner."

Chief Medical Examiner, Max Arnstein pulled back the sheet. The detectives got a look at the dead pastor, who was wearing plaid pajamas and a gray flannel robe, both drenched in red body fluid, as was the hardwood floor. Dan looked to Arnstein, and said, "What do you see?

"Two shots to the chest. Close range. One straight to the heart."

Dan shook his head. "Why the hell is it always two shots?" The detective saw yellow markers numbered one and two. Eying the shell casings, he said, "Looks like twenty-twos."

The crime scene crew continued searching for DNA. "Who's the man over there?" Syms asked, pointing to the right rear corner of the church, where an elderly man was sitting with a paramedic and patrol officer.

Arnstein said, "The janitor. He's the one who called it in."

Syms said to his detectives, "Go check him out."

A gray blanket had been placed around the man's shoulders covering the top of his night garb. Dan and Scotty neared him. The female paramedic said, "He's disoriented."

Dan saw the oxygen line running from the man's nose. "Has he said anything?" Dan asked.

"He was babbling incoherently when we got here."

"Got a name?"

"Benedict, Hernan Benedict. It's taped to the back of his medical device. He looks to be well into his seventies, maybe eighties."

A second EMT wheeled a gurney toward the man and Dan knew there was no questioning the janitor now.

Scotty pointed to an open door at the rear left corner of the church. "I'd say that's Jonathan's living quarters."

"Let's take a look," Dan said.

Syms walked back outside as the detectives went to the rear of the church and entered Jonathan's private space that consisted of a kitchen, bedroom, bath, and study, all neatly kept. Books lined one wall of the large study where a leather recliner, sofa, roll-top desk, as well as flat-screened TV were in the room. Scotty peeked into the bedroom where the bed was unmade. "I don't see anything unusual in here," he said.

The detectives kept searching for clues but came up empty. "I think we're done for now. Let's come back later with fresh eyes," Dan said.

They joined Syms, and Ramirez outside where the crowd had dissipated. "What the hell happened here? Who was shot first?" Dan asked.

Ramirez said, "Hard to say, but my guess would be the Pastor. Hardison never got out of his car."

"Judging by the hat in his car, he was still in uniform, but why?" Dan asked.

"Doesn't make sense," Scotty said.

"I don't get it," Syms said. The captain looked up at the street sign. The corner of Clarkson and Eastland was only three blocks from where Wallace had shot Jerricks. "What the fuck was Hardison doing down here?"

"Someone set them up. Somehow, the chief was called down here and was ambushed," Dan said.

Syms took out his phone and called the hospital for an update on Hardison. The news was unsettling. "He's still in surgery," The weary captain said.

Dan spotted a tow truck. Minutes later, the blood filled Lexus was up on the flatbed and gone from the scene.

Arnstein had Pastor Jonathan taken to the University morgue where an autopsy would be done. The EMTs transported the janitor to Woodland. Ramirez and the rest of the uniforms left the scene at 2:52 a.m., while the distraught detectives headed home.

▲

Earl Hardison came to Hartford nine years ago from Harlem where he was the assistant Chief of Police. One year later, his wife, Edna had a stroke and died.

He'd been raised in the Bedford-Stuyvesant section of Brooklyn. His father passed when Earl, an only child, was ten. His mother never re-married, raised her son alone, and she succumbed to cancer a dozen years ago at the age of seventy-one.

Earl had worked his way through college and married while serving a stint in the army, sixteen months of which were in Viet Nam. He and Edna had two sons, Terell and Jalen. The boys couldn't have been more different. Terell was much like his father, having graduated from CCNY, and serving in the army. He married his high school sweetheart and moved to California where he, his wife, and three boys reside.

Jalen had always been trouble, having been expelled from high school and indulging in drugs. Earl pushed him into the army, where two years later, Jalen was dishonorably discharged, wound up living in Chicago with low-life friends, and never held a decent job. He'd secretly married, was quickly divorced, and it wasn't known to the family if Jalen had ever fathered a child, but with all the women he'd been with, they never discounted the possibility.

Now, the wounded chief was in Woodland Hospital, fighting to survive the gunshots that had penetrated his body.

CHAPTER 27

D an got home and rather than waking Phyllis, he went into the den and sat in his recliner, resting his head on the back. His eyes were open; all he could see was Hardison's Lexus. Two hours later, after he'd managed a cat-nap, Phyllis entered the den. The clock read 5:25 a.m. The exhausted detective said, "Didn't want to wake you."

"The alarm went off five minutes ago. Kids have to get ready for school. I heard snoring down here. What happened last night?"

He turned on a lamp, took her hand, and breathed hard. "Hardison was shot."

Phyllis gasped. "Dead?"

"It's serious. He was ambushed in his car, and he was hit at least twice. By the time I got there, he was already in surgery at Woodland. I have to get cleaned up and go to headquarters. Syms was going to keep tabs."

Dan went upstairs, showered, put on fresh clothes, and came downstairs a half-hour later. Phyllis had made coffee and poured him a cup. "Thanks," he said as he picked up his cell phone and called the captain.

Syms answered. "Dan. I'm at the hospital and spoke with the doctor. Hardison was moved into the Surgical ICU unit. He had significant blood loss. They removed a bullet from his neck that had missed a main artery, and another from his shoulder." Syms took a breath. "He's hooked up to a ventilator and monitors."

"Doctor say anything else?"

"He said Hardison could be out for days, but hopefully the chief will stabilize."

"I couldn't sleep," Dan said.

"Obviously, I didn't get any. I'm leaving here soon. Meet me at headquarters."

"I'll be there in a little while."

Kate and Josh came downstairs, dressed and ready for breakfast as Dan was about to leave. He hugged his kids. "Have a good day at school," the loving father said. He kissed Phyllis. "Could be a long day," he said as he headed out the door.

With his headlights on, and little traffic to delay him, the detective drove to headquarters unable to rid his mind of Hardison's blood soaked vehicle.

Dan looked for Syms, but the captain's office was vacant, and then the yawning captain entered the room. "I paced the floor at Woodland all night. Didn't even think about trying to sleep."

"I can use more caffeine," Dan said. "You want to go to the caf?"

"You go. I might take a nap in my office."

As Dan neared his cube, Scotty appeared. "How's the chief doing?"

"No change, Syms just got back here from the hospital. He's beat. Hang up your jacket and let's go to the caf,"

There was no hiding the angst in the cafeteria as news about the ambush had spread fast. A somber buzz filled the room and the detectives decided to grab their coffees and head back upstairs.

Dan set his cup on Scotty's desk and started walking toward the captain's office. "I'm going to raid his Advils." Dan entered Syms's empty workspace and he saw flashing red lights on the phone. Tempted to pick up the main line, he chose not to answer, and grabbed the ever-present pill bottle, put a couple of tablets in his hand and returned to the squad room where he downed the tablets before sitting beside Scotty. "I don't know where he went. Maybe he went up to Hardison's office."

"What the hell happened?" Scotty asked.

Dan yawned. "We know what happened. What we don't know is why it happened. I want to know what the hell Hardison was doing down there, in uniform, at that late hour. I'm thinking Pastor Jonathan must have called him, but why?"

Syms entered the room. He was carrying clean clothes. Dan said, "I borrowed a couple of your pills."

"All those frickin' red lights on my phone still lit?"

"Like a Christmas tree."

"I'm gonna go to the gym, take a shower, and put on these clean clothes." The captain sighed. "I have to call Hardison's kids. Last I knew, Terell was in California. I think I have his number. Not sure where Jalen is, but Terell should know."

"I want to get the crime scene report from Dixon, and we'll probably go back to the church," Dan said.

He knew the incident report was only going to tell him the specifics of the time of the first call, everyone who responded to the scene, time they arrived, and whatever details Ramirez had noted. Dan was hoping someone had witnessed or heard something useful, but he also remembered Ramirez had said no one had made any statements.

Dan knew this was a neighborhood that had been rocked by the Wallace shooting. The detective was concerned somehow these two incidents may have been related, either gang retaliation for Jerricks' death, or someone with a grudge and a need to make a statement by targeting Hardison. Was Pastor Jonathan a pawn who was played in order to isolate Hardison? Or was Jonathan targeted too, but why?

The detectives entered Dixon's office. "How you holding up?" Dan asked.

"Been through a lot of shit, but nothing like this. I sent a couple of my guys to the hospital to keep an eye on Hardison, and I sent Ramirez home after he finished his report."

"We're going back to the church to take another look around. Mind if we see the incident report?" Dan asked.

Dixon reached into his tray. "I just read it." He handed it to Dan.

The detective browsed it. "I didn't think it would tell us much," he said as he passed the report to Scotty who also read it, and handed it back to Dixon.

"You guys should go across the hall and check with Garcia," Dixon said.

"Good idea," Dan replied.

The detectives crossed the floor, entered the gang unit room, and headed for Garcia. "We need to talk," Dan said.

"What was Hardison doing down there last night?" Garcia asked.

The detectives pulled up chairs. Sitting across from Garcia, Dan said, "We need to find out. It's strange. He was in uniform too." Garcia bowed his head, and Dan asked, "What can you tell us about gang activity around Clarkson?"

"We know the Knights have been quiet, and that rest usually means something is up, but my guys can't figure it out. There hasn't been a run-in with the Sultans in a while."

"Think either gang could have done this?"

Garcia rubbed his chin. "It doesn't fit. The Knights are mostly petty thieves, vandalizers, and yeah, they've got weapons. Word is they've been recruiting and they want to get in on drugs. That's the Sultans game. Last time the Sultans were down there, it was a drive-by and the Knights retaliated. There's always bad blood, but this shooting doesn't make sense."

"You don't think, in any way, this is tied to Wallace and Jerricks?" Dan asked.

Garcia pondered that question. "Hard to say. As we discussed earlier, Jerricks was an outcast and was doomed." Garcia paused. "If it was gang related, it's more likely the Sultans. I doubt the Knights would shoot up their own neighborhood, and they surely wouldn't have targeted Pastor Jonathan."

Dan rubbed his tired eyes. "So why would the Sultans pull this off?"

Garcia said, "Think about this. What if they wanted it to look like a Knights hit?"

Scotty said, "Are you serious? If that gets out there'll be a gang war."

"Right. Meantime, my guys will be snooping around too."

"Thanks," Dan said as he and Scotty exited Garcia's office.

▲

When Dan and Scotty entered the captain's office, Syms was standing, wearing clean clothes and staring out his window at the blue dome atop the sprawling building a few blocks away. Syms turned and said. "Samuel Colt made a lot of guns over there. I bet he never thought his factory would spit out weapons that so many times, ended up in the hands of so many bad people." He paused. "Talked to the mayor. She's concerned about another uprising. I'm more concerned with the neighborhood turning into a shooting arcade. If the deceased pastor couldn't maintain level heads down there, then no one could." Syms eased into his chair. "Arnstein said it appeared Jonathan had been shot at close range."

"He's the expert. Looked that way to me," Dan said.

"I agree, but Hardison was shot in the neck, and a second bullet pierced his left shoulder." Syms paused. "Those shots don't sound like close range to me."

"Think we have two shooters?" Dan asked.

"Could be."

"Listen," Dan said. "We spoke with Garcia. He's got eyes and ears in the gang sector. He can't say if this was a gang-related shooting or not, but we can't rule it out."

Syms picked up his trusty bottle. "I don't buy it. To me it looks more like an individual or two who had a vendetta."

Dan put his hands on the desk. "I think that's more likely too. The incident report said exactly what I thought. We're going back to check out the church again. Maybe we'll find something. I wish that janitor had been able to talk to us."

"I wish Hardison was able to talk to us," Syms said.

"Amen," Dan replied. "Let's get down there, partner.".

"Good luck," the tired captain uttered.

Chapter 28

A patrol car was parked in front of Pastor Jonathan's church where yellow tape had sealed off the area. Still, neighbors passed by, placing flowers and wreaths on the moist grass. An older couple, both wearing raincoats, had stopped to pray for the pastor as Dan and Scotty walked toward the church. "Excuse me," Dan asked, "Are you members of this congregation?"

The teary-eyed woman looked at Dan. "Known Pastor Jonathan since he opened the doors." Clutching the shaking hand of her husband, she uttered, "Praise the Lord. God be with the pastor."

The husband put his arms around his wife. "A shame, a shame. He was such a good man."

Dan said, "We're going to catch the person who did this. Peace be with you."

Approaching the policeman at the door, Dan said. "Looks like a lot of people have been by here."

"A steady stream," the officer said. "I've been here since five. They keep coming."

Scotty opened the door and stepped inside with his partner. The lights were on. "This is a nice little church. Didn't notice the mosaics last night," he said.

"Last night? Earlier this morning is more like it," Dan replied as he studied the chapel. "Check the pews on the left. The lab guys have the casings. Maybe there's something they missed." Dan went up and down the pews on the right. "Nothing but a few hymnals," he said, his voice echoing in the open space. "Let's check the living quarters again."

The detectives went to the rear of the church and entered Jonathan's private area. In the den, Dan noticed an array of photos, framed pictures of young boys that were spread across the credenza. Windows in each room were draped and wooden crosses hung on the walls.

Dan joined Scotty in the study where an antique-looking roll-top desk was in the middle of the room. He slid the top back. "Bills like the rest of us," Scotty said.

A pad on top had writing on it. Dan flipped through it. "Looks like he was in the middle of composing a sermon. You see a phone?"

"On the table next to the desk."

"What about a cell?"

"Haven't seen one."

Dan thought for a second "Maybe it was in his robe pocket," he said. Sifting through a journal, Dan saw names of people he assumed were parishioners. Stars were next to several of the entries. "Wonder what the stars next to these names mean? Let's get out of here."

When they got outside Dan said, "I'm a little bothered by the cell phone. Maybe it *was* in the robe pocket. Feel like a ride to the see Arnstein?"

"If we must. That place gives me the creeps."

"Yeah, like the ones the Giants give the Patriots."

"You mean like the Bruins give the Rangers."

"Wouldn't know about that, pal. Not a hockey fan. If it doesn't have a ball it isn't a sport."

"So skating isn't a sport?"

"Neither is skiing. Speaking of ice, wonder how many Arnstein has in the cooler."

The detectives entered the building that was becoming all too familiar. They marched toward the morgue and Scotty said, "There are more dead people here than live ones."

"Imagine slicing them up and exploring their innards?" Dan said.

"Thanks for that image."

Dan rapped on the glass window outside Max Arnstein's office. The gray haired-bushy-browed coroner opened the door. "You guys get any sleep?" he asked.

"Look at my chin. This should be a clue," Dan replied as he pointed to his razor nick.

"I don't think any of us got much rest," Arnstein said.

"We know what killed the pastor. Did you find anything in his robe or pajamas? A phone maybe?' Dan asked.

We have the robe and cut off pajamas, but we didn't find anything inside the pockets, except a hanky."

Scotty peered into the brightly lit examining room where a technician was preparing a female for examination. The naked woman's body was prone on a steel table as the team washed the corpse with a shower-like spray hose. "Jesus, just like the carwash," Scotty said.

"She was found in the woods near a lake in Milford," Arnstein said.

Dan looked through the glass window and saw the victim. "What's her name? What Happened?"

Arnstein replied. "Christ, she was half-naked, sexually assaulted, and strangled. Her name is Heidi, thirty-four. According to the Milford police she was divorced and lived with her mother. A waitress at a local restaurant. No kids."

Dan looked back at Arnstein. "Did you see Hardison?"

Arnstein shrugged. "He had been taken to Woodland by the time I got there. I only get to see the dead ones."

Dan turned to Scotty. "Let's check with Aki as long as we're here."

The detectives went upstairs and Dan opened the office door. Aki said, "Good timing. I was about to send you the report on Cassandra Biaggio."

Expecting to hear the prints matched the Marley CD, Dan didn't like what he heard. "They don't match," Aki said.

"Another miss. Damn it."

"You want the cards back?"

"I'll take them," Dan said. "Thanks for the bad news."

"Bad news?" Aki said. "What the hell happened last night? Arnstein was beside himself when I saw him earlier. A pastor and Hardison?"

"We were just downstairs," Dan said. "The pastor was killed in his church. Hardison is on life support at Woodland. Still too early to say if he's going to make it. We'll get the bastard who shot them."

Chapter 29

Dan barely touched his breakfast. Having sent the kids off to school, Phyllis prepared to leave for work. "Not hungry?" she said to her troubled husband.

"No. I keep thinking about us. I keep thinking about Hardison. I keep thinking about when I was shot. My stomach is churning."

She placed his hand in hers. "I hate to see you like this," she said. "You have to stop thinking. We both know your job is dangerous. You took a year off and couldn't stay away. I worry every day, but you're a strong man, and you know you love your job. We'll pray Hardison is okay, but if the worst happens, you'll only be at peace once you've captured his —"

Dan released her hand and raised his, stopping her from saying the word *killer*. "You're right," he said. He stood and kissed his devoted wife. "Have a good day, hon."

Phyllis kissed him on the cheek. "See you later."

Finishing his toast and coffee, he took a deep breath, and called Syms. "Any news on Hardison?"

"I'm at the hospital. Got here about an hour ago. He's still in ICU hooked up, hasn't opened his eyes yet."

Dan asked, "You heard anything about the janitor? Is he still there?"

"I think so. I'll check. Hernan Benedict wasn't it?"

"Yeah. With any luck he'll be coherent."

"I'll let you know."

"Okay, see you later."

As soon as he got to the squad room, Dan stood at Scotty's desk. "Syms is at the hospital. Nothing new on the chief," he said. "I won't rest until the bastard who shot Hardison is in jail, or dead."

Scotty looked up. "We won't rest."

An hour later, Syms entered the room and marched to his office. Dan and Scotty followed him down the hall. "Have a seat boys," the captain said as he sat in his chair. "Nothing more I could do at the hospital. Hardison is in good hands."

"You talk to the janitor?" Dan asked.

Syms leaned forward. "I did. He's being discharged later. His daughter was there and he's going back to her place."

"Was he any help?"

"It seems the pastor was a gracious man who paid him to clean the chapel. Jonathan had even fixed up a room for him. Hernan stayed twice, sometimes three nights a week."

"So he sounds pretty coherent," Dan said.

"Not really, his daughter told me that, but he did talk a little. Says he was awakened by a loud noise he thought was a car backfiring." Syms paused. "Cars don't backfire these days, so I'm sure it was the first gunshot he heard. A second loud burst got him out of bed so he went into the chapel, the lights were on, and he saw Jonathan on the floor with blood everywhere. The rest is blank."

"Did he remember calling for help?"

"No. He remembers sitting in a chair and an EMT asking him questions. Next thing he remembered was being in the hospital. His daughter said he's been in and out and she's heard him say the word scooter, but she thinks he's trying to remember the shooter."

"I thought he said he didn't see a shooter," Dan said. "He heard the gunshots and came out only to see the pastor had been shot. And how did he manage to call for help?"

"He pushed the button on his medical alert gadget."

"I wonder if he did see the shooter and it's lodged somewhere in his memory. We might want to talk to him later." Syms nodded and Dan asked, "Have you checked out Hardison's office?"

"Not yet." Syms rocked in his chair. "That morning, I had an appointment with him, first thing, but when I went up to his office he was gone. I know he'd been in. There was a nearly empty cup of coffee on his desk. Not like him to just disappear, and certainly not like him to leave the cup there."

"Mind if we go up there?"

"Go. I have to give Terell another call. When I got in touch with him before he said he was going to get up here, and he'd try to contact his brother who was in Chicago."

The detectives walked up a flight and headed toward Hardison's office. "Don't see you up here often," Human Services officer Gracie Hammonds said.

"I think that's a good thing," Dan replied. "Don't you?"

"Probably. Guess it means you're staying out of trouble. You heard anything?"

"Not really," Dan replied. "The chief is still holding on."

Hardison didn't have a secretary, and his office door was shut, so Dan turned the doorknob and entered the room with Scotty, who flicked on the light, and said, "It's too neat." He moved to Hardison's computer and turned it on. "He has it password protected. It's locked. If we need to get a computer guy to get in we can do that."

Dan saw the cup still on the desktop and checked inside the desk where everything was stashed away in an orderly fashion. Checking the calendar on the chief's desk, Dan saw several appointments slotted over the past few days, none setting off any alarms, except the one with Syms's name that had a pencil line drawn through it. "Wonder why he cancelled and didn't bother to tell Syms?" Dan said. "Obviously something came up, and the chief left." Dan noticed a notation. "He penciled in '*Cubs*' at the bottom. You see an address book?"

"No, you?" Scotty replied. "Wait, there's a Rolodex on the credenza." He flipped the Rolodex and snapped out the white card with Terell and Jalen's information. "Didn't Syms say he couldn't locate Jalen? Here's a card with both son's info."

:Grab it and give it to Syms.".

The detectives exited the chief's office, Dan turning off the light and closing the door. They stopped at Gracie's desk. "You guys have any luck?" she asked.

"Tell me something," Dan asked. "Were you here that morning?"

"I'm here every morning. I have a perfect attendance record."

"Did you see him leave here?"

"No. He wasn't here when I arrived at eight. First time I saw him was about ten." Gracie thought for a second and then said, "There was someone who came to see him around two. A thin black man who was wearing a leather jacket and baseball cap."

Dan looked at Scotty. "Cubs?" Turning to Gracie, Dan asked, "Do you remember what the cap said?"

"No, I just remember it was blue," she answered.

"Thanks," Dan said.

As the detectives walked away from Gracie, Dan said to his partner, "Let's check something else out." .

"Where we going?' Scotty asked.

"Down to the lobby."

Dan knew all visitors had to enter the building through the main lobby. He also knew there were cameras that took videos of everyone coming through those doors. He knew too that all visitors had to sign in, so he thought he'd be able to identify Hardison's guest.

The detectives entered the lobby. Inside the police station main entrance there was a window where the uniform assigned to check-ins maintained a visitor list. Two such lists existed: one was for people who came to visit detained suspects, the other was the one Dan was interested to see. He stood at the window with Scotty

131

where cute, short-haired brunette, blue-eyed Ashley Marholan said, "Haven't seen you two in a while."

"True, it's been too long. You still single?" Dan asked.

She smiled. "You still married?"

"My wife says I'm a happily married man."

"Do you have the list of visitors from the day Hardison was shot? Someone came to see him that afternoon, and I want to find out who it was," Dan said.

Ashley paged through the log and saw three visitors were listed, but none had come to see Hardison. She showed the detectives the page. "This is odd," Dan said.

"Wait a second," Ashley said. "There was a guy who came in here, never signed in. He was wearing a baseball cap and he asked to see the chief. He said he had an appointment. I directed him to the phone on the wall where he called Hardison's office. A minute later the chief called down and said to buzz the visitor in."

"So he was never logged in?"

"No. Hardison said to let him in."

"The cap. Do you remember if it was a Cubs hat?"

"You know. I think it was. The video will tell you for sure."

Dan knew he'd broken a few rules in his time, but Hardison had broken a cardinal one.

"I need the video from that afternoon."

"I'll take care of it," Ashley said. "Check back in the morning?"

"Thanks. You're a sweetheart. You never answered my question. Still single?"

"And happy. Nothing but jerks out there."

Dan said with a wry smile. "Can you wait a couple of years? My kid will be out of college, and he's better looking than me."

"See you, Dan. Bye, Scotty."

The detectives headed to the captain's office where Syms was sitting with his back to the door as he stared out the window. "You spend half your day looking out that window. Seen any UFOs? " Dan quipped.

Syms swiveled around. "No, but I'd like to know what planet you two strange looking characters came from. What have you got?"

Scotty handed the Rolodex card to the captain. "Found this in Hardison's office. You said you couldn't reach Jalen. Check this number."

Syms glanced at the card. "That's what I have. I talked to Terell again. He'll be here soon. Jalen is still out of the loop. Terell said they hadn't spoken in a while and he can't locate his brother."

Chapter 30

Hoping to identify the man who had visited Hardison, Dan made his way to see the young officer he'd pictured as his future daughter-in-law. "Morning sunshine," he said to Ashley.

"Hi Dan," she said as she handed him the lobby video.

"You sure you don't want to see Mike's picture? Got a nice one in my wallet."

"You're dying to show me, so go ahead."

Dan opened his wallet and waved the photo at her. "You're right about one thing," she said. "He's better looking than you. Don't lose the tape, Dan."

Heading toward his cube with the video in hand, Dan grabbed Scotty and they marched into Syms's office. "Here's something we need to look at," Dan said. "This is the lobby tape from the day Hardison was shot. Gracie said the chief had a visitor that afternoon who was wearing a baseball cap. Ashley said the visitor never signed in because he went to the wall phone and a few seconds later, Hardison called her and told her to buzz the guy in. This should tell us who he was."

"Dan placed the video into the machine in back of the captain's desk. The detective then proceeded to a chair with the remote in his hand and started the tape. Watching intently, they all saw the visitor appear. "That's the guy, Cubs cap," Dan said.

"Can you zoom it?" Syms asked.

Dan froze the video on the image and zoomed in. "Jesus, could be anybody, but he knew Hardison well enough to not have to sign in," Syms said.

"The Cubs hat," Dan said. "Didn't you say Jalen Hardison lived in Chicago?"

"That's what Terell said. If it's Jalen, what the hell was he doing here? And why the secret? I know Hardison shunned me that morning, but I would have thought he'd have told me if his son was coming."

Dan restarted the video. "He's leaving. Looks like he was here for about an hour."

"Shut it down," Syms said as he reached for his desk phone. "I'm calling Terell again." On the second ring, Terell answered and Dan heard. "Terell, this is Captain Syms." There was a long pause and Syms spoke a little louder. "Didn't you tell me Jalen was living in Chicago?" Another pause and Syms said, "Let me know when you get in. I'll have an officer down in the baggage area waiting for you. You have my number?" Seconds later the call ended and Syms looked at his detectives. "He's about to board a plane. He's on his way here."

"What about Jalen?" Dan asked.

"Terell said he still can't reach him."

Dan said, "I need to see Ashley again. "There should be another video of the parking lot."

Down in the lobby, a woman stood beside a stroller and nervously paced the floor. Her purse was dangling from the child's seat as the baby slept. Dan saw two packs of cigarettes inside the unzipped diaper bag. After checking the young mother's ID, making her sign in, and inspecting her purse, Ashley advised the visitor she'd have to leave her belongings at the check-in window. A uniformed officer escorted the visitor into the cellblock, while another officer stayed in the lobby with the small child.

Dan smiled at Ashley. "Me again," he said. "I need another favor. Can you get me the video of the visitor's lot from the same afternoon as the other one?"

Ashley smiled back. "I'll get a copy for you. How's a couple of hours?"

"That's fine. Thanks doll."

Dan got back upstairs and Scotty was at Luke's desk. "Hey big guy," Dan said. "You had a chance to talk to your neighbor?"

"Hell yes. He's a Jets fan. I told him I was too. What a crock. I'm a Giants fan like you. Anyhow, I started talking about Joe Namath. Believe it or not, my father went to the Football Hall of Fame in Canton when Namath was inducted. My dad brought home a signed jersey from him. I told Ed that, and he's excited to see it, so he's coming over to watch the Jets game."

"Nice work," Dan said.

"Nice? Crap nice. I'm gonna miss the Giants and Cowboys."

"I'll tape if for you,"

Luke stared at Dan. "Tape, my ass. Nothing worse than watching a taped football game. You're gonna owe me big time."

Dan patted Luke on the shoulder. "Thanks big dude for taking one for the team."

Luke shook his head. "Is it too late to ask for a trade?"

Dan and Scotty retreated to Dan's desk. "Ashley getting the other video?" Scotty asked.

"She should have it soon. What do you think of her?"

"Cute, real cutie."

"Yeah, good personality and I keep trying to get her interested in Mike. I showed her his picture."

Scotty chuckled. "I thought Phyllis was the matchmaker. Remember when she wanted to fix me up with your neighbor, Terry?"

"I sure do. You were hot on Sally and I had to tell Phyllis about her. Only mistake I made was saying how gorgeous Sally was. Never tell a woman how good looking you think another woman is."

"So what's with Ashley?"

"You know, she kind of reminds me of Phyllis."

"Hey, Mike's what? Nineteen? He's probably getting more ass at college than you can imagine."

Dan grinned. "You're probably right."

A few minutes later, Dan heard unfamiliar footsteps. He turned and saw Ashley, all five feet-two inches of her. "This is a surprise," he said.

"Hi, Scotty," Ashley said.

"Hi, Ashley. How are you?"

"Great, but your buddy is quite persistent you know."

"Yeah, he's a royal pain."

"Okay," Dan said as he held out his hand. "That was quick. Promise I'll lay off the Mike stuff."

Ashley winked. "I have magical powers. I will admit Mike is good-looking, and I do have a younger sister."

"Really? Think she'd be interested?"

She handed Dan the video. "If he can wait … She's eleven."

Dan smiled at her again and pointed to the photos on his desk. "Then there's Josh, he's twelve."

Ashley again returned the smile. "Hope this helps you guys."

"Thanks for the visit," Dan said. "Have a good one."

The detectives headed back to the captain's office and Dan presented the new video to him. "Put it in," Syms said.

With the tape rolling, Dan said, "There he is getting out of a silver Malibu and heading toward the lobby. There's someone else in the car. Looks like a female."

Dan fast-forwarded the video to the point where the visitor walked out of the jailhouse and got back into the vehicle.

Focusing on the rear license plate of the sedan, Dan wrote the numbers on a pad. "Florida. It could be a rental."

CHAPTER 31

Terell Hardison was on his way to Hartford, leaving his wife and three children behind. It had been two years since he'd seen his dad, and that Christmas was also the last time they'd had any contact with Jalen.

Landing at Bradley Airport at 2:30 p.m., Terell exited his American Airlines flight and walked with his carry-on to the baggage area, where he stood and watched luggage circle around the conveyor. Finally, he grabbed his blue Tourister from the moving belt and wheeled the bag toward the transportation area. Ramirez held a sign that had Terell's name on it, and the younger Hardison approached the officer. "I'm Terell," he said.

"I'm Charlie Ramirez. My car is right outside. How was your flight?"

"Long. How far do we have to travel?"

"About fifteen miles."

Twenty-five minutes later, Ramirez and Terell were inside Syms's office. The captain stood, and shook Terell's hand as Ramirez set the luggage in the corner. "How was the flight?" Syms asked.

"Long, and stressful. At least they served food." Terell placed his tan sport jacket in his lap as he sat. "What's the latest on Dad? I can't wait to see him."

"He's still in the ICU, but he's improving."

"If you guys need me, I'll be down with Dixon," Ramirez said as he left the office.

Terell's eyes welled up as he reached into his pants pocket for a hanky and wiped his tears. "Dad's a strong man. He can't die. I need to see him."

"We'll get you over there, but there are a couple of things I want to show you first. Let me get detectives Shields and Scott in here."

The detectives entered the office and introduced themselves to Terell. "We've come up with a couple of videos you need to see," Dan said. "As we understand it, you haven't been able to locate Jalen."

"True. He hasn't been in contact with us in two years."

"And as far as you know he's in Chicago?" Dan asked.

"That's the last I knew."

"Sit back and watch."

Dan picked up the video from Syms's desktop, and placed the lobby tape into the video player. "Take a look," Dan said as he started the tape. "Tell us if you recognize anyone."

Terell's jaw dropped as soon as he saw Jalen. "What? Are you serious? He was here? When was he here?"

"The afternoon your father was shot," Syms said.

Terell's head sank toward his knees. "Why? Why would he come here? Do you think he had something to do with it?"

Syms leaned back. "I don't want to stretch that far, but what can you tell us about Jalen?"

"Can I have a drink of water?" Terell asked.

Dan filled a cup, and Terell drank the whole cupful. He closed his eyes momentarily, and then said, "I don't know where to start. Damn it. Jalen was always hard to deal with, got into a lot of trouble. Dad had little tolerance for Jalen's defiance, especially when my brother was expelled from high school. Jalen was also doing drugs, so Dad made him enter the service. Jalen was pissed. He never forgave Dad. Jalen ended up in Iraq. Once he got back home, he got sent to the brig twice for disrespecting his superiors, and ended up with a dishonorable discharge."

Terell breathed deep and continued. "I enlisted before Jalen went in. Dad was proud of me. Jalen withdrew from all of us after he got out of the army." Terell stopped and dropped his head in his hands.

"It's okay," Syms said. "Get him another cup," he said to Scotty.

Terell took the cup and drank more water. With sweat beading on his forehead, he wiped the drops with his hanky. "Jalen went to Chicago. A service buddy talked him into coming home with him. Soon after, we found out Jalen was again doing drugs and running with the wrong people. He even got married, didn't last long, never met her or even knew her name." Terell briefly smiled. "Funny, a couple of years ago, we thought he might have turned himself around because he came to California and celebrated Christmas with us and Dad. My brother looked good too, but that was only a façade. To this day, I don't know what made him spend time with us. Like I said before, that was the last time we saw him."

Syms reached for his Advil and picked up the bottle. "You said he hung with the wrong people? Like how wrong?"

"Bookies, money lenders, junkies, and drug dealers."

"Got ya," Syms said. "He have any kind of rap sheet?"

"I don't think so."

"There's another video I want you to see," Syms said.

Dan switched tapes and ran the second one. "That's him getting into the silver car. Notice the passenger seat. There appears to be a woman in the car."

"I see. Haven't got a clue. God, don't let him be connected with the shooting," Terell lamented.

"We hope not, but the timing of his visit and their secret meeting is curious. I'm thinking Jalen might have been in some kind of trouble," Syms said.

"Could have been. I'd have no idea. How about taking me to the hospital?"

"Sure," Dan said. "I'll take you and drop you off at the hotel later."

"Thanks. I'm staying at Dad's house. I spoke with his neighbor. He has a key."

Dan had called Phyllis, informing her he'd be late because he had to drive Terell Hardison to the chief's house in Bloomfield.

It was a little after seven p.m. when Dan finally pulled into his garage. Connie had gone home. Phyllis was in the kitchen. "Hi, hon," he said.

She kissed him. "There's beef stew in the fridge."

Dan opened the refrigerator and smelled the cool dinner, as Phyllis handed him a bowl. "Put some in the microwave," she said.

Dan did as she suggested and a minute later he removed the bowl, grabbed a spoon, and sat at the island. Phyllis poured him a glass of water as he began to eat, and she sat beside him. "How is Hardison doing?" she asked.

"He's stable. I guess that's good news. Where's the kids? They go to bed early?"

"Hardly, I sent them to their rooms after they ate. Seems they were in the den and were teasing each other when Connie was doing her new puzzle. Kate apparently nudged the table and several pieces fell on the floor."

"Connie get mad at them?" Dan asked, as he shoveled stew into his mouth.

"They all picked up the pieces, but Connie told them she wasn't making brownies for them, as she had promised. I told the kid's you would have a chat with them."

As soon as Dan finished eating he said. "You want to get them?"

Seconds later Kate and Josh entered the room. "Hey. I heard you guys knocked over Connie's puzzle," Dan said.

Josh pointed to his sister. "She did it."

"Did not," Kate spouted as she kicked Josh's leg."

"Hey, hold it right there," Dan said as he stood between the dueling siblings. "You two behave, or I'll make sure you never have brownies again. Go upstairs and get ready for bed."

The kids raced upstairs with Phyllis not far behind. "I'll be back."

Ten minutes later, she returned. "You know, sometimes I think they need a session or two in my office."

"I need a hot shower. I'm beat. Terell Hardison is a nice guy, cut from the same mold as his father. I wish he didn't have to see his dad hooked up to all those machines."

"Go shower. I'll be up soon."

"I'll probably be out like a light."

"And snoring too."

CHAPTER 32

Yesterday's visit with his father had been more upsetting to Terell than he'd imagined. The vision of his dad, unable to communicate, deeply bothered him. He'd hoped things would be different this morning.

After having a rental car dropped off at the house, Terell drove to the hospital, but upon entering the ICU unit, he sensed there was little or no progress. The chief was still intubated, and hooked up to the same monitors. Helplessly touching his father's hand, Terell whispered, "Love you Dad. Don't leave us now. I'll be back."

Exiting the room, Terell looked at the nurse tending the unit. "We're taking good care of him," she said.

"Thank you," he replied.

Leaving the hospital after his short visit, he headed to police headquarters. Parking in the visitor lot, he entered the lobby where he signed in before Ashley allowed him upstairs to see Syms.

Dan and Scotty were sitting in the captain's office when Terell walked in. Syms said, "Have a seat."

"I just came from the hospital," Terell said. "He's still hooked up. Nothing I can do. They're taking care of him."

"We're all praying," Syms said. "We have to think the best."

Dan said. "He's a strong man, He'll pull through." Dan paused. "You were at the house last night. Did you notice anything unusual, any notes?"

"No. I spent a lot of time looking at family photos. My grandmother, mother, him, me, and Jalen. I have to say, my father keeps a clean house. I wonder if he has a helper."

Dan said, "You wouldn't wonder if you saw his office. Neat as a pin."

Terell stood. "Mind if I go to his office?"

"Sure," Syms said. "Scotty will escort you up."

"Know what? I really should go back to the hospital. I have to be there, even if the worst happens. I need to be at his bedside, but I would like to sit in his chair for a few minutes."

"Understood," Syms said.

Scotty took Terell to the chief's office. Fifteen minutes later Terell was ready to go back to the hospital, so Scotty led him down to the visitor's entrance.

A

Dan had remained in the captain's office. "Gotta find Jalen," he said.

"No shit," Syms replied. "Go find him."

Scotty returned. "Terell went back to the hospital."

"Do you think Jalen could have shot his father?" Dan asked.

Syms grimaced. "I'd like to think not, but then again, there are people like the Menendez brothers."

Returning to his desk, Dan opened his drawer and retrieved the piece of paper on which he had written the license number of the vehicle Jalen had gotten into. It didn't take the detective long to trace the Malibu to the Alpha Car rental company. He got up and tapped Scotty on the shoulder. "Come on, we're taking a ride to the rental place by the airport."

It had been a while since their last visit to the airport and Dan remembered seeing the Alpha location on the road leading into Bradley International. "There it is," he said as he drove up to the office. Once inside, they walked to the counter where a young man, clean cut, who appeared to be only a couple of years out of

144

high school, greeted them. "Good morning. How can I help you?" he politely said with a smile.

Dan presented his badge to the employee. "Can we see the manager," he asked?

"I'll tell him you're here."

The balding, middle-aged manager wearing his red company-issued shirt came to the counter. He slid his wire-rimmed glasses down. "What can I do for you?"

Dan flashed his badge and placed a piece of paper on the counter. "We tracked this car here and we need to know who rented the vehicle."

The manager asked, "Why do you want to know?"

Dan replied, "There were two people in the vehicle who may have committed a crime and you can help us greatly."

"What kind of crime?"

The quick thinking Dan lied when he said. "There is a video of them leaving a gas station without paying."

The manager placed his elbows on the counter. "You know I'm not supposed to give out private information. You have to subpoena the rental agreement."

Dan said, "Look. I know the info is right there in your computer."

The manager whispered, "I've been here nineteen years and I like helping cops. Done so a few times, so I'm doing you a favor."

A few seconds later, the detectives had a name, address and contact number written on a pad. "Can you print out the agreement?" Dan asked.

"If you want it, you'll definitely have to get some papers."

"We probably don't need it. Thanks, we appreciate your help," Dan said.

The detectives got into Dan's car. Scotty said, "Nice one. Gas station?"

"Hey, I could have said bank robbery. Would that have made you happy?" Dan looked at the information he'd obtained. "Shelaine Eppington. Lives in Chicago. It's no surprise she rented it, not Jalen. When we get back, let's check for a criminal record for both of them."

Scotty said, "If I call Shelaine, you think Jalen might answer?"

"Good idea. It's worth a shot and if she answers, that's good too."

Scotty took out his cell and punched in Shelaine's number. The call rolled to voicemail. "Nothing. Voicemail. It was a woman's voice."

Chapter 33

Dan saw his partner who was toting a Tupperware container. "Muffin man is here," Scotty yelled. "Come and get them."

Stripping off his jacket, he placed the container on the small table inside his cube. Dan, Landry, and Luke were quick to surround the table as the baker lifted the lid.

"Any nuts?" Dan said.

"You have to ask every time?"

"I kinda do. Hard to know if I may have pissed you off."

Grabbing a muffin, Luke said, "Caf anyone?"

"Not us," Dan said. "We have a lot of work to do."

"Okay. See you later," Luke said.

"Sally give you the kitchen back?" Dan asked.

"She let me borrow it. Her oven is baking a new muffin."

Dan wasn't sure how to perceive that remark, and then he grinned. "You devil. She's pregnant?" he uttered.

"She is."

"You the father?"

Scotty snatched the half-eaten muffin from Dan's hand. "I'm hoping," he said with a wry smile.

"Welcome to my world. Three kids and broke. Maybe now you'll get that vasectomy."

"Know what? You should be the poster boy for male snipping."

"Hey, if the pay is right, I'll take the job."

Scotty handed his partner back the muffin. Dan took a bite and then said, "How about checking the criminal data base for Shelaine Eppington, and Jalen?"

Scotty sat and turned to his computer, accessing the criminal data base known as NCIS and searched the names Shelaine Eppington and Jalen Hardison. "Nothing, they're clean. I suppose that's good news," he said.

Garcia stormed past the detectives and went straight into Syms's office.

"What the hell is that all about?" Dan said. "Let's go find out."

The detectives followed Garcia and seconds after the gang unit leader entered the captain's office, so did the detectives.

The gang unit leader said, "Damn it. Just what we need."

Dan asked, "What's happened?"

"It keeps getting deeper around here," Garcia said. "There was a drive-by last night on Clarkson. Sultans shot two Knights. One of the victims is Skeeter Hantoras. Ring a bell?"

Dan shrugged. "Should it?"

"Christ sakes. Hantoras is Julio Vegas's half-brother," Garcia said.

"What?" Dan said. "I didn't know Vegas had a half-brother. His other brother Santiago was killed in a drive-by several years ago, and Julio was killed last year."

"Yeah," Garcia said. "Guess what? There was another half-brother named Caesar Ortiz, and he was a Sultan."

"Brothers in rival gangs?" Dan said. He looked at Garcia. "What do you mean was another brother?"

"It's like this. Skeeter's alive and he's at Woodland, but the other Knight died. And later Caesar Ortiz was found dead in a car. Shot several times."

Great, Dan said. "I guess it was only a matter of time before the gangs would get back at it."

Garcia turned toward the door. "I have to meet with my unit."

"Keep us posted," Syms said. The captain turned to Dan. "He has his hands full."

"We do too," Dan said.

Syms leaned forward. "So what have you got?"

Dan said, "We have info on the rented vehicle. It was rented by a female named Shelaine Eppington. We have her number and tried to contact her, but the call rolled to voicemail, so Scotty didn't leave a message. But I have a hunch she might pick up a call from Terell. We need to get him down here." Dan paused, "She should recognize the name Hardison. If Jalen picks up, that would be great." Dan eyed the phone on Syms's desk. "How about giving Terell a call."

"I just talked with him. I'm going to join him at the hospital," Syms said. "I'll get him back here."

About two hours later, the captain and Terell entered the squad room and headed to Syms's office. Dan and Scotty followed them. "How's the chief doing?" Dan asked.

"Nothing has changed," Terell said. "Dad's still hooked up to machines and he hasn't opened his eyes yet."

They all sat and Dan said, "We did some checking and as we suspected, the vehicle Jalen drove here was a rental, but he didn't rent it. A female named Shelaine Eppington did, and we have her phone number. Does that name ring any bells?"

"No."

"We've tried to call her, but I don't think she'll respond to us. She might answer if she sees your name. And there's a chance Jalen will answer. I'd like you to call her using your cell."

"Really? Shelaine who?"

"Eppington. She lives in Chicago."

Terell took out his phone. "What's the number?"

Dan read it and Terell made the call. "She's not answering. Voicemail, should I leave a message."

Before Dan could respond, Terell hung up. "I should have told you before you made the call," Dan said. "Try it again and tell her your name, and say you need to talk to your brother."

Terell re-dialed and this time when voicemail kicked in, he left a message along with his phone number. Now what?" he asked.

Dan replied, "If he calls, talk to him."

Terell got up and his phone vibrated. He answered. "Hello." He nodded and the detectives heard. "Jalen. Where are you?"

Syms, Scotty and Dan listened. Dan whispered. "Put him on speaker."

Terell did so. "I'm where I belong," Jalen said. How'd you get this number?"

"What's that matter? Where the hell are you?"

"I told you. I'm where I belong."

"Come on, Jalen, be real. Where the hell are you?"

"Chicago."

"Who's Shelaine?"

"I still want to know how you got this number, and how'd you know about her?"

"Come on, Talk to me. You went to see Dad, didn't you?" There was silence on the other end. "Talk to me Jalen."

"Look. I don't know how you got this number, but lose it."

"Hold on Jalen. You can diss me all you want, but what about our father?"

"What about him?"

Terell realized Jalen didn't know. "You know where he is?"

"I know where he is."

"I don't think you do. He's in the hospital, shot up and dying. I'm here and you should be here too."

There was a short pause. "Shot up?" Jalen said. "Won't bother me if he croaks."

"You bastard. You fucking moron. What is it with you?"

"You wanna know the truth? He could give a shit about me. You want to know the truth? I came to see him, okay? He turned his back on me, like he always did."

"Slow down. What the hell? He tried to set you straight more than once, and you know it."

"Straight? Yeah straight to the fucking army, straight to Iraq, straight to Chicago, straight to drugs and street hoods, straight to gambling, and straight to hell."

"So why were you here?"

"None of your fucking business. How'd you know I was there?"

"You're not invisible you know, the cops know you were here. You want me out of your life too? What the hell did I ever do to you? I always had your back, and you know what? I still do. So what were you doing here?'

"Damn you, Terell. I got myself in a little trouble here and my girl is havin' my baby. I got to settle a debt with a bad dude. I owe him fifty-grand."

"Oh my lord. Are you straight these days, drugs?"

"Yeah. I been clean for a while. My girl's clean too. I may have to get out of here."

"So, if I get this right, you came here to get fifty-grand from Dad."

"Yeah, but he turned me down. Told me to get a job and a life. Called me a no-good son."

Dan, Scotty and Syms intently listened and they were hearing an ear full. "Listen to me you idiot," Terell shouted. "Don't turn your back on blood."

"Me turn my back on blood? I think *your* father is the one who turned his back on blood."

"And he may be dead soon." There was silence and a click. "Jerk hung up," Terell uttered. "I need some water."

Dan left the room and returned with a cup of water. He handed it to Terell who let out a huge sigh and then drank the entire cupful. With a tear in his eye he said, "Jalen's really screwed up."

Dan asked. "You need more water?"

Terell winced. "No thanks. You heard that shithead. He called Dad … *My father*! Asshole brother. I'm not finished with him."

Syms stood and put his arm around Terell's shoulder. "Go get some air."

Dan watched the visibly shaken Terrell exit Syms's office. "What do you think?" Dan asked.

Scotty shook his head. "I don't know. Sounds like Jalen was mad enough to kill his father, but it also sounds like he didn't know about the shooting."

⚓

Terell walked out of the police station with steam coming from his ears and got into his rented vehicle. He couldn't forget Jalen's words about blood. It was sacrilegious. If Jalen were standing beside his brother right now, Terell would beat him to a pulp. Still parked in the police visitor's lot, Terell called Shelaine's number again and Jalen answered. "What do you want now?"

"It's not over, Jalen. It's not over. You need to get your head straight."

"Damn you. Who the hell are you to tell me what to do?"

"Shut up you ass. I'm blood, same as *our* father. Listen up. Nobody is to blame for your screw-ups but you. You made your life what it is. You want help. I'm here. I don't know why, but I still love you."

There was a momentary hush, and Jalen said, "Damn you. You were always a goody two-shoes. Lily white, and for a black man, that's a laugh. Always did things by the book. Daddy's little disciple. That's not me."

"No shit. You said you have a baby on the way. You telling me straight you're off drugs?"

"I swear I am." There was a brief silence and then Jalen said, "I'm sort of clean. I'm trying. I'm in deep shit. I have to settle my debt real soon, or we have to get the hell out of here. I lied to dad. I said I needed fifty-grand. I need thirty. I wanted to have a little left over for me, Shelaine, and the baby."

"You know I shouldn't do this, but I can send you thirty. How did you get yourself in this bind?"

"Let's just say I lost a bet. He's already got my car, and he won't wait much longer before he sends his guys after me. I been sort of running, moving around the city. Right now we're in a motel in Rockford, about ninety miles out of Chicago."

"Everything in her name?"

"Yeah. I even ditched my phone."

"Can you make it back here? I'll pay. I'll give you my Visa number and you book a plane. I'll have the money wired here so you can have the cash."

"Really, Terell?"

"Really. You get back here and come to the hospital with me. I want you here when Dad opens his eyes. I think it will mean the world to him."

"What's the story? Who shot him?"

Terell told what he knew to his brother.

"Damn, Terell. You really doing this?"

"We're brothers aren't we? Get your ass back here. Hey, tell me something. Where'd you go after you left Dad's office?"

Jalen proceeded to tell his brother what happened later.

"Call me when you get in," Terell said.

Re-entering the lobby, he approached Ashley. She called Syms to let him know Terell was back.

A few minutes later he was in the captain's office with Dan and Scotty.

Terell said, "I couldn't let it rest. I just got off the phone with Jalen. He's coming back here and I'm bailing him out of his debt. It seems he came here to ask Dad for the money. I should say he came here to get the money. He had called Dad and told him a story about the debt, but he lied about one thing. He said he needed fifty-grand, but he only owed thirty. He wanted some for himself, Shelaine and the baby."

"Did he say where he and Shelaine went when they left here?" Dan asked.

"You're getting ahead of me," Terell said. "Dad had gone to the bank to get the money that morning … A bank check. He decided to treat Terell and Shelaine to dinner where he was to hand over the money. They met at a place called Justine's."

"Justino's," Dan said. "Nice place."

"They met at around eight-thirty. Things went well and they were enjoying dinner. Dad sensed Jalen was high, and pushed the issue. Dad went ballistic when he realized Jalen had lied to him about being off drugs. That was it. Dad pulled the check back. That was the last time he saw Dad." Terell paused, "Oh, yeah. Jalen said Dad had gotten a call during dinner and had to meet someone later."

Dan said, "The Pastor."

"Jalen didn't hear who it was. He swears he and Shelaine went to a motel near the airport and turned in the car in the next morning. Then they flew back to Chicago. That's it. Syms stood and said to Terell, "Let us know when he gets in."

CHAPTER 34

Justino's was in the south side of town, not far from Frankland Avenue where Javier Ibanez had been killed. The detectives entered the establishment. A host approached them. "Two?" he asked.

Dan displayed his badge. "Wish we could say we came to eat, but we'd like to talk to the manager."

"I'll get him," the host said.

Dan eyed the interior and saw shell-shaped sconces on the walls and silver candle holders on each maroon-linen-draped table. He also spied a wine cabinet that was stocked with dozens of bottles, and a bar with huge TV screens, one on each end.

The host returned. With him was a tall man who looked thirty-something. His head was shaved and an earring hung from his left ear. He extended his hand to Dan. "I'm Alton Vick. I understand you want to talk to me."

"I'm Dan Shields and this is Joe Scott."

They all shook hands and Dan said, "Can we sit for a minute?"

"Sure," Alton replied as he guided them to a table toward the rear of the restaurant. "What's this about?" he asked.

"It's about police chief Hardison, who was shot several days ago."

"I heard about it."

Dan said, "We have reason to believe he was here the night he was shot."

"Really? What makes you say that?"

"His son told us."

"Wait here. Jessica was on that night."

The young waitress came to the table with her boss. Dan asked her, "Do you remember the police chief being here a few nights ago?"

"There was a police officer who was wearing a uniform. I do remember him," she said.

"Was he with anyone?"

"I remember a man and a woman. She might have been pregnant. They were sitting with him."

"Did you happen to hear any of their discussion?" Dan asked.

"No, but the couple tore out of here before they finished eating."

"Do you remember if the police chief made any phone calls?"

"No. It was quite busy that night."

"Did you see him leave?"

"No, but he left a nice tip."

"Thank you," Dan said as he turned back to Alton. "We think he may have made a call or received a call from here, but his cell is missing."

Alton rubbed his chin. "Wait a minute. There was one found in the bathroom. It was turned in to me by the cleaning crew."

"Do you still have it?" Dan asked.

"I do, but the phone is inoperable. The case is broken, and the glass is shattered. I was hoping someone would come back and ask about it. Do you want it?"

"Yes. Can you get it?"

Alton stood, walked away, and returned a minute later. He handed the broken phone to Dan. "I was told it was in a stall. One of the cleaning crew stepped on the phone and you can see the damage."

Scotty looked at it. "Looks pretty useless."

Dan handed his card to Alton. "If by chance someone does come looking for the phone, call me."

Leaving the restaurant as two patrons entered, Dan said to Scotty, "So far, Jalen's story holds."

When the detectives returned to headquarters, Dan showed Syms the shattered phone. "You recognize it?"

"Really? Looks like an elephant stepped on it."

"The manager at Justino's said it was found in the bathroom. A waitress also verified Jalen's story. This has to be Hardison's phone."

"Nice deduction Sherlock. You tried to call it?" Syms asked.

Dan placed the phone on the desk. "Try it. See if it rings."

Syms took out his cell and called Hardison's. The phone vibrated. "All I hear are cracks and pops, but it's his."

Dan leaned on the desk. "I was thinking. You had a conversation with Hernan Benedict. I'd like to give it a shot. Maybe he'll remember more now."

"Not a bad idea," Scotty said.

"You have his daughters address and phone number." Dan said to Syms. "How about letting me have it. I'll give her a call."

"Syms wrote the information on a piece of paper and handed it to Dan. "Good luck."

An hour later Scotty and Dan were on their way to Stone Village, a community of three-hundred units north of downtown. "That's it, the green one, number ninety-seven," Scotty said.

Dan squeezed his Accord into a spot barely fifteen feet from a hydrant and the detectives walked up to the front door of the brick two-level unit. Scotty rang the bell. Ernestine clad in a brown house dress opened the door.

"Thanks for allowing us to stop by," Dan said.

"Come in. My dad is in the den watching Wheel of Fortune. I'll get him."

The detectives sat in the living room and waited. The small home's living and dining rooms were combined. A kitchen was to the right of the dining area and a hallway led to the den and what Dan assumed were the bedrooms and bath. It appeared the fireplace hadn't been used in quite a while, if ever. No wood or logs of any kind were in sight. Ernestine escorted her father into the room. He wore his pajamas under a red plaid robe and sat on the couch beside his daughter.

"Hi, Mr. Benedict," Dan said. "We met briefly at Pastor Jonathan's church."

"The church. Poor pastor. I don't remember you."

"I didn't think you would. It was very upsetting." Dan sat forward. "Mr. Benedict. Do you remember talking with Captain Syms at the hospital?"

He nodded. "I think so."

Dan noticed the medical emergency device strung from a chain around the man's neck. The detective was hopeful of obtaining more info, and he got the feeling the old man seemed to remember more now than he had before. "Do you remember who the last person was, besides you, who was at the church that day?"

The Janitor held his daughter's hand. "He loved those kids,"Benedict said before becoming silent and staring at the wall.

"Mr. Benedict," Dan said. "You started to say something about kids."

The man continued. "Oh, them. He was like a father to them."

Once again, he looked off into space. "Mr. Benedict," Dan said again. "You were saying."

"Oh yes. He liked that new kid. Can't remember his name."

Dan thought for a second. "Does the name Devon McCray ring a bell?"

Benedict nodded. "That's the one. He was there until we had supper."

Dan asked, "Do you remember what they talked about?"

"No, but I do remember the kid running out as if his pants were on fire."

"Was there an argument?"

"The pastor never argued."

"Why do you suppose Devon McCray was so upset?"

"Can't say."

"You mean you don't know?"

"That's what I said, can't say."

"Did he come back again later?"

Benedict was silent. Ernestine looked at Dan. "I think he's tired," she said.

The detective turned to her. "When he talked to my captain at the hospital, your father said something about a scooter or shooter."

"I think he's trying to say the shooter was a kid."

Benedict uttered, "I heard a loud bang." He momentarily closed his eyes, and then reopened them. "I came out and saw the pastor. He was face down on the floor."

Dan sensed Benedict was holding back something that the old man couldn't quite get out. "Did you see the shooter?" The detective asked.

Benedict became quiet again. A few seconds later, he mumbled, "Shooter, scooter."

"What are you trying to tell us?" Dan asked. "Did you see the shooter?"

The janitor closed his eyes. "He's exhausted," Ernestine said.

The detectives rose and Dan handed Ernestine his card. "Thank you. If he should say something else that might help us, please call me."

CHAPTER 35

Dan felt a chill in his bones, and it wasn't the cool weather he was feeling. As soon as he arrived at the police station, he headed for the holding tank. Stopping before opening the outer door, he thought twice about going inside, but his inner-voice kept talking, and he continued his morning journey. He stepped to sergeant Denine's desk. "Let me in," Dan said. "By the way, it smells in there."

"It's not nearly as bad as the old place though," Denine said. "The house is nearly full."

Dan walked down the corridor and saw three unoccupied cells. The rest had tenants. As he strolled toward the rear of the tank, he heard a whistle, and then a voice. "Psst. Dan."

The detective looked to cell thirteen on his left. "Curly, what's the story this time?"

"Bar fight and public intoxication. I sober up quick."

Curly Cornwall liked a good fight every now and then, and at six-three, two-sixty, he'd won more than a few. "I busted up a guy pretty good." Curly showed his arm muscle. "Not much of a struggle, mother-fucker tried to blindside me, but I saw his fist coming, and I went bam. His sorry ass is in the hospital. Hey, can you get me a pick? My afro needs attention."

Dan eyed the hair. "That thing is as high as I've ever seen it. Makes you look about six-six, and you look thin. Been eating lately?"

"Hell, I'm short on coin, but I got a job coming up."

"You? A job? Like what?"

"Bouncer. The guy at the club liked my work." Curly shook his head. "That Pastor Jonathan. I knew it would be a matter of time."

Dan's ears perked up. "What did you say? What do you mean? You know anything about him?"

Curly backed away from the bars. "Not really."

Dan didn't like that response; he knew it meant Curly knew something. "Tell me what you know Curly, and don't fuck around."

"Whoa, I don't know nothing."

Dan glared at him and raised his voice. "Come on, Curly. I said don't fuck around with me. What do you know? Get your ass back here."

Curly took two steps and drew closer to Dan. "Look. All I know is, word's getting around he was mentoring the kids."

"We know he was. What's wrong with that?"

Curly moved up to the bars and wrapped his hands around them. "You know what mentoring is, right?"

"What are you saying?"

"Man, you're pretty straight."

"Come on, Curly."

"Okay, rumors have it he'd been mentoring the young boys in sex."

Dan's jaw dropped. "Are you saying he was a predator?"

"Got that right."

"You know that for a fact?"

"Hey, it's what I heard."

Dan was stunned, and he stood in silence for a few seconds before backing away from the bars. "Nice to see you Curly. I need to get to work, and I don't know whether to hope you're right or wrong."

On his way up to the squad room, Dan thought about Curly's comments, and the detective remembered seeing pictures of young boys on the pastor's wall and credenza. What Curly had told him fit. Boy's pictures, no girls, only boys.

Dan strode heavily into the squad room.

"What's eating you this morning?" Luke asked.

Dan ignored the question and rushed to Scotty. "Let's go, you gotta hear this shit."

Dan tossed his jacket on a chair, and barreled into Syms's office with Scotty right behind him. Syms immediately grabbed his pill bottle. "You're hyper. What's on your mind?"

Dan leaned on the desk. "Shit, a lot of shit. You know who's downstairs? Of course not. Curly Cornwall, and he told me a mindblower. Pastor Jonathan was a predator."

Syms stood. "A what? You fucking joking? He mentored those juveniles."

"Really? Well his mentoring apparently included having sex with them. It fits. There are photos of at least a dozen boys in his office."

Scotty was speechless until Dan finished spewing out the news. "You sure Curly is telling you the truth?"

"I think it's true. Curly might be a street menace, but he's always been straight with me."

Syms sat back with his jaw wide open as Dan continued, "We're gonna go tear that church apart."

"Jesus," Syms said. "I haven't seen you like this in a long time."

"Well. I don't like cops getting shot, especially Hardison, and me of course. And I sure as hell don't like child molesters."

Syms said. "Wait a minute. "What happened with Benedict?"

Dan said, "We talked to him and he told us Devon McCray had stormed out of the church." Dan pounded his hand on the captain's desk. "You know, I was never sure of that McCray kid. Know what? Sasser turned over a weapon the kid gave him, but how do we know it was the gun Jerricks had on him? That store video is fuzzy. I want another look at it when we get back."

Dan and Scotty headed to the church after obtaining the keys from Dixon. Upon arriving, the detectives found several fresh flower arrangements and signs on the lawn and front steps.

Entering the church, Scotty turned on the lights. "Cool in here?" he said.

Walking past the chapel into the pastor's quarters, Dan turned on the light and he eyed all the photos in the room. "What do you think? Ages what? Ten, twelve, fifteen? "

"Sixteen pictures," Scotty said.

Dan studied the photos. "McCray would make seventeen," Dan replied. "Hey, remember the list of names you found. I'd bet the names of those kids are on it."

Scotty found the list. "Seventeen names with stars next to them, all boys. The last one starred one on the list is Devon McCray." Inside the desk drawer, Scotty spotted a key. "Look at this."

Dan noticed a few panels, one with a keyhole. "Try it."

Scotty inserted the key, opened the compartment, and pulled out the contents. "Jesus," he said. "Take a look. Porn … Stacks."

Dan eyed the videos. Names on hand printed labels were on each one. "He had sex with all these kids."

"Got a cell phone." Scotty said as he searched the contents. "Look at this. Texts, and pictures. Kids naked. He clicked on a video. "Jesus, Dan. He's pleasuring himself." Scotty handed the phone to his partner. "Take a look."

Dan shoved the phone back into Scotty's hand. "What the hell do I look like? A pervert? I'll take your word, pal." Dan spotted an empty waste basket, and pointed to it. "Put that shit with the videos in there. We'll take that stuff back with us."

Scotty dumped the evidence into an empty wastebasket. "You know, someone is going to have to view these."

"It won't be me. Grab the basket. Let's get out of here."

The detectives returned to headquarters and stormed into the captain's office. Scotty placed the bucket of porn on the floor. Dan pointed to it. "It's all in there," he said. "Videos of the pastor and all those victims."

Syms threw his plastic pill bottle against the wall. "Damn it!" he yelled. "You look at those?"

"No, but Scotty got a glimpse of him masturbating."

"Holy shit. Keep this crap in-house." Syms said.

"Pick up your pills." Dan said. "We're gonna view that convenience store tape again."

The detectives headed back to Dan's desk to retrieve the tape. Something had bothered Dan from the beginning about the McCray kid and how he was near enough to Jerricks to grab the gun. What was he doing there? And having heard from Sasser, that the kid had a prior for robbery, further interested Dan. He grabbed the tape. "Come on. The conference room has a player."

Dan and Scotty entered the room where a long table with ten chairs around it took up most of the space. A tape player was attached to the TV in the far corner. Scotty turned the light switch and closed the door behind them. Dan inserted the tape of the robbery. "Here we go," he said as he started the video. "Cheap crap. Fuzzy as hell."

The taped angle was from behind the counter and showed Moses Sterling handing money to Jerricks. That part was unmistakable. Dan noticed someone crouched behind a row of shelves. The barely visible person wearing a blue hoodie darted out of the store "The blue hoodie," Dan said. "That's Devon McCray. He was with Jerricks."

"Makes sense," Scotty said.

Dan replied, "As soon as Jerricks was shot, the kid swooped in, took that gun, and grabbed the paper bag. I think McCray may have been a lookout, and he may have had his own weapon."

"What about the gang crap? Jerricks was a Knight. As far as we know the kid wasn't a member."

Dan removed the tape. "Not yet. Ever heard of gang initiations?"

"What are you getting at? You think robbing a store with Jerricks was a test?"

Dan shook his head, paused, took a deep breath and looked at Scotty. "No, but I think Pastor Jonathan might have been."

"Holy Jesus," Scotty said with his hands in the air. "But what's Hardison got to do with it?"

"Good question," Dan replied. "The pastor was shot at close range and Hardison was hit from a distance. I'm sure there were two shooters. We need to get the ballistics report?"

"Let's go see Garcia."

The detectives walked down a flight of stairs and went to Garcia's office. The gang unit leader was pacing in his office and Dan asked, "What's buggin you?"

"The gangs are at it. Two Sultans died last night. We need to keep units on alert," Garcia said.

Dan said, "Tell me more about Jerricks. You said he was on the outs with the Knights."

"He was, but according to one of my guys, he was trying to make amends and smooth things out," Garcia replied

"How so?" Dan asked. "I hardly think robbing a convenience store would be the resolution." Dan stared at the wall in back of Garcia, and then said. "Could he have been asked to do a favor in order to get back in good straights?"

"What kind of favor?" Garcia asked.

"The kind involving bringing young blood into the gang?"

"Could be. We know they're recruiting," Garcia replied.

"I'm thinking the store robbery was a warm-up for Devon McCray. I think the kid wanted into the gang and after Jerricks was shot, the kid had to earn his way in another way. Here's a bombshell. Pastor Jonathan was a predator. We're sure he molested, or tried to molest McCray."

"What?"

"You heard me. Curly Cornwall is downstairs and he told me. We have evidence from the church. Porn, kiddie porn with all those kids he mentored. We're also sure Devon McCray was the last person to see Pastor Jonathan alive, and the janitor at the church told us the kid had left in a fit of rage that night," Dan said. "We think he came back later with another shooter whom we suspect shot Hardison. We're gonna check ballistics to see how many weapons were fired."

The detectives went directly to Syms's office. Dan asked. "You ever get a ballistics report on the weapon that killed the pastor and wounded the chief? I'm sure there were two guns."

Syms rocked in his chair. "I'll get on it."

CHAPTER 36

Dan was at his desk and his cell vibrated. He looked at the text he'd received from Scotty.

Sick as a dog. Stomach thing. Was up all night.

Dan texted back.

I'll tell Syms.

Dan saw the empty captain's office, so he called Syms's cell. "Where are you?" the detective asked.

"On my way to see the chief."

"Scotty's sick. Stomach bug. I'm coming to Woodland."

"Hey," Syms said. "I got the ballistics report last night. It's on my desk. It confirms what you thought. Two weapons."

"I knew it. See you in little while."

As Dan headed out of the building, Garcia was entering. "How's it going?" the gang unit leader said.

"I'm on my way to the hospital. Hardison's still out."

Garcia said, "I hear Skeeter Hantoras is going home soon. Looks like he's the lucky one."

When Dan arrived at Woodland, he took the elevator up to the Surgical ICU unit and when he stepped out, he saw Syms who was standing outside a room on the opposite end of the floor. The captain had tears in his eyes. "What happened?" Dan asked.

"He's awake, off life support. They moved him to this stepdown unit. Terell, Jalen, and Shelaine are here."

Dan walked into the multiple-bed unit and saw the chief, who had been extubated, but still had a finger monitor on his hand and an IV hookup. "Hi Terell," Dan said.

Terell introduced Jalen and Shelaine while Dan stood at the chief's bedside. The detective smiled at the patient. "I knew you'd come around. You'll be back in no time."

Struggling to speak, Hardison winked at him. Dan winked back, stepped away and whispered to Terell, "Have you talked with the doctor?"

"Let's step out," Terell said.

They joined Syms. "It was a miracle," Terell said "I think it's a message from God. Jalen brought a miracle with him. I came back here late yesterday afternoon and held Dad's hand. I told him Jalen was sorry and he was coming here. All of a sudden, Dad's eyes opened. The doctor came in, examined him, and told me if Dad was stable in the morning, he'd be moved over here." Terell paused. "He may be here a few days and then he might go to a general nursing unit and private bed."

"That's great," Syms said.

Terell shook his head. "It's amazing. I think Jalen has seen the light.We're going to be family again. I'm helping him out of his jam and he's coming to California with Shelaine."

"Great," Dan said.

Syms added, "I'm so happy."

Dan took a deep breath and leaned into Syms. "We have to talk. Listen, the ballistics report indicates two different weapons. We know Devon McCray was the last person to see Jonathan. I think Hernan Benedict keeps trying to say McCray was the shooter, and it's clear he wasn't alone." The janitor's words were ringing loud and clear in Dan's ears: *Shooter, scooter, scooter, shooter*, and the detective's eyes opened wide.

"What's wrong?" Syms asked.

Dan realized what Hernan Benedict was really trying to tell him. *Son of a bitch is here too.* "I have to do something," he said to Syms. The detective turned and walked quickly down the corridor.

Dan was on a mission, and marched downstairs to the admitting desk, every step heavy with anticipation. Standing at the front counter with fire in his eyes, he asked the clerk. "What room is Skeeter Hantoras in?"

The clerk entered the patient's name into her computer and said, "Two-fifteen."

"Thanks," Dan replied as he strode toward the elevator. He entered the empty car and pressed the level two button. *Scooter my ass. Skeeter ... That fucking thug is mine now.*

The short trip seemed longer than it actually was, but before stepping out, Dan buttoned his sport coat, keeping his itchy trigger finger from his weapon, and with purpose in his strut, he neared room 215.

The riled detective stopped at the medical station in the center of the floor where he saw a nurse and a doctor conversing. "Excuse me," Dan said.

The young physician turned to him. "Yes, sir."

Dan showed his badge. "I'm here to see Skeeter Hantoras in two-fifteen."

The doctor said, "He's being discharged. He would have been out of here earlier if he'd had clothes. Someone dropped off a set a little while ago."

"Someone was up here? Do you know who it was?"

"No. Whoever it was gave the clothes to an administrator downstairs, and an orderly brought up a bag to give to him. That's all I know. We need to bandage him again, let him dress, and get him pain pills to take home with a prescription."

Dan glanced at room 215 where the door was shut. "Do me a favor, doc. I need to talk to him in private. All I ask is that you let me finish talking with him. If you hear loud conversation, don't panic. Please stay out, okay?"

"Go ahead. He was a lucky guy. The shot that hit him missed a main artery by an inch."

"I'll keep that in mind."

Dan took several steps, aching to pull his weapon from its holster, and he barged into the room, shutting the door behind him.

Still in a hospital gown, the startled Skeeter said, "Who the hell are you?"

Eying the approximately five-nine hoodlum, who was sitting on the edge of the bed, Dan said, "Interesting question. I'm your worst nightmare."

The gang member whose tattoos covered his visible skin from his shaved head to his neck got off the bed and tried to stare Dan down. "Who the fuck are you?" he yelled, moving the empty IV pole out of the way.

Dan stared back, and showed his badge. "Sit, you bastard. Now you get me?"

Skeeter sat in a chair beside the bed. "Fuck you. I'm outta here."

Dan's cold eyes stared into his captive's eyes. "Let's gets one thing straight from the get-go." The detective moved closer to Skeeter and raised his voice. "Neither one of us is leaving this room until I get what I want. You understand me? And don't bother trying to call the nurses station."

"You don't scare me?" Skeeter said.

"We'll see about that. Let's start with this." Dan stared into Skeeter's eyes, and harshly said, "I'm the cop who fat-ass Biggie shot a few years ago. I knew your half-brothers, Santiago, and Julio. Some family you got."

Skeeter tried to get up, and Dan shoved the hundred-sixty pound thug back down into the chair. "Ouch, God damn you bastard!" Skeeter yelled. "That's a fucking bullet wound. Keep your fucking hands off me!"

"Okay you scumbag. Chief Hardison is still upstairs. Pastor Jonathan is dead, and Devon McCray is free and loose. And your boy Jerricks is dead. Did I mention your other half-brother Caesar? It's like this. I know McCray was with Jerricks committing that convenience store burglary." Without missing a breath, Dan continued. "I know they both had weapons and I know McCray had been getting mentored by the pastor. You get where I'm going?"

Skeeter placed a hand over his throbbing wound and began to sweat. Dan saw him eying the buzzer. "Bastard, you can't keep me here," Skeeter said as he tried to get up again.

Dan held both hands up and menacingly glared at him. "Oh yes I can. I can even rip that bandage off your chest, so you're going to hear the rest … Whether you like it or not."

"You're fucking crazy. I'm getting out of here."

Dan shoved him back down with more force than last time. The detective's face was red with anger as he said, "McCray wanted into the Knights, didn't he? He came to you and you ordered him, as an initiation, to gun down the pastor, especially after Devon had told you the pastor had molested him."

Skeeter swallowed hard. "Bullshit!"

Dan leaned in close to Skeeter's face. "Oh, I know you did. I also know there was a second shooter. You were there to see he finished the job. I'm *dead right* aren't I? Somehow Hardison showed up shortly after the church shooting, and you put a couple of bullets in him. Why?"

"Get out of my face you fucking maniac!" Skeeter screamed.

"That's not going to help, Skeeter. You want out of this room, you tell me where I'm wrong. Only thing I don't get is Hardison."

Skeeter squinted. "You can't talk to me without a lawyer."

"Who says? We're talking right now aren't we? Like I said, you aren't leaving here until I get what I want. So why Hardison? You bad guys trying to make a statement? Kill the head and you fuckers can run the city?"

Skeeter didn't say anything.

"You don't have to say anything asshole. I'm going to let them re-bandage you and let you finish getting dressed. As soon as you've signed the release forms, we're going downtown."

"You can't arrest me. You have no proof of anything."

"You're under the influence of drugs."

"You're crazy."

"No I'm not. I'd say you're on pain meds, and I bet you'll have some Oxy or Percocet on you before we leave. That's why we're going downtown where you can wait until we bring Devon McCray in. I'm sure he'll talk. He's still a juvie. He'll get a lesser sentence."

"Horseshit! He won't tell you anything?"

"I think he will when I explain his options to him. Where does Devon hang out?"

"The community center. Go find him. He's not ratting."

"By the way. Why did the Sultans target you?"

Skeeter blurted out. "Cause' I talked Caesar into splitting and coming over to us, but my dumb-ass brother couldn't keep his mouth shut."

"Thanks for the chat. I think we understand each other. I'm going to let the nurse wrap you again, and when you're dressed, we're leaving together."

Skeeter stood. "Open the fucking door," he said.

Dan stared at his prey. "One last chance, Skeeter. Why Hardison?"

Skeeter didn't say a word. Dan, still peering into the attacker's eyes said, "That shit look on your face tells me everything I need to know. If you think it was rough here, wait until we get downtown. I'll be right outside this door."

While waiting as Skeeter's wound was being freshly dressed, Dan called Syms. "Hey, something came up. I'll see you in the morning."

CHAPTER 37

D an saw the note Syms had left on the detective's desk.
Get your ass down to my office ... NOW!

As soon as the detective stepped inside the captain's office, he saw the look on Syms's face. The angered boss pointed at his prized lieutenant. "What's this shit you pulled at the hospital?"

Dan moved close to the desk, placing his palms on top. "It's hardball. Good old-fashioned hardball. Skeeter Hantoras is downstairs. I'm going out to find Devon McCray."

"Slow down."

Dan sat in a chair.

"I said slow down, not sit down. Get up."

Dan stood.

"Sit down. What the hell did you charge him with, and what the hell did you do? You just walk in with him and take him to the tank?"

"Pretty much."

"You can't fucking do that, and you know it!" Syms yelled. "Tell me again. What exactly did you charge him with? And where the hell is the paperwork?"

Dan knew whatever he was about to say wouldn't satisfy his boss. "Possession of drugs. He had Oxy and no prescription when we left the hospital. Haven't officially filed charges yet, but he thinks I have."

"What?" Syms said as he held his hands in the air. "Damn it. We can't hold him. Get your ass downstairs and have him set loose. If the DA hears about this one, we're toast. And I know damn well the doctor handed him a prescription."

Dan stood. "Right. I said he didn't have one when he left the hospital. It must have fallen out of Skeeter's pocket."

"Jesus Christ!" Syms yelled.

"He needs to be locked up," Dan hollered. "He shot Hardison."

Syms uncapped his Advil bottle. "What? How'd you get that?"

"It was what Hernan Benedict was trying to tell us. The words he kept saying, shooter, and scooter. I realized he was trying to say Skeeter and it all fit. He heard the McCray kid shouting Skeeter."

Syms sat back and grabbed his head. "So go get some real evidence and a warrant. Damn it, until then, he has to be out of here. You get your ass downstairs and set him free."

The detective had his orders. "Okay, but you can be sure, I'll have a short leash on that bastard."

Dan hastily left the captain's office as Scotty entered the squad room. "Where you off to in such a rush?" Scotty asked.

"Damn it. I have to go release a prisoner."

"A what? What the hell did you do?"

"Tell you when I get back. Your stomach okay? You off the crapper?"

"Pepto works wonders."

"Stay away from Syms."

Dan obeyed orders and then headed back upstairs. He filled Scotty in on Skeeter Hantoras and the unofficial arrest. "Let's go make someone happy."

Scotty eyed his partner. "I thought you said to stay away from Syms."

"I did, but this won't take long."

Dan and Scotty entered Syms's office. "He's out. Happy now?" Dan said.

"Me? You should be happy you're not in the tank." Syms eyed Scotty. "You okay?"

Scotty replied, "I am."

"Good. Keep a tight rein on your partner. What's with the juvie?" Syms asked.

"We'll have a chat with him. Skeeter told me where to find Devon."

"Take a black and white. Go get Ramirez."

Dan went downstairs and asked the sergeant to come with them. Ramirez picked up the keys to a cruiser and the three officers got into the vehicle. "You think the kid is carrying a weapon?" Ramirez asked.

"Could be," Dan said.

The squad car pulled into the Uccello Community Center at the corner of Early and Barber. Ramirez and Scotty stayed inside the vehicle, while Dan got out and entered the facility. A counselor with long dreads, who appeared to be in his mid-twenties, approached as the detective walked down the corridor toward the gym. "You looking for someone?"

Dan peeked inside the gym at the basketball game in progress as he flashed his badge. "Devon McCray. I hear he hangs here."

"Haven't seen him in days. Might be home with his disabled mother."

"Disabled?"

"Dee, nice lady. She's been in a wheel chair ever since that fucker of a husband shoved her down a flight of stairs. You tried the house?"

"Thought I'd try here first. What the hell happened?"

"To Dee? Asshole was always drunk, and I guess they got into it one night about a year ago. He took off and no one's seen him since."

Dan started to turn around. "I can't remember the address."

The counselor crossed his arms. "You fish?" he said. "I know you just tossed out some bait."

Dan opened his wallet and handed the man a twenty. "I need the address."

"Now that's nice bait. So what's Devon done?"

"He might be in a little trouble."

"Trouble? Listen, he's a good kid, but you know something?" the counselor said as he pointed down the hall. "A lot of kids here are troubled, but this place isn't a hangout. We keep them busy. There's a computer room and a library down there. Take a look at all the kids in there. Basketball and the gym are what most outsiders focus on, but damn it, it's about time someone gives a shit about these kids. You didn't see any bikes out there right? I mean motorcycles. There are bicycles, and I guarantee not one is stolen. Look around, you won't find drugs in here either."

Dan asked, "Did you know Pastor Jonathan?"

"Not really. I know some of the kids have been mentored by the man."

Dan held back the truth. "I do need Dee McCray's address. I want to talk with Devon."

The counselor gave Dan the address and then he handed the detective back the twenty-dollar bill. "I hope you learned something."

Dan shook the man's hand. "What's your name? Ever thought of being a cop?"

"It's Taylon, and I spent five years at the corrections center before deciding I wanted to help these kids from making the same mistakes I made."

"I'm proud to have met you, Taylon. Keep up the good work."

Dan got back into Ramirez's car. "Let's go to the house. Devon wasn't there, but I got the address. His mother's name is Dee and she's disabled because the kid's father threw her down a flight of stairs."

A few minutes later, Ramirez's car was parked in front of the house. The uniformed officer said, "I'm coming with you guys."

The two-family residence had side-by-side doors. As the trio walked up four steps onto the front porch, they couldn't tell which unit was the McCray's. Dan found it odd there was only one mailbox between the units and he looked at Scotty. "Your guess is as good as mine."

Ramirez stepped forward. "Wait a minute. Didn't you say she'd been pushed down stairs?"

Dan said, "Good thinking. Upstairs it is, ring the bell."

Ramirez pressed the white button and they waited. No one came down to open the door. He pushed it again as Dan peeked into the side glass window, and he saw a door at the top of the stairs open. Seconds later, a voice said, "Leave my medicine by the mailbox."

Dan banged on the glass to get her attention. "Dee. We're police. Please let us in."

"Police? What do you want?"

"We need to talk to you."

"Hold on. I'll buzz you up. Is my medicine down there?"

"No," Dan said. He heard a buzz and Ramirez opened the door. The lawmen entered the house and marched upstairs where Dee greeted them. She was standing behind her walker and wearing a green and yellow house dress, curlers in her hair. She straightened her oval-shaped glasses.

"What's this about?" she asked. "Have you found my no-good husband? Hope he's dead somewhere."

They entered the living room. The walls were painted dark blue, and unmatched end tables were on each side of the long couch that appeared to be on its' last legs. The police officers sank into the soft cushions. "Is Devon here?" Dan asked.

"In his room. Why?"

Dan didn't want to hide anything. He said, "Actually it's quite serious. Devon may have been involved in a convenience store robbery."

"A what?" Dee said.

Dan told the mother about her son's involvement with Vandor Jerricks. "Devon's not a bad kid," she said. "A little lost since his father left. That son of a bitch would have beaten the crap out of Devon had I not gotten in the way. Bastard pushed me down those stairs and I spent a month the hospital with a broken hip and leg. I'm lucky I can walk with this walker."

Before Dan could tell Dee about the pastor, there was a noise coming from the kitchen that sounded like the back door opening. Dee shouted, "Devon, don't you leave. You get in here."

The boy, wearing his blue hoodie, shut the back door and entered the living room. "These police want to talk to you," she said.

Devon shrugged with his hands in his pockets and stood beside his mother.

Dan looked him in the eye and the boy looked away. "We need you to level with us. We have your friend Skeeter in custody. He told us a lot of stuff. We know you were with Jerricks. What ever happened to the brown bag? I bet you spent the money from the robbery."

Dee's eyes opened wide and she glared at her son. "Tell them," she said.

Devon said nothing.

Dan looked at Dee. "There's something else you need to hear. It's very serious," he said. Dan turned to Devon. "Look at me and listen. Skeeter nailed you as the person who shot Pastor Jonathan."

Dee bowed her head and her face drew tight with surprise and anger. "Devon. Is this true? Answer the man."

He still didn't speak.

Dan said, "Devon. "Tell us about the pastor."

Devon cast his eyes on his mother, but couldn't speak. "Dee. You need to hear this." Dan turned to the boy. "We know the pastor molested you, didn't he?"

Devon nodded as he stared at the uniformed officer's handcuffs.

Stunned, Dee said, "This is true?"

"Sit down Devon," Dan said. "I want to make this easy on you. We know you wanted into the Knights, and we know Skeeter made you pull the trigger on the pastor. We also know Skeeter shot the police chief." Devon's face filled with fear and he crept close to his mother. "Tell us we're right and we can cut you a deal."

"What does that mean?" Dee asked.

Dan said, "I'm not going to sugar coat this. Devon is in a lot of trouble. He's still a juvenile and we can get him a reduced sentence if he cooperates." Dan leaned close to Devon, who now seemed to realize he was trapped. "I need the gun you shot the pastor with."

Devon slowly walked to his room, Ramirez by his side. They returned to the living room with Ramirez holding the weapon. The scared boy stood beside his mother again. "Listen closely," Dan said. "I need Devon to sign a sworn statement implicating Skeeter Hantoras as the co-conspirator in Pastor Jonathan's killing, and the sole shooter of Police Chief Hardison. Hantoras will get a first-degree murder charge. The charge for Devon will be the same, but his court-appointed attorney will petition for a lesser sentence. Devon will likely go to a juvenile detention center for a period of time. Skeeter will go to prison for life."

Dee was shaking. Dan took a breath. "I said I wasn't going to sugar coat it. Devon could go away for a while, or if he doesn't cooperate, he could go away for a long time."

Dee hugged her son. "I think you better cooperate," she said.

Devon, his head down, held his hands out. "We don't need cuffs," Ramirez said. "But you do need to come with us."

"When will I see him?" Dee asked.

"It depends," Dan said. "He's not under arrest right now, I want him to sign the statement, and then he'll be formally arrested and arraigned. My guess is the judge will set bail, and you can get him out upon payment. Devon will be released to your custody until the hearing. It could be twenty-four to forty-eight hours. We'll let you know and if we have to, we'll send a car for you."

"Go son. I love you. I'll see you soon. Do as they say."

As they walked down the stairs, a delivery man stepped onto the porch. "I'll take that prescription," Dan said. He took the bag and brought it up to Dee. "Here's your medication."

With tears in her eyes, Dee said, "Thank you. Take care of Devon."

Dan walked back down the stairs and got into the squad car. Scotty sat with Devon in the back seat. As they rode back to the jail, Ramirez whispered to Dan. "You sure you can get him a reduced sentence?"

Dan whispered back. "No. Just hoping to get him tried as a juvie. Bail is another story."

CHAPTER 38

Chaos greeted Terell when he entered his father's hospital room. He saw a frantic nurse and heard her shout, *Code blue!*

Startled, Terell asked, "What's happening?"

"Cardiac arrest. You better step back. It's going to get crowded in here."

Terell momentarily froze, and then he stepped back as response team members entered the room with a crash cart. One responder grabbed the backboard, and with the help of another nurse, they rolled Hardison and placed the board underneath him. Immediately, the doctor in charge began compressions and a respiratory therapist inserted an endotracheal tube, securing it in place. "Adrenaline," the doctor ordered. He continued compressions, stopping every few minutes to check the monitors. With no change, the doctor shouted! "Stand by for defib."

With pads placed on Hardison's chest, the doctor said, "Get ready to shock. Two hundred joules."

A nurse handed paddles to the doctor and he called out, "Clear."

The team stepped back, and an electrical jolt hit Hardison. The lines on the monitor didn't move. "Again!" The doctor shouted.

Terell's face was flush and he began to sweat as he watched.

Still the monitor didn't move. "Three hundred," the doctor ordered. The third jolt was administered, and a nurse said, "Got rhythm."

The doctor, breathed easier as did the rest of the skilled team. "Good work," he said as he turned to the head nurse. "Stay with him."

Terell gasped. "Is he okay?" The dazed son asked.

The doctor said, "That was close. We'll stabilize him. I think he'll be okay."

Terell studied his father, and then stepped out to call Syms. The captain answered. "How's it going?" Terell was breathing heavily. "What's wrong?" Syms asked.

"Dad … He had a heart attack. They brought him back. I saw the whole thing."

"Oh my God."

"They're taking care of him, but I have to get out of here."

"Where are Jalen and Shelaine?"

"I took them to the airport this morning before I came here. I need to call him. I can't believe this is happening. We can't lose Dad now."

"I hear you. Keep the faith, and keep me posted."

⋏

Dan saw Syms approaching. The captain had a sullen look on his face. "What happened?" Dan asked.

"Terell just called. The chief had a heart attack."

"What?" Dan said. "He was doing so well."

Scotty jumped up from his desk. "Are you serious?" he asked.

"Terell said he's in good hands. All we can do is wait. How'd you guys make out with the McCray kid?" Syms replied.

Scotty said, "It was tough. His mother uses a walker and she knew nothing about the robbery, the shooting, or the pastor."

Dan said, "The kid nailed Skeeter Hantoras, signed a confession and we charged Devon with premeditated murder. He spent the night in juvie detention. Should be arraigned later today." Dan paused. "I kind of told him and his mother he'd be tried as a juvenile, but that's not cast in stone. I'm hoping for reasonable bail."

"Neither one of those things are likely with premeditated," Syms said as he turned toward his office.

"Tough one," Scotty said.

Dan rose. "I need to run it by our friend Sasser. He knows the ropes. I'm calling him."

The attorney answered his phone. "What's happening, Dan?"

"I have some disturbing news. Hardison had a heart attack this morning."

"You serious?"

Dan told Sasser everything he knew. Then he said, "I need a favor."

"Do tell, my friend."

"We have Devon McCray in custody, and he signed a confession to killing Pastor Jonathan. I have the murder weapon, and he identified Skeeter Hantoras as Hardison's shooter"

"What's the charge?"

"Premeditated. Here's the glitch. I sort of promised the kid and his mother he'd be tried as a juvie and receive a short sentence."

"You did what?"

"It was the only way. I had to. Who's prosecuting these days?"

"I hope it's not Middleton. If he's at the arraignment, that's bad news. He's a shit ass DA, by-the-book guy, probably will argue for no bail. When's the kid being arraigned?"

"Later this morning."

"Hopefully Bainbridge is presiding. I know him well."

"So we heard."

"Good guy. Know what I mean?"

Dan snickered. "Yeah. I hear he has nice lined pockets in his pants."

"Big pockets too. I'll get to the courthouse."

"Thanks, Sass."

There was something else bothering Dan. "Come on partner. We need to see Garcia again."

183

The detectives entered Garcia's office and before Dan told the gang unit leader why they were there, he informed him of Hardison's heart attack.

"I'm curious," Dan said. "As far as we can tell, no gang members ever came to see Skeeter while he was in the hospital, but someone dropped off clean clothes before he left. Any idea who that might have been? I checked with the front desk. They had the bag of clothes sent up to him. The clerk couldn't tell if the person was male or female, so it appears he has at least one friend."

"We know he's got a girl and we know where he usually hangs. My guess is she brought him the clothes."

"What about this girl?"

"Gang member, low profile, we don't even have a name. It's only recently that he's been seen with her. So what the hell did you do to Skeeter Hantoras? Denine said you hauled him in here from the hospital and had to let him go."

"I did, but now we need to get him. We have a confession from Devon McCray and a sworn statement that Skeeter shot Hardison." Dan clasped his hands. "I want Skeeter's ass bad. You know where he is?"

"My guys have eyes out for him."

"Let us know when you locate the bastard."

As soon as Dan got back to his desk, his phone rang. It was Sasser. "I'm at the courthouse. McCray was just brought here from juvie detention. He's next up."

"Bainbridge presiding?"

"Alcott. Last time I saw him it didn't go too well. He's a prick."

"Call me later."

"What's happening?" Scotty asked.

"Let's go see our favorite captain," Dan said as he stood and led the way into Syms's office.

Syms said, "What now boys?"

"Listen," Dan said. "Sasser is at McCray's arraignment. Alcott is presiding and Sasser will call me later. In the meantime, I talked to Garcia and his guys are on Skeeter. I want to bring that bastard in as soon as possible."

Syms turned to Scotty. "Don't you let him do anything stupid."

Scotty nodded. "You got it. I have him on a leash."

The detectives returned to their cubes and Dan's phone rang again. "We got a problem," Sasser said. "Judge Alcott set bail at an even mil. That ass of a prosecutor, Middleton falsely sang about the kid's gang affiliation. I argued the kid had been abused by Pastor Jonathan, but Alcott turned a deaf ear. The judge recently had a gang member skip town and didn't want to make the same mistake. That shithead prosecutor doesn't want to entertain a plea deal either. He's gonna go for the full adult conviction."

"Fuck. Got hearing date?"

"Next week, and I'm sure Middleton will be at the top of his game. Bad shit."

"Listen," Dan said.

Sasser cut him off. "No way am I posting bail."

"Any way to get at Alcott? How about calling Bainbridge? Can't you talk to him?"

"Bainbridge?"

"I thought you had him in your back pocket?"

"He was, but I'm sorta low on funds. No pay, no play. My pockets were full then. Not so much anymore."

"Yeah, but you could blow the whistle on him, if you wanted."

Dan heard Sasser mumbling to himself. "You crazy? I want to hang onto my balls."

"Any way to get to Middleton?"

"Like I told you. He's an ass. We have our hands full."

"Jesus. I don't know what to tell Devon's mother," Dan said.

"Me neither," Sasser replied.

"Try to come up with something, Sass. I need you to work it."

"Me? You got us into this mess. Hang tight. I'll see what I can do."

Chapter 39

Dan had Devon McCray and Skeeter Hantoras on his mind. As the detective walked up the back stairs toward the squad room, he heard Garcia yell. "Dan."

Stepping into the gang unit leader's office, he saw Chaser Castillo, a broad shouldered veteran sitting next to Garcia. "Good timing. We know where Skeeter Hantoras is," Chaser said. "Last night he made a quick stop home and took off in his truck. Potter spotted him this morning at a motel in the Meadowlands."

Dan asked, "Is Skeeter armed?"

"Can't say for sure. My guess is he is?" Chaser replied.

"Is he alone? What about the girl?"

"Not sure."

Dan turned to Garcia. "I want to go get him now."

The unit leader looked to Chaser. "Call Potter."

Chaser phoned the lookout.

Dan listened and Chaser gave him a thumbs-up. "He's there. River Meadow Motel."

"The girl?" Dan asked.

"Potter didn't see her."

Dan said, "I saw Scotty's car in the lot. I'm gonna grab him and let Syms know what's up."

"You guys can ride with me," Chaser said.

"I'm gonna get Ramirez too," Dan said. "We'll all ride with you."

Dan went upstairs, stopped at Scotty's cube, and grabbed him by the arm. "We're going to get Skeeter Hantoras. Syms has to know." The detectives hurried down the hall to the captain's office. "Garcia's guys have Hantoras in sight. Now is our chance to bring him in," Dan said.

"Where is he?"

"River Meadow Motel. I gotta get Ramirez."

Once the capture team was together, they hopped into Chaser's unmarked vehicle.

"What about back-up?" Scotty asked.

"I'll get on that, if we need it," Ramirez said. "Been to that motel several times. It's two levels, and wraps around in an L-shape. Rounded up more than a few hookers and dealers there."

Dan fidgeted in the back seat as they approached the seedy section of the city where four motels, two strip clubs, and several bars existed within a two square-mile radius. "Can't wait to get my hands on him again," Dan said.

"There's the motel," Chaser said. "That's Potter's car across the street."

Chaser stopped his vehicle and rolled down his window as he pulled up to Potter. "He's still here," Potter said. "His truck is the black pick-up near the back of the lot."

"Got a room number?" Chaser asked.

"Not positive. "Twenty-three, or twenty-one." Potter replied.

"Follow me," Chaser said.

The neon sign outside the motel office flashed *Vacancy.*

"Stop here," Dan said. "I'll get the room number from the desk clerk."

Seconds later, Dan got back into the car. "It's twenty-one, but we got a problem. Skeeter checked in at two a.m. The girl is with him. I don't trust the desk clerk. He better not tip Skeeter."

"Shit," Ramirez said. "What about the girl? What now?"

"We have to get him. I hope he has the balls to leave her out of it," Dan said.

"I'm gonna park behind the red Audi," Chaser said as Potter followed, stopping his unmarked vehicle next to Chaser's car.

The foursome exited Chaser's vehicle, and Potter joined them. Dan scanned the motel complex. It appeared to him that several rooms were occupied. He peered into the window of twenty-one. "They're in there," Dan said. "I saw someone peeking out at us. Fucking office guy tipped him."

Ramirez said, "I'm calling for back-up."

"I don't want to wait," Dan said.

"Protocol partner. I think we should wait," Scotty said.

"Your call," Chaser said to the lead detective.

"Let's go now," Dan said.

The law enforcers, guns drawn, approached the ground-level room and Dan knocked on the door. "Skeeter. We know you're in there. Open up."

Dan heard the TV, but he also heard something else … A sound that alarmed him. "Shit. A baby. I hear a baby." He knocked again. "Open up, Skeeter."

A young woman holding a diapered two-year-old in her arms opened the door. Dan and Chaser entered the room. "Where's Skeeter?" Dan asked.

"Not here," the nervous girl said.

Dan saw in her eyes she was lying. "Where is he?"

"Not here," she repeated.

Noticing the open back window, Chaser yelled. "He went out there!"

Scotty heard someone running, turned around, and saw Skeeter getting inside the pick-up. "There he is!" Scotty shouted.

Potter quickly got into his vehicle and hemmed the truck in. He swiftly hopped out with his gun pointed at Skeeter. The truck's engine was running. "Shut it down and get out!" Potter loudly commanded.

Dan and Chaser ran to Potter, and the officers surrounded the truck, while Scotty stayed with the young mother and child. Three guns were aimed at Skeeter. Dan demanded, "Get out!"

Skeeter stayed inside the locked vehicle, ignoring the order. Dan repeated, "Out now Skeeter!"

Two back-up cruisers arrived. Several motel patrons had opened their doors, and a few more looked out from balconies to see what the trouble was. Ramirez again loudly repeated, "Get back inside your rooms! This is a police situation."

All but one bearded man in a Patriot's sweatshirt did as they were told. Ramirez pointed to the man whose cell was aimed at the truck and taking a video. "You too. Get back inside."

The man reluctantly tucked his phone into his sweatshirt pocket and went back inside his room. Several sets of eyes were watching from motel room windows.

Skeeter wasn't acknowledging Dan's commands. "I don't think he's coming out, not alive he isn't," Dan said. "If he shows a weapon, he's dead meat." Dan barked at Skeeter, "Get out of the truck now with your hands up!"

Four uniforms rushed out from the two black and whites and closed off the perimeter. Flashing lights now lit up the parking lot.

Skeeter continued to ignore Dan's commands. "Have it your way, Skeeter. Last chance to end this peacefully. Open up or we're coming in to drag you out ... Dead or alive!" Dan shouted. "One minute and it's over, Skeeter. We're smashing the window and dragging you out."

Sixty seconds passed and the officers waited. "What do you think?" Dan asked Chaser.

"We can wait him out. He isn't going anywhere."

Dixon's car pulled in and he and approached the engaged officers. "He isn't surrendering. There's a girl and baby in room twenty-one. Scotty's in there," Dan said.

Dan saw a crazed look in Skeeter's eyes as the disobeying target appeared to be reaching into a jacket. Without hesitating, Dan fired a shot through the driver door window. Skeeter's head flew to the side, blood gushing from the bullet's entry. The recoil from the gunshot left Dan's hand tingling.

Loud screams came from inside room twenty-one. Scotty stood by the girl who was on her knees crying uncontrollably, the baby still in her arms.

Hearing the gunshot and screams, several motel guests again came out of their rooms and Ramirez yelled to the crowd, "Get the hell back in your rooms! We'll let you know when it's okay to come out."

Chaser opened the truck's door, his weapon pointed and ready. Next to Skeeter's slumped over bloodied body was a handgun. Lowering his Smith and Wesson and placing it back into its holster, Chaser said, "Nice shot, Dan." Picking up the dead man's gun, he handed it to the detective.

"Thanks, I'll get this over to ballistics so they can make a positive. This has to be the gun he used to shoot Hardison."

Dixon had called for an ambulance. When it pulled into the lot, Dan directed the EMTs to the girl, while the officers waited for the crime scene unit and the coroner to arrive.

Dan had one piece of unfinished business and said to Ramirez and Dixon, "I'll be right back." The detective walked to the motel office and stormed through the door. He pointed at the sweating Middle-Eastern looking clerk. "I told you not to tip Hantoras, but you did. You want a ride to jail? " the angry detective said.

"No, sir."

Dan looked into the man's eyes. "You ever pull shit like that again and you'll be in cuffs. Got it?"

"Yes, sir."

Leaving the clean-up work to the EMTs and crime scene crew, Dan returned to headquarters with his partner, Ramirez, and Chaser. With blood figuratively on his hands, and his once fired weapon now in evidence, he sat in the quiet squad room reflecting upon his deliverance of a bullet into Skeeter's forehead. The shooting made Dan sick to his stomach; he'd never shot, let alone killed a suspect until a couple of hours ago.

Scotty tried to console him. "Drink some water. You had to do it. Skeeter might have shot at you if you hadn't fired first."

"I know you're right, but it all happened so fast. I killed him. I killed the bastard who shot Hardison." Dan chugged the rest of the water, turned to his computer and said, "Syms is gone. I need to do the incident report. Why don't you go home? I'll leave when I'm done."

"Are you sure you're okay?" Scotty asked.

"First time I ever killed someone," Dan said. "I guess I signed up for this a long time ago, but never had to pull the trigger. Go home, pal. I'll finish up here."

Scotty left, but finishing the report didn't erase Dan's vivid picture of Skeeter's bloodied body.

CHAPTER 40

Dan entered his house and hung his coat inside the foyer closet. Still thinking about the moment he fired the fatal shot, he placed his empty holster inside the special compartment.

Walking slowly into the kitchen, he heard voices coming from the den. He entered the room and forced a smile. "What's going on?" he asked.

Phyllis turned to him. "Last few pieces of the puzzle that Mike had sent."

Dan couldn't hold the happy face and exited the room. Phyllis followed him out. "What's wrong?" she asked.

"I'll tell you later. I'm going upstairs and will be down in a while. You and the kids finish the puzzle with Connie."

"Something happened today didn't it?"

Dan looked into his wife's eyes. "I shot and killed a suspect."

She took his arm. "I can see you're not okay. Talk to me."

"I will, hon. Right now I need a long hot shower."

Twenty-five minutes later, after toweling off, he put on a pair of sweats and placed his body on the bed. He stared up at the ceiling, and thought about that young girl and the baby. Dan's weary eyes closed, and when he opened them, the clock on his nightstand read 8:17 p.m. Dan got out of bed, and went downstairs.

Connie had gone home, and the kids were getting ready for bed. He hugged both children, and then waited as Phyllis took Josh and Kate to their rooms.

Dan opened the fridge, took out his dinner, and warmed the meatloaf and potatoes in the microwave.

Phyllis returned and stood by his side. "What happened?"

"I'm okay now," he said as he took the food out and placed it on the table. "I shot the thug who put Hardison in the hospital. I was with the gang unit. I know it comes with the territory, but it's funny in a way. I'll never forget when I was shot, but shooting and killing someone was something I'd never had to do before and it just hit me in an eerie way. I'm okay."

"Really? Your hand is shaking."

"Probably from the recoil." He stared at his dinner, took a bite and pushed the food aside.

"Your face has pain written all over it. I think we need to have a long chat. Let's go into the den."

Dan stopped her from saying anything further. "I get it. I can't eat right now anyway."

Dan lay on the couch as if he were in her work office. She slid a chair over and held his hand. "I may have to bill you, you know. So what happened?"

Dan took a deep breath. "We all had our guns aimed at the thug who was inside his truck. It looked like he was reaching for a weapon, so I shot first. It was instinctive. I had to shoot. Turns out he was going for his gun."

Phyllis interjected. "Isn't that what you were trained to do?"

"Training is one thing, but doing it is another," he said as he sat up. "What I didn't tell you is," Dan hesitated. "There was a young girl, maybe twenty or so, and a baby in his motel room. It's them I keep thinking about. They're with Social Services."

Phyllis looked him in the eyes. "How would you feel if you knew they might be in a better place now?"

Dan sighed. "I guess that would square things a little." Dan sat up and looked at the clock. It was nearly ten p.m. when the session ended. "I feel better, he said. "Thanks, hon. You're a damn good therapist. I might become a regular patient."

She kissed him. "Got news for you. You've been my patient for several years. Go eat something. I'll toss the meatloaf. How about a couple of eggs?"

"Thanks. I am hungry now. I'd like toast and coffee too."

"I'll make decaf."

Dan gave her a big hug. "So when do I get my bill?"

"You can't afford me on your salary."

Dan smiled. "We'll work it out."

CHAPTER 41

Dan walked toward his cube and Scotty said "How are you doing, pal?" You were a little shaky when I left here."

"I was, but I'm good now. Phyllis made me talk it out with her. If you ever need therapy, I'll set you up with her."

Syms came down the corridor and stood at Dan's cube. "You okay? Garcia told me about Hantoras?"

"Yeah," Dan said. He turned to his computer, printed the incident report and handed it to the captain. "I wrote it up before I left here yesterday."

Syms grinned. "You actually followed procedure?"

"Miracle isn't it?"

Syms scanned it and then said, "You know the last time I fired my gun? It was my second year on the force. I shot a suspect in the leg. Four years later I had to shoot again. This one was fatal. It was him or me. I remember how it felt pulling that trigger for real."

"I wonder how long my gun will be kept for evidence," Dan said. "I kind of feel naked without it."

"So did I, but it wasn't too long."

Dan said. "Take the incident report back with you. We have to see Garcia."

The detectives neared Garcia's office. Chaser was sitting opposite the gang unit leader. He turned his head and said, "How's it going guys?"

"Good," Dan said.

"Sit," Garcia said as he looked at Dan. "We're discussing your expert marksmanship."

"Thanks," Dan said as he and Scotty took seats beside Chaser. "Tell me what you know about the girl. I was a little distracted after the shooting. What's her story? Is the baby Skeeter's? All I got was her name, Charisa Morales."

Garcia sat back. "Charisa was taken to a safe house. Social workers have talked to her. Sit tight, you're not going to believe this." Garcia leaned forward. "Skeeter was doing a good thing. He was taking her away from the gang."

Dan shrugged. "You kidding me? So the baby is his?"

Garcia took a deep breath and let it out. "She has no idea who the father is. She's nineteen and got initiated into the gang two and a half years ago. You know what I'm telling you? She was sexed-in."

"Jesus Christ. How many raped her?" Scotty asked.

"She doesn't remember. Social Services is going to find a place for her and the baby."

"At least one good thing came out of this," Dan said. "I can't believe that bastard was saving his girl and the baby from gang life."

▲

Hardison had no idea who had shot him, nor did he know his ambusher was dead. Dan knew he'd have to tell the chief what had happened the night of the shootings.

The detective entered Syms's office and he noticed a smile on the captain's face. "Good news?" Dan asked.

"Terell called earlier and informed me that the chief is much improved. They moved him to a private room. Terell is there now, but he's going home later."

"I'm going to Woodland," Dan said. "I have something I need to discuss with the chief."

When Dan entered the hospital, he realized he didn't know what room the chief was in, so the detective stopped at the information desk and obtained the number. He got into the elevator and exited on the fourth floor. Dan approached the door of room 403 and saw Terell coming out. "Hey," Dan said. "I heard the old moose is doing well."

"I'm so elated. He'll be fine. I'm going to the airport to catch a flight back home. Thanks for your support."

Dan shook Terell's hand. "Have a good flight. We'll keep your dad on his toes."

"Thanks."

Entering the room, Dan saw the chief who was sitting up in bed with the TV remote in his hand. "Hi, Dan."

"You look good. You've got your color back."

Hardison pointed the remote at his smart detective. "Now I know I'm still alive. Black is black, there's no changing from light black to dark black, or any other color. Sit down you clown." Dragging a chair from the other side of the bed, Dan sat beside Hardison. "Ever seen this People's Court? Never seen a judge as good looking as her," the chief said.

Dan grinned. "Now I'm sure you're still alive. You eating okay?"

"Hard to ruin oatmeal and Jell-O. I eat what they give me. You couldn't sneak in a good burger could you?"

"Next time."

"You know they want me to go to rehab when I get out of here. I don't know about that. I been up walking around. I might be a little weak, but I'll be okay. I don't think I even need the walker they want me to use."

"Syms will be here later."

"I know. Talked to him a few minutes ago. So you're all over the news. Give me the dirt."

"It's a little complicated. What have you heard?"

"Heard this Skeeter guy was a gang banger with a long list of priors."

"Listen. Some of this you might not believe, but it's true." Dan paused. "Skeeter was the thug who shot you."

Hardison put the remote down and lifted a glass of water from the table next to his bed. "Why? How'd you nail him?"

"I am a detective, remember? Here's the part that's hard to swallow. Remember Devon McCray?" Pastor Jonathan was mentoring him." Dan paused. "Jonathan was a predator. He'd molested dozens of boys. McCray was the last."

Hardison turned off the TV. "A what did you say? A predator, child molester? "Are you telling me, the juvenile shot the pastor?"

Dan looked Hardison in the eyes. "He did. We have him in custody awaiting arraignment." Dan moved closer to the chief. "I gotta know one thing. Who called you at Justino's when you were dining with Jalen and Shelaine?" We know you dropped your phone in the bathroom, where a cleaning crew member found it. Bad news is he stepped on it and smashed it to smithereens."

The chief closed his eyes and then opened them. "Oh my God. It was Pastor Jonathan who called me. He said he had something important, very personal to discuss. I never got to find out what that was, but I think you just told me. You never know, do you?" Hardison sighed. "I can't believe it."

Dan bowed his head. "We have videos in evidence."

The chief eyed Dan. "Skeeter. What's his story?"

"Turns out he was on thin ice with the Knights and was recruiting to try to restore his status. He put McCray up to killing the pastor as an initiation. Jonathan was the perfect target, since Skeeter knew the pastor had molested the kid. You were collateral damage. While McCray was inside the church, you showed up. Skeeter was playing lookout and when he saw you pull up, he opened fire."

"Jesus, talk about being in the wrong place at the wrong time."

Dan's cell rang. "I gotta take this call." He stood and answered his phone. Sasser said, "I tried Bainbridge, but he shot me down like a Russian Mig."

"You talked to Devon's mother?"

"Yeah, she's really upset."

"I can imagine. I'm with Hardison. He's doing well. Talk to you later." With the phone back inside his pocket, Dan turned back to the chief.

"What was that all about?" Hardison asked.

"That was Hancock Sasser. He's representing Devon McCray whose arraignment didn't go as well as we'd hoped. Alcott presided and a shithead prosecutor named Middleton got a high bail set. The kid is going to juvie detention until his hearing." Dan sat back down. "Damn it. I told the kid's mother he'd be home. No way can she put up bail. Middleton will be lobbying for McCray to be tried as an adult when they appear at the hearing."

Hardison shook his finger at Dan. "Know what? Alcott owes me. I'll let you in on a secret. Last year his wife, get this, she's half his age. Only twenty-eight. She was stopped for a DUI, got a hefty ticket, her car was towed, and she spent a few hours drying out in the dungeon. Funny thing was that he was out of town and she couldn't reach him until morning. He called me, didn't want anyone in the judicial branch to get wind of the charge, so he asked me to get the ticket torn up and erase any records of the incident." Hardison smiled at Dan. "As of right now, I'm officially back on the job."

CHAPTER 42

Hardison had given Dan good vibes, and the detective felt like he might be able to keep his promise to Dee McCray. It all hinged upon the chief persuading Judge Alcott to reconsider the bail decision.

Feeling the need for caffeine before heading upstairs, Dan entered the cafeteria. He saw his partner in line to cash out and caught Scotty's attention. "Grab a table," he said. Dan joined him a couple of minutes later. Taking a sip of coffee, Dan sat and set his hot cup down. "I told the chief about Skeeter Hantoras."

"Scotty drank from his cup and then said, "What'd he say?"

"I told him the whole story about the pastor, McCray, and Skeeter. The chief was shocked, but he told me it was the pastor who had called him. That's why he went to the church."

"I'm sure the predator stuff jolted him."

"While I was there, Sasser called and said Judge Alcott set high bail for McCray. I told Hardison. He then told me a story about Alcott. We may have a shot at getting Devon McCray's bail rescinded."

Scotty listened as Dan recited the story about the judge's wife. "That's a great one."

The detectives finished their coffees, dumped the cups in the trash, and headed upstairs. As soon as he got to his desk, Dan said, "I have to call Sasser."

The lawyer's voice-mail kicked in. "Hancock, call me as soon as possible." Dan said. "We may be able to get Alcott to reverse his decision."

"Thirty seconds later, Dan's phone beeped. "What's up Houdini? You got a story?"

"I got a whopper." Dan heard traffic. "You on the road?"

"Good guess."

"Listen. Hardison has one-up on Alcott and the chief is going to bend the Judge's ear."

"What kind of shit does he have on him?"

Dan filled the attorney in, and Sasser said, "You realize, the best the judge can do is to get me and Middleton in a room together and hope to arbitrate a plea and back off trying Devon as an adult. If we can reach a plea deal, that's the best of both worlds. He won't even go to trial."

"What about bail?"

"That's something Alcott can waive. Hope Hardison can get the judge to take immediate action. If it happens, Alcott will have to call me. That prick, Middleton will be pissed."

"Speaking of pricks, what have you been doing about Biaggio?"

"Funny you should ask. I'm filing a wrongful death suit against him. I spoke with the Ibanez's, and they're in."

"You what?"

"It was Biaggio's car that killed Javier, wasn't it?

"Yeah. Can you really file a lawsuit?"

"Anyone can file a lawsuit. The court system is full of trivial suits."

"Can you win it?"

"Beats me. Can't win if you don't play. Know what I mean?"

"Keep me posted," Dan said.

"Ditto."

Turning to his partner, Dan said, "Sasser is filing a wrongful death suit against Biaggio on behalf of the Ibanez family."

"Can he do that?"

"That's what I asked him. He can."

Dan sat at his desk and thought about Sasser's wrongful death suit against Biaggio. Although Hancock Sasser had chased his share of ambulances, it was beyond the detective's comprehension how the sly attorney came up this tactic. Wanting to learn more about the pending action, as well as personal injury claims, Dan had to meet with the slick lawyer, so he pulled out his cell and called him again.

Sasser answered. "Dan, what now?"

"Hey, good buddy, I need to see you this morning."

"Got an important appointment."

"I want to talk about Biaggio. Who you meeting with?"

"I gotta talk to someone about a suit."

"You going to see the Ibanez's?"

"I'll be done by eleven-thirty."

"Then meet me for lunch at noon."

"Where? You paying?"

"If you tell me what I need to know?"

"Can't make no promises. Meet me at Babe's."

"Babe's? The barbecue place?"

"What's wrong with a little home cookin'? You ever had their ribs?"

"You got somewhere else?"

"That's the deal, Babe's. Somehow I talk better when I'm there. Meet me at twelve sharp."

Turning to Scotty, Dan said, "I'm meeting Sasser for lunch at Babes."

"You shitting me? You hate smoked food."

"I'll have to bear with it for a while. He says he talks better there. While I'm with him, how about taking a shot at finding some of Biaggio's personal injury cases? Look for small payouts … Ten grand or so. Start with Burgess."

Scotty laughed. "Babes huh. I'll get on the paper trail."

"I gotta see the captain," Dan said.

When he got to Syms's office, the captain smiled and said. "I talked to Hardison. He told me about Alcott. Funny story."

"I'm gonna have lunch with Sasser."

"Where at?"

"Don't laugh, Babe's."

Syms broke a big grin.

"I said don't laugh."

Syms laughed. "You hate barbecue."

"I hate Biaggio more. Win some, lose some. How bad can it be?"

"Hope you don't puke."

"Hey. I'll force down what I have to."

"You want me along? I love smoked stuff."

"This one is solo. Go have a cigarette with Landry."

"Nice, that guy's gonna have lung cancer soon. Last butt I had was in high school."

▲

The yellow awning with a plate of ribs sketched on it was unmistakable. As soon as Dan got out of his car, the aroma of pungent, charred food attacked his senses. Taking a deep breath, which was a mistake, he inhaled a dose of smoked food.

Once he was inside, the annoying smell was even stronger. He saw Sasser at the end of a long line of hungry customers. "Take a tray," the attorney said. "Try the pulled-pork sandwich with collards, beans and corn bread."

"Any burgers on the board?"

Sasser smirked. "Danny boy, put some hair on your chest. I'm telling you the pulled pork is to die for."

"Right. In my case it's probably something to die from."

"You act like you don't barbecue ribs in your yard."

"I don't. Burgers, dogs, and steak. That's it." Dan ordered what Sasser had recommended and the detective paid the cashier for both meals.

The attorney led Dan to a checkerboard-clothed table toward the rear of the restaurant. Placing his tray on the table, Sasser said "So what's on your mind?"

"Tell me more about the wrongful death suit. Can you really win?"

Sasser held a forkful of collards near his mouth. "Win? Hell, I don't even know if I can really file it yet. Sometimes they have to be filed after a criminal court case, but sometimes they don't. I'm grabbing at straws, filing for funeral expenses, pain and suffering, lost wages. I'm shooting for fifteen-million."

Dan reluctantly picked up his sandwich, swallowed a bite, and said, "Lost wages? He was a kid. He had no job."

"Right. Getting killed deprived him of the opportunity to go to college and earn a living."

Dan took a second bite, this one bigger than the first.

"You should try the collards," Sasser said as he filled his mouth.

"I prefer the corn bread. The beans aren't bad," Dan replied. "Let's get on to ambulance chasing. You told me a little, like when you were a runner."

"Hey, keep it down. I got a reputation."

He was right. A tall, muscular man who appeared to be about forty stopped at their table. The obviously much younger woman with him had braided hair, and her long brightly painted nails were attention getters. "Hey, Sass. How's it going?" the man asked.

"Good, Bails. You staying out of trouble?"

He pointed to his friend. "She's got me straight man."

Sasser eyed her hands. "Nice nails. You do those? What's your name, doll?"

"Felicia. My sister did these. She's a manicurist."

"Nice to meet you," Sasser replied. "Good to see you too, Bails."

"See you around, Sass," Bails said as he and Felicia exited the restaurant.

"Bails?" Dan said.

"Long story. That guy has a list of DUI and B and E arrests as long as my arm. Pretty ironic, he worked for his brother as a bail-bondsman."

Dan looked at his plate and held off taking in more disgusting food. "So about personal injury," Dan asked.

"Right. It's easy if you have your network set."

"I know Biaggio has a repair shop involved."

"That's a pretty good one, but most guys simply have runners or they might respond themselves. I knew a tow truck company that was on the take. Hell, all it takes is a fender bender, a police report, a lawyer, doctor and insurance company. It's a mill, a well-oiled machine. Once the lawyer has his mark and convinces the willing participant to perpetrate the fraud, it's a matter of a visit to a doctor. Might be a few weeks of going to a chiropractor, and sometimes you don't even have to show up."

"What a racket," Dan said before he tried the greens. "Not exactly broccoli, green beans, or asparagus."

Sasser took a bite of his sandwich and Dan began feeling more uncomfortable with the smoke odors in the room, but he couldn't simply get up and leave Sasser who was still enjoying the meal. The fast-thinking detective, who'd had enough disgusting smells enter his sinuses for one day, pushed his pulled-pork sandwich aside and then pretended gagging.

A startled Sasser yelled. "What's wrong? You choking? Water?"

Dan faintly uttered, "Allergic to the sauce." He reached into his coat pocket and pulled out his EpiPen.

"Need help?" Sasser said as other patrons began staring at their table.

"I know Heimlich," one man shouted.

Dan placed the EpiPen at his hip and pretended to inject himself. "No, thanks. I just need my pen." He placed the device down and sat back. "It's working, but I have to get out of here now."

"Drink some water," Sasser said as he handed Dan a full glass.

Dan drank it and put the unused pen back into his pocket. "I'm okay, this stuff works fast, but I really need to go." Dan got up and Sasser stood. "Finish up," Dan said. "I'll talk to you later."

"Okay. I gotta go over and have the Ibanez's sign the papers."

Pretending to still be a little light headed, Dan said. "I thought you said you were going there earlier?"

"You said that. I said I had an appointment about a suit. Needed to see my tailor to get fitted."

Dan walked out and got into his car. With the smell of smoke gone from his senses, he took a deep breath. *That EpiPen sure came in handy.*

He had escaped Babe's, but there was another issue he had to deal with, and he knew he might have to calm himself once he got home.

This was the day Phyllis was to take the kids to the orthodontist. Although he opposed the braces, his inner voice told him not to do battle with his wife. He'd already strongly expressed his thoughts about the subject he still regarded as one big scam.

He saw Phyllis's SUV, and he knew she was home. Dan drove his car into the garage and exited his Accord. He hit the wall button, closing the garage door, entered the mud-room and placed his shoes on a mat, before stepping into the kitchen.

Phyllis, who was still dressed in her gray pant suit said, "You're a little early."

"Hi, honey," he said with a smile.

She kissed him. "The kids are upstairs."

"Where's Connie? I didn't see her car."

"I told her not to come today because of the orthodontist appointment." Phyllis picked up a piece of paper from the counter. "Take a look at this," she said as she handed it to Dan.

He held it and took a long look at the bottom line, before placing it back on the counter. Trying hard not to overreact, he said, "Thirty-five hundred! Just for Josh?"

"That's what it costs these days."

"I have to digest this … That's a lot of money. Are we sure about this? You know what I think."

"I know what you think, and I'm thinking our children should have nice teeth."

"They have nice teeth." Dan saw the look in Phyllis's eyes and calmed down. "All right, what kind of payment plan does he have?"

"We can make monthly payments, no interest, but if we consent to both Josh and Kate, he'll cut the price by five hundred dollars."

Dan grimaced. "Some deal. I still think it's a scam."

She took his hand and squeezed it. Smiling at him, she said, "I knew you'd agree."

Dan gave her a mock smile. "I call it blackmail, sweetie. I like the bed I sleep in and the warm body next to mine. So when does Josh get his braces?"

"We have to go back in two weeks so the doctor can take impressions and then about a week later, he'll put the braces on."

"How long did he say Josh would have to wear them?"

"About twelve to fifteen months and then we'll be ready for Kate."

Dan smiled. "Can't wait," he said as he kissed her on the lips.

Phyllis detected an unusual odor. What have you been eating?"

Dan laughed. "Long story, hon. I had lunch with an attorney at Babes." He took his EpiPen from his pocket. "This saved the day."

"You had an allergic reaction?"

"Tell you what? I'll brush my teeth, and later we can put our pillows together and I'll explain."

"Maybe you should shower before we *talk*. I just changed the sheets."

CHAPTER 43

Dan sat in his cube never expecting to hear what Hancock Sasser was about to tell him. The detective's desk phone rang and he answered the lawyer's call. "Hey Dan, It's me. Got a little problem you need to know about."

Rolling his eyes, Dan said, "What now my trusted friend?"

"It's your other friend, Mr. Biaggio. He's pulled a fast one."

"What the hell does that mean?"

"Seems the ambulance chaser sent a couple of messengers to see the Ibanez's. I'd visited the house after I left Babes, and then went to the courthouse to file the suit. Mr. Ibanez just called me. Last night, two guys representing Biaggio came to their place, shoved fifty grand into the couple's pockets, and had them sign off on any claims involving Javier's death."

Dan stood and pounded the-desk top with his fist. "What?" He shouted. "How the hell did Biaggio know? And who were his guys?"

"He must have someone at the filing office. Mr. Ibanez's described the men as one big guy, and one small guy."

Dan thought. "Holy Jesus. I know those goons. The big guy's name is Vincenzo."

"Yeah. He said Vinnie."

"So now what?"

"Now I'm a fish out of water. Biaggio didn't leave me bait to catch any. That *no-claim* document trumps everything."

"Slick, a very slick move. Hang in there. I'm going to have another chat with Mr. Biaggio."

"Good luck, Danny."

Dan hung up and rapped on Scotty's cube. "What was that all about?" Scotty asked.

"It was about shit hitting the fan. Biaggio's thugs got to the Ibanez's and paid them off. You and I have another unannounced lunch date with Biaggio at Cefalu."

"What have you got in mind?"

"Won't know until we get there, but I sure as hell want to rattle the guy."

Scotty said, "Guess what I learned? Personal injury cases are not public record. We're shit out of luck on that one."

Dan shrugged. "Figures." The detective knew he had to watch his steps before the sly Biaggio decided to pull ranks with some judge. "Let's go ruin that bastard's day and spoil another meal."

▲

At ten minutes past noon, the detectives entered Cefalu as the lunch crowd filed in. Dan looked to the rear of the restaurant and he saw his prey. Biaggio with the same two goons, sitting where they had been the last time."

The host said, "Be right with you."

Dan said, "We came to see Mr. Biaggio. I have an urgent message for him. We'll just be a few minutes."

"I'll tell him you're here."

"That won't be necessary, he'll be more than happy to see us," Dan said.

The detectives approached the lawyer. Biaggio dropped his fork on his plate as Dan and Scotty stood at the table. Wiping his face with a linen napkin, Biaggio said, "So what is it this time? You enjoy ruining a good meal don't you?"

"I have to talk to you," Dan said.

"Make an appointment. You know where my office is."

"This won't take long, sir."

"What the hell are you doing here? Shouldn't you be out tracking down criminals?" the lawyer barked.

Dan stared at Biaggio and the detective held back his raw anger. "Doing our best, sir."

Vincenzo stood. "You fools need to take it outside," he said.

"Thanks for the offer, Vinnie. It's a little chilly out there," Dan sternly replied. "We'll keep our jackets on, but I have a hunch it's going to get warmer in here."

Scotty eyed the short associate with the funny nose. "I don't believe we got your name."

The sidekick stared at Scotty. "What's it to you? They call me Pug."

Biaggio's eyes fill with rage as he sneered at Dan. "You've got some set of balls. This better be short."

Dan looked at the two other men. "Would you mind if we chatted with Mr. Biaggio in private."

The lawyer waved to his associates. "Go get a drink," he said to them. He looked at Dan. "You've got five minutes, then my friends will be back to escort you two out. You got it?"

"That's fine," Dan replied.

Vincenzo and Pug vacated their seats while and Dan and Scotty sat on either side of the lawyer. "So shoot," Biaggio said.

Dan glared into the man's eyes. "There's something you should know." The cagy detective glanced at the painting behind Biaggio. "Is that from the Godfather?"

"Cut the crap. Get to the point."

"Sorry. I think we have a lead on who stole your Jag. It turns out there was a camera in the school lot where the car was found."

Biaggio's eyes widened. "Really? So you want to know if I can ID the suspect?"

"That won't be necessary and, interestingly, the lab had forgotten to tell us they obtained DNA from hair follicles found on the driver's seat. Anyway, I wanted to let you know that we expect to have a warrant soon."

"I want that video," Biaggio said.

"You'll see it in time. We can't give it to you now because we haven't made an arrest yet."

Biaggio looked at his Rolex. "You have to go now,'" he said as his associates made their way back to the table.

Dan grabbed Vincenzo's arm. "By the way, the Ibanez's appreciated your visit."

Vincenzo looked at Biaggio, and the lawyer said. "Hold it Mr. Shields."

"Sorry, we have to go now to nab a few criminals. Thanks for your time," Dan said.

Vincenzo held his hands out to stop the detectives. "Sit down," Biaggio said to Dan and Scotty. "What the hell do you care if I gave the poor kid's family money to cover their expenses and more?"

Dan looked straight into the lawyer's eyes. "Interesting timing. Pretty surprising to me, since you hardly even seemed to know the Ibanez's names before. And with your generosity, you had them sign a *no-claims* document?"

Biaggio looked at Vincenzo. "Get these two gumshoes out of here."

Dan said, "And who is it you have working at the courthouse?"

"Get out!" Biaggio ordered.

"Okay," Dan said. "We'll leave. But you can bet you haven't seen the last of us."

"You come here again and I'll—"

Dan cut him off. "You'll what? Croak on your meatballs?" he said.

"Get the hell out now, smart ass."

The detectives headed back to the Accord and Dan said, "He's sweating. He knows we're going to get the truth sooner-or-later, and Humpty Dumpty is going to take a fall."

"What kind of bull was that about a video?" Scotty asked.

"If he buys it, I expect him to get busy."

A

As Dan and Scotty headed to the door, Biaggio turned to his associates. "Says he has a video of the parking lot. I think he's bluffing." He eyed Pug. "You wiped the Jag down, right?"

"Yeah, no way. It was late and pretty damn dark."

Biaggio picked up his fork and resumed eating. "I don't buy it. That frickin' wise-ass detective is blowing smoke up mine."

Chapter 44

Dan saw Luke, who was standing at table next to the water cooler, and walked up to the big guy. The hulking detective was chewing on a doughnut while making a cup of coffee. He pointed to the note on the chalkboard above a new coffee maker.

Be careful. Don't get used to the donuts.

"What have we got here? Looks like Syms finally felt guilty," Dan said. "Looks like you got the only chocolate one, big fella. How'd you make out with your neighbor?"

"I don't think he's talking, and I'm not watching another Jets game."

"Seen Scotty?"

"He's in with the man. You having any?"

"Already had coffee. I'll pass on the goodies."

Without stopping at his desk, Dan proceeded to the captain's office where Scotty was sitting across from Syms. The captain gave his brassy detective a sour look. Raising his voice, he said. "What the hell is this shit about having a video from the lot where the Jag was found?"

Dan remained standing. "Biaggio called you?"

"Hell no." Bainbridge did. He said if we have video evidence, then we need to turn it over to Biaggio. So do we have evidence?"

Dan leaned on the desk. "No. I wanted to make the no-good lawyer sweat, and I knew telling him that crap would stir up a reaction. What did you tell Bainbridge?"

"You think I'm stupid? I know you too well. I told him I'd talk to you about it."

"So you didn't say we didn't have a video?"

"No, you dip. Sounded like one of your shenanigans … And what the hell are you two doing popping in on him again at Cefalu? He's tired of you disrupting his lunches."

Dan nodded. "Meant to tell you about that. Amazing coincidence. We were having lunch there and we happened to run into him and his friends."

Syms eyed his bottle of pills. "Right, got any other bull stories?"

"Not right now, and this is no shenanigan. This is a game."

"So now you're playing Clue?" Syms sat back and paused. "Okay, have it your way. Now sit down."

"So when is Hardison due back?" Dan asked.

"I talked to him. He expects to be back soon."

"What's with the doughnuts?" Dan asked.

Syms shook his head. "I suppose you already grabbed one."

"Nope. I'm all business. Don't have time for coffee breaks."

Scotty laughed. "Speak for yourself. I'm going to take advantage of the captain's generosity."

Syms pointed to the door. "Out. And the treats are today only."

As soon as he got back to his cube, Dan's cell rang and when he answered, he heard Hancock Sasser. "You won't believe it, but we did it. Hardison got Alcott to hold a pow-wow. We just finished … Should have seen that shithead, Middleton."

"What happened?"

"It's done. We got a plea deal. Middleton opposed it, but Alcott squeezed the prosecutor's nuts and the DA caved. Devon won't stand trial. He'll get a sentence Alcott will determine later. My guess is five."

"What about bail?"

"Alcott is rescinding bail. The kid will be released later today. I'll pick him up and take him home."

"Sasser, you're the frickin' man. Thanks, good buddy."

Dan went to Luke's desk. "By the way," Luke said. "I got a call from Cassandra Biaggio. She left a message. She has another place to show you guys." He looked at Dan. "Should never have let you use my phone."

"I didn't expect that," Dan said. "I told her we'd contact her if we saw another place we liked."

"Well, she's hot after a sale and as far as she knows, you two are one happy couple looking for a house."

Scotty joined the conversation. "Don't look at me," he said to Dan. "It was your idea."

Dan eyed Luke who said, "Oh no."

"Oh yes," Dan replied. "Hand it over."

"For what?"

"I have to call her back and make another appointment. I'm not ruling her out as the Jaguar driver. Hand it over." Luke pulled his phone from his pocket and gave it to Dan. "Here goes nothing," Dan said as he returned her call. "Voicemail," he whispered before leaving a message.

"Now what?" Luke asked.

"She'll call back."

"She better make it quick. I need my phone."

"Go get another doughnut. This is official police business. I'm confiscating your phone."

"Funny, Dan, real funny." Luke's phone rang. "It's her," Dan said as he answered the call. A few seconds later, he looked at Scotty and said, "We're on. We're meeting her in an hour at two-nineteen Starsdale."

"Nice area," Luke said. "My phone?" Dan handed the phone back to him.

⋏

Starsdale was a quiet West End street. Dan maneuvered around a UPS truck and saw a large, beige colonial with a three car garage. Dan turned his Accord into the driveway and his eyes lit up like a pinball machine. "Are you serious?" he said to Scotty. "It's the Jaguar."

The duo exited Dan's vehicle, and they studied the sporty car. "Looks good. The repair shop did a nice job," Dan said.

The front door of the house opened and Cassandra waved the detectives into the home. "Nice to see you again," she said. "I wanted you to look at this house. I think you'll like it."

"Thank you," Dan replied.

She guided the two men through the residence, and ended her tour with the spacious garage. "Very nice," Scotty said.

"This is another one I don't think will stay on the market long," she said.

"You might be right," Dan said. "I couldn't help noticing your car. I love Jags, and yours looks brand new."

Cassandra clutched her purse. "It's fairly new, but it was stolen recently and the front end was damaged. I just picked it up from the repair shop."

"Really. They did a great job. Who fixed it?"

"Foreman Auto Body."

"Where was it stolen from?"

"My husband said it was taken from the lot in back of his office."

"Is he in real estate as well?" Dan asked.

"Hardly. He's a lawyer, but he had a court case today, so I had my older son drop me off at the body shop to pick up the car."

Dan realized he couldn't tip his hand by letting Cassandra know he and Scotty were detectives. "Lucky the car wasn't wrecked," Dan said. "I had mine stolen once. It was a Mustang. I loved that car. Unfortunately, it was involved in an accident much like the one the other day that took the life of a young kid." Dan turned to Scotty. "What's his name?"

"Javier something," Scotty said.

"Yes," Dan said. "I was lucky the woman my car hit wasn't killed, but my sweet Mustang ran into a tree after the car struck the lady. I never got the car back."

Dan saw Cassandra's eyes start to well up. "I saw it on the news," she said as she sighed. "I feel so sad for the boy and his family. I have two teenage sons and couldn't imagine losing either one."

Dan caught himself before he could blurt out that he had a teenager and two smaller children. "I'm sure that would be very devastating," he said. Focusing on his job, he asked, "How long was the Jaguar missing, and where'd they find it?"

"It wasn't gone long. I don't know where they found it. All I know is that it had a scratched fender." Cassandra squinted. "You're beginning to sound like police officers."

Dan said, "I've been told that before. I'm just the curious type."

"So what do you do?"

Scotty said, "Actually, we're with the Umbrella Insurance Company, claims adjusters, and we're familiar with Foreman Auto. They do great work."

Cassandra checked her watch and got back to business. "What do you gentleman think? Would you like to make an offer?"

Dan eyed his partner and Scotty said, "We do like it. Can we get back to you later?"

She handed Scotty another business card, and then went into her high-pressure sales tactic. "I hope you decide to make an offer soon. It's a hot market. I know this beautiful residence won't stay listed for long."

"I'm sure you're right," Dan said. "By the way, if you were to make an offer, what would you suggest?"

"I sense this seller would accept something under the asking price. It doesn't hurt to come in low and negotiate."

"Thanks for the suggestion," Dan said. "We'll get back to you soon."

The detectives followed her out and walked to Dan's car. Cassandra got into the Jaguar and both vehicles backed out of the driveway, heading in opposite directions.

Dan said, "Interesting. But I'm certain she wasn't the driver. She expressed real heart-felt passion for Javier and his family." Dan gave Scotty a thumb's-up. "Nice save, pal. Never been a claims adjuster before."

CHAPTER 45

Dan couldn't believe his eyes when he got to his cube and looked down the hall to Syms's office. Sitting in a chair was Chief Hardison.

Dan entered the captain's office. He shook Hardison's hand, but the detective saw distress on the chief's face. "Shut the door and sit," the captain said. "This isn't good. No one's heard from Jalen."

Hardison said, "Terell gave him the money. Jalen was supposed to go back to Chicago and pay off the debt. He promised Terell that he and Shelaine would come to California after settling up. He swore he'd get off drugs and enter a program out there. No one's heard from him. The only number I have is hers...And that phone might be dead. So might she and Jalen."

"Have you contacted the Chicago police?" Dan asked.

"I did, but do you know how many homicides, missing persons, and shootings there are in that city? All they can do is wait for a body to show. I regret treating Jalen like dirt."

Syms sighed. "You can't blame yourself. Maybe he'll show up."

Hardison stood.

"Are you going upstairs?" Dan asked.

"Already went up there. By the way, don't spread the news about Jalen."

Hardison opened the door and exited the office. Dan remained with Syms. "The chief might be right. Jalen may not show. It sounds like he got in way over his head, and those mobsters don't fool around. No one's ever found Jimmy Hoffa," the captain said.

Dan said, "Listen. There's good news. Sasser got a plea deal for Devon McCray. The kid is probably going to get five, but the most he'll do is one in juvie. With good behavior, he could be out in six months. If he needs a counselor, Phyllis can help him."

"Hardison must have really put it to Alcott."

"I guess so. That Sasser. He's good, isn't he? If I ever need a defense attorney, I know who to call. So get this. Biaggio had two of his goons visit the Ibanez's. The messenger's gave them fifty grand to sign a *no-claims document*, and Sasser is pulling the unlawful death suit."

"You serious?"

"Dead serious, but we're going to get Biaggio. Another interesting tidbit. Scotty learned personal injury settlements aren't public information."

"So where does that leave you?"

"Good question. I think we'll start at the body shop and begin to unravel Biaggio's scams."

"Syms stared at his detective and pleaded, "Play by the book this time, okay?"

"Absolutely," Dan said as he headed out the door. He turned back and eyed Syms. "Just which book was that?"

Syms picked up his pill bottle, stood and pretended to throw it at his always scheming detective.

Dan walked back to the squad room. "Hardison stopped to say 'hi' to us," Scotty said.

"He had a pained look on his face though," Landry uttered.

Dan replied. "I know. He's still a little weak."

"Blues?" Luke said.

Dan shook his head. "Me and Scotty have to visit an auto shop."

"Okay," Luke said. "See you later."

"Grab your coat," Dan said to his partner as he donned his own jacket. "Time to see what Foreman is all about."

As they headed to the auto repair shop in Dan's car, Scotty said, "So what's really going on with Hardison?"

Dan took his hand off the wheel and pointed at Scotty. "You know, I think you have been around me too long. Look, I'm not supposed to say anything, but I can't bullshit you either. Keep this under your hat."

"I knew it wasn't good," Scotty said.

Dan recited the story Hardison had told.

"Yikes. That's a hard one to swallow, but I can see why he had that ugly look on his face."

Auto body shops all looked the same to Dan. He noticed at least two dozen damaged cars in the lot. He parked his vehicle outside the office that had a red canopy over the front door. The rest of the sprawling one-level brick building was divided into work bays. Dan eyed eight garage doors, one was open and the rest were shut. A Honda, very much like his was backing out of bay three, and he watched as the car was driven into a gated area reserved for completed jobs.

The detectives entered the office where an employee behind the counter was helping a customer. With a pen tucked behind his ear and a clipboard in his hand, the worker came out from behind the counter. "I'll be with you gentleman in a few minutes," he said to Dan and Scotty. "I need to write up this man's estimate."

The customer, who appeared to be in his mid-thirties followed the estimator outside.

Several minutes later, both men re-entered the office where the detectives had waited. As the customer turned for the door with his copy of the paperwork in hand, Dan stopped him. "Can I talk to you for a minute," the cagy detective said.

The man said, "I'm waiting for a ride. I have to pick up a loaner."

"I understand," Dan said. "This will only take a minute. Let's go outside."

221

They stopped a few feet from Dan's car, and the detective pulled out his badge.

"Cops? I'm innocent. I was rear-ended."

"I believe you, sir," Dan said. "We want to know if any lawyer has contacted you."

"No, why? I gave the guy inside my insurance information. He's handling the repairs."

Dan took out his card and handed it to the man. "Do you mind telling us your name?"

"Matthew Greene."

Dan said, "Mr. Greene. This is important. If an attorney calls you and tries to convince you he can get you money by having you fake an injury, please call me immediately. It's a scam and you can help us. If you accept his deal, you can be arrested, so it's imperative you cooperate with us. Would you mind giving me your number and address?" Dan took out a note pad and wrote down the information as the man recited it. "By the way, did you call the police? Were they at the accident scene?"

"Yes. She got a ticket, and her car was towed. My ride is here."

"Thank you," Dan said as Greene got into a Volvo sedan driven by a female. "Let's go back inside," Dan said to his partner.

He and Scotty walked to the counter. "What was that all about?" the employee asked. "I'm Dave. You need an estimate?"

"I thought I recognized Mr. Greene," Scotty said. "I was wrong, half wrong. I used to work with his brother, they look a lot alike."

At that moment, Dan thought the better of his plan to talk about Biaggio with Dave. "We're cold calling. I see your ads and we're wondering who takes care of the advertising?"

"I couldn't tell you. I'm sure one of the Foreman brothers can."

Dan pretended to feel the vibration of his cell phone and faked answering a call. "What," he said. "Are you okay?" He turned to Scotty. "We gotta go. My wife's car was hit by a pick-up. She's okay, but they're taking her to Woodland as a precaution." Dan put the phone back in his pocket and he threw his hands in the air.

"Strange day," he said to Dave. "Probably be back with my wife's SUV."

The detectives got into Dan's car. Before he buckled up, Scotty said, "What the hell was that crap all about?"

Dan peeled out of the driveway. "I think Biaggio is going to call Matthew Greene. I realized it would have been a mistake to talk to Dave. He might have tipped the lawyer that we were snooping."

Chapter 46

Dan knew he was gambling, but he figured his odds were good that someone at Foreman would contact Biaggio about Matthew Greene's accident and dole out all the details. He also presumed the lawyer would obtain the police report that citied the other driver. What Dan didn't know, and he didn't really care, was how much the ambulance-chasing attorney dished out to Foreman for each referral.

Dan realized he'd only told Greene half the story. He neglected to tell his mark that he would be asked to follow Biaggio's instructions. At the same time, Dan hoped Luke would be willing to give Burgess one last shot at turning on Biaggio.

The holding tank always piqued Dan's interest. He never knew who he would find locked up. Entering the facility once again, he stopped at Dom Denine's desk. "How's business?" he asked the gatekeeper.

"Pretty good. Wish I got a commission."

"Let me in. Can't wait to see who's here," Dan said.

Dom laughed. "One of your best buds is in there. Wanna guess?"

"I have so many friends. Let me be surprised."

Dan opened the metal door and walked down the center aisle, peering from left to right, and when he looked into cell eight, he rapped on the bars. "Jesus Christ. Hampton, get up!"

The veteran car thief rose and stepped to the cell door. "Jeeze, Dan. It's not easy to get sleep around here."

"Can't wait to hear this story."

"You know what? That Lincoln you had me steal wasn't worth diddly. I only got three hundred for it. Did Sasser ever get his computer?"

"Gee, thanks for asking. Yes, I got it back to him through Dewey."

"Dewey? Man, I ain't seen him in a while."

"No shit. He doesn't take hot cars in trade. So what's it this time?"

"God damn Ferrari, a hell of a ride. Got it up to one-ten on ninety-one."

"So the State Troopers got you? What the hell are you doing here?"

"Hell no, they never saw me. Wasn't 'til I got off on Lederer Road. I made an illegal uey and a black and white stopped me. Damned Ferrari showed up stolen, and I was so close to the chop shop."

Dan chuckled.

"You laughing?" Hampton said.

"What the hell am I going to do with you?"

"Beats me. I'm living paycheck to paycheck. I was stupid this time. That Ferrari would have netted me at least a grand and a half, maybe two."

"You gonna make bail?"

"Always do."

"Get some rest. I'm sure I'll see you again soon."

"Stop by the doughnut shop."

Dan walked upstairs, and Luke yelled, "Need to see you. We got a problem."

Dan stood at Luke's desk. "Don't we always?' Dan said.

"It's Burgess," Luke said. "I went to see him and the son of a bitch told me he'd called Biaggio."

Dan tapped the padded wall. "He did what?"

"No shit. He talked to the freakin' lawyer and told him I was asking questions about his personal injury case. Burgess mentioned me."

Scotty entered the squad room and joined the conversation. "This looks like trouble," he said.

Dan said, "The worst. Burgess called Biaggio. The lawyer knows about us digging into his ambulance chasing." Dan shook his head. "You know something, maybe we got lucky, Luke. We have another potential whistle blower. Found him at Foreman Auto yesterday."

Syms stood outside his office and shouted. "You three, in my office now! And I mean now!"

Luke and Dan hurried down the hallway as Scotty hung up his coat, and followed behind. They entered the captain's office. "Sit your asses down, while you're still employed." Syms took two pills from his already opened Advil bottle. He eyed Dan. "Biaggio? That name ring a bell? Shut up. Hardison called me last night. Guess who called him? Don't bother. Judge Bainbridge, and guess who called the judge. I don't think I have to tell you, now do I?"

Luke looked at Dan as Syms kept talking. Dan saw the anger in the captain's eyes, and said, "You look like your head is going to burst."

"Did I tell you to talk? Shut the hell up." Syms looked at Luke. "What's this I hear about you posing as a home buyer?

"Uh," Luke uttered.

"Shut up. Funny thing though, Biaggio's wife described two gentleman who looked at a couple of houses. Neither one was tall and muscular." Syms eyed Dan and then turned to Scotty. Okay blondie, how did you and Dan like those houses Cassandra Biaggio showed you?" Syms said, staring into Scotty's eyes. He paused long enough to swallow two pills, then he shifted back to Luke. "Who's this neighbor you've been bugging that called Biaggio?"

"He's a guy who got a settlement from a P.I. scam Biaggio talked him into."

Syms stood and pointed to the door. "Great. Three fuck-ups. Dan, you stay for a minute. You other two get out."

Scotty and Luke returned to their cubes while Dan remained in Syms's office. "Damn it, Dan. I know you want this guy bad, but he's slippery and powerful. I'm not saying don't try to take him down. Watch your step, or heads will roll. Got me?"

Dan stood. "Got it," he said as he exited the office.

Stomping back to his desk, Dan kicked his chair. The noise prompted Scotty to jump up and check his partner. "Calm down, Dan."

"Me? I'm calm. I'm cool. I'm gonna drop in on that dirty lawyer."

Scotty held his hands up. "Whoa. That guy has some heavy ammo. We'll get him."

"The damn personal injury scam is one thing, but it's about Javier Ibanez and who ran him down. And we know Biaggio is running from the truth. We both know that Jaguar wasn't stolen. The driver was someone he knew. Should have known Biaggio had Bainbridge in his back pocket too." Dan sat back and took a deep breath. "Biaggio is really sweating, isn't he? I'm not afraid of him, or his friends." Hey Luke, Dan yelled. "Are you gonna talk to Burgess again?"

"Yeah. I'm gonna tell him he can stick his Jets up his ass."

Dan rubbed his chin, turned to Scotty, and said, "Speaking of asses, Biaggio's is going to get a hard kick. Let's go to Cefalu for lunch."

"Wait," Scotty said. "We go to Cefalu again he'll have us thrown out, maybe arrested."

Dan smiled. "We'll see about that, but first I have another idea. He pulled out Cassandra Biaggio's card? I'm gonna call her and set up another appointment. I want to level with her and push hard. She knows something."

"I'm sure she does," Scotty said. "But she'll tell her husband, and we'll be out in the cold."

"Sit back, pal. I'm calling her."

Cassandra answered. "Hello," she said.

"Mrs. Biaggio, this is Dan Shields." He heard car noises and assumed she was in her vehicle.

"What the hell are you calling me for? My husband told me all about you. What was that charade you and your partner tried to pull?"

"Listen. I apologize, and obviously your intuition was correct, we are detectives. We know your husband's Jaguar wasn't stolen and we need to know who drove the car. You know Javier Ibanez didn't have to die."

Dan heard her sigh. "I'm almost at my appointment, but I can't help you. I have no idea."

"But you do know it was his Jaguar … Right?"

She hesitated before answering. "Look. You have my husband all wrong, he's a good man. If he says the car was stolen, it was stolen. Now leave me alone."

"Think about it, Dan said. "I could tell you have real compassion for Javier Ibanez and his family. You have my number on your cell. Call me if you want to talk."

Dan heard silence and the call ended. He said to Scotty. "She knows. Time for lunch."

The brazen detectives entered Cefalu and Dan immediately spotted Biaggio, Vincenzo, and Pug who were seated at the same spot they always seemed to occupy. The host led the detectives to a table on the opposite side of the dining room away from Biaggio.

Dan opened his menu. "Think he saw us?" Scotty asked.

"Not sure, but I can fix that," Dan said.

"You're not going over there are you?"

"Hell no, but you have to go by him to get to the men's room, and I don't think he'll miss me passing by." Dan got up. "You order. Whatever you get, same for me."

The confident detective walked slowly toward the bathroom and he saw Biaggio who was eyeing him. Dan waved as he passed by on his way to the lav. He went in and while washing his hands, the door opened. Vincenzo entered and stood beside him. "What are you doing here?" the big man grunted.

"Pissing and washing my hands. Something wrong with that?"

"Smart ass. I suggest you leave right now."

"Relax goon. My partner and I are having lunch. Then we'll be on our way. Tell Mr. Biaggio we send our best regards, and tell him his wife is a very good real estate agent, and she was very helpful."

Dan shut the water, wiped his hands, slipped past Vincenzo, and headed back to join Scotty. "I certainly got his attention."

"I guess so. That big lug went in after you. What the hell went on in there?"

"Nothing. Just a little chit chat."

Minutes later, as the detectives were enjoying lunch, Biaggio and his associates approached their table. Biaggio gave Dan a menacing look, "Stay away from me, and my wife. I thought I made that perfectly clear," he whispered while eying Scotty. "You don't look as stupid as him? Are you?"

Scotty kept silent. "Funny." Dan said as he looked up at Biaggio. "Just how deep are Bainbridge's pockets? Maybe I should tell you that he's about to be exposed and his clout isn't what it used to be. He's going down, same as you, and you can take that to the bank."

Biaggio stuck his face within inches of Dan's. "I'm telling you one last time. Back off. I'm warning you!"

Dan looked him in the eyes. "You don't scare me."

"Have it your way," Biaggio uttered, as he and his men exited the restaurant.

The detectives stayed and finished their meals. Dan picked up the tab and took out a credit card. "Expensive way to make a man sweat," he said as he paid the seventy-six dollar tab.

Biaggio's remark stuck in Dan's head all the way back to headquarters, but he didn't let on to Scotty that it bothered him. Dan sat and contemplated the seedy lawyer's warning. Was it only idle chatter intended to make him back off? Or was it some sort of real threat? Either way, the detective didn't like the strong words. He got up, grabbed his coat and stood at Scotty's cube. "Come on, let's get out of here."

Chapter 47

Shortly after pulling out of the headquarters lot, before entering I-91, Dan noticed in his rear-view mirror a black sedan that seemed to be keeping two car lengths back. It followed him onto the highway, and when he pulled out to pass, so did the other car, and when he moved back to the right-hand lane, the other vehicle did the same.

Dan slowed to let cars pass him, and sure enough, the black sedan slowed as well. In his rear-view mirror, he could tell there were two people in the suspicious car. Nearing his exit, Dan signaled with the following sedan maintaining its distance.

At the bottom of the ramp, the Accord turned right as did the other vehicle. It was clear to Dan he was being followed. *Biaggio wants to play games, but he's not getting anywhere near my house.*

Approaching a yellow light about to turn red, Dan kept going and the sedan following him switched lanes to make it through the traffic signal. *Okay, pal. Let's go for a ride.*

Dan turned right at the next corner in the opposite direction of home and called Phyllis. "Hi, hon, something came up. I'm gonna be a little late. Don't worry, see you soon."

Approaching the drug store where he'd purchased his EpiPens, he pulled into the lot and parked in a spot close to the front door. Casually exiting his car, Dan spotted the sedan as it nestled into a space toward the rear of the store. Glancing back, he got a glimpse of the vehicle, a Cadillac. He was sure the occupants were

Vincenzo and Pug. *Let's make this interesting, fellows. Time to up the ante.*

The fast-thinking detective entered the drugstore and strode to the pharmacy counter where Sarah was still on duty.

"Hi, Dan," she said. "Am I supposed to have something for you?"

"No," he said. "I need a favor. You have a back door I can use?"

"What? Why?"

"I spotted a couple of suspicious kids outside in the lot. I want to check them out."

"Robbers?"

"Maybe. Keep calm. I need to get out now. I'll be back."

Sarah pointed to the door, and the detective exited the pharmacy.

He knew he'd lied to Sarah, but once he was outside, Dan slowly walked between two rows of cars and stealthily made it to the rear of the parked Cadillac. Glad to have his Smith and Wesson back, he crouched, then stood and rapped on the driver's window. With his gun pointed at Vincenzo, Dan said, "Roll it down."

Startled, Vincenzo turned to face the detective. "What the fuck?" he shouted. He eyed the weapon and did as he was told.

"Funny meeting you here. Place your hands on the wheel. Pug. Put yours on the dash now." Dan saw a fob that was sitting in the cup container between the front seats. "One hand off the wheel, Vincenzo. Hand me the fob and unlock the back door." Vincenzo handed Dan the fob and the detective tossed it into the bushes behind the vehicle. "Hands back on the wheel, you big ass," Dan said as he hopped into the back seat with his gun still pointed at Biaggio's protectors. "Looks to me like your boss is sweating bullets? I can have a black and white, in fact several here in two minutes, so both of you keep your hands where they are and don't turn around or give me a reason to shoot. I fired this recently, and I'm trigger-finger itchy. I know you're both carrying, so either of you reach for a weapon there will be more blood on the windshield than in a Red Cross bank."

"Stick it up your ass," Vincenzo said. "The boss told you to back off and we're making sure you heard him."

"Really? You think you were coming to my house? You or your boss even think about that, and I won't be as polite next time. You give Biaggio a message. I'm gonna get his ass and he can't do anything about it."

"Real tough cop," Vincenzo said. "Biaggio will have your badge before he's done with you."

"Thanks for the warning, goon. Tell me. Who the hell was driving the Jag? Who the hell is he protecting?"

"Wouldn't you like to know? Fuck off cop!" Vincenzo yelled.

Dan smelled marijuana. "You guys have a few joints in here?" Vincenzo started to turn his head. "Keep your eyes in front," Dan ordered. "I think we're done. I'm calling for a unit. I think you bozos will enjoy the new holding tank."

Dan called Dixon. Minutes later, black and whites rolled up, lights flashing, and four uniforms got out. Dan exited the Cadillac. "I was waiting until you got here," Dan said to the uniforms. "These two are armed and they were planning to rob the drugstore. There's pot in the car too."

With several weapons pointed at the two men who were still inside the car, one uniformed officer ordered Vincenzo and Pug out of the vehicle.

"You guys can take it from here," Dan said. "I have to go back inside."

He reached the pharmacy and smiled at Sarah. "Thanks for your help. I was right. They were planning to rob you, but they're in custody. Have a good night."

The intuitive detective exited the drugstore and he saw the two handcuffed suspects being shoved into a squad car. Satisfied, Dan got into his car and headed home.

Entering his house, he followed his routine of safely stashing his weapon away. Dan stepped into the kitchen. "Hi, hon," he said.

"I'm late because I stopped a robbery at the drugstore. Waited for the uniforms to haul two thugs to jail."

Phyllis looked at him. "You did what?"

"Nothing dangerous. A couple of harmless juveniles."

"We already ate. Kids are upstairs. I'll heat up your pasta, and I'm going to take a bath. Haven't had a good soak in a while."

Dan ate, cleaned up and headed to his lounge chair in the den, where he picked up the remote and turned on the TV. An hour later, his phone rang, and Syms shouted, "What the hell did you do now?"

"What are you talking about?"

"You know what I'm talking about. I got a call from Hardison, and he's livid. It seems two of Biaggio's associates got arrested for robbery, possession of marijuana, and carrying concealed firearms. They're downtown, sitting in the tank."

"That's a shame."

"Don't get smart. What were you doing with them?"

"I'll tell you in the morning. Long story."

"Long story? It better be damned good! Biaggio is going to night court to get his friends out."

"Calm down. I'll be in early."

"Early? You be in my office at six a.m. sharp."

Chapter 48

Dan was on his way to headquarters where he expected a confrontation with Syms. The captain's door was open and the clock on the wall read 6:02 a.m. "You're late. I said six sharp. Sit your sorry ass down."

"Looks like we've got the place to ourselves," Dan said.

Syms had his pill bottle in his hand. He put his feet on the desk and leaned back. "I'm trying to be calm. You know, you're gonna get us all fired someday, and that day may be soon. Biaggio got his guys out last night. So what's the story?"

Dan told the captain exactly what had happened. Dan grinned. "I think Biaggio understands me better now."

Syms laughed, took his feet off the desk, and leaned forward. "Amazing, just fucking amazing. How the hell do you do it?" Sitting back, Syms said, "Go get him."

Dan rose and said, "I'm sure he's going to demand a refund for getting the car towed to impound."

"Way ahead of you on that. He already did. Dixon is heading to the lot to personally release the car."

An hour later, Dan saw his partner enter the squad room. Scotty was toting a Tupperware container. He hung his jacket and started walking to the coffee maker with the container. "Muffins?" Dan asked. "Yeah, dig in before they're gone."

The detectives poured coffee and grabbed muffins before sitting at Scotty's desk. "Got a hell of a story to tell you," Dan said. "I nabbed a couple of robbers last night."

Scotty nearly spilled his coffee after taking a sip. "Robbers?"

Dan recited the tale of his evening's adventure, and Scotty said, "Are you shitting me?"

While eating his muffin, Dan's cell vibrated. His jaw dropped when he saw the caller ID and he turned to Scotty. "Holy shit. It's Biaggio." Dan let it ring three times before answering. "Hello."

"Okay, Shields. It's time to stop playing games," Angelo Biaggio said. "Meet me for lunch. You know where. And come alone."

"What about you? Your goons?"

"Funny, Mr. Detective. I don't think you'd be too happy to see them again. I'll be alone. Eleven-thirty sharp. I'm buying."

"You're on."

Dan put the phone in his pocket and shrugged as he turned to his partner. "Guess who's having a free lunch with Biaggio?"

Scotty's eyes widened. "Us?"

"Close. The guy wants to have a one-on-one with me. I gotta tell Syms."

Dan entered the captain's office. "Now what?" Syms asked.

"Our friend, Mr. Biaggio just invited me to lunch at Cefalu. This should be interesting. I'll let you know how it went when I get back. Scotty's staying here."

Syms stood. "Be careful. I mean be real careful."

"I will. My gun will be loaded and on the table."

"Cute. Get out of here!" Syms said.

Dan knew Biaggio was up to something. Was the lawyer going to say who was driving the Jag and confess it wasn't stolen? One thing was for sure. This meeting wasn't about a free lunch, and the cagy detective knew he had one place to visit before he headed to Cefalu.

▲

At ten before noon, Dan walked into the restaurant and strode right to Biaggio who was seated alone at his favorite table. The lawyer uncharacteristically stood and shook the detective's hand. "Thanks for coming," the brassy attorney, dressed in an expensive looking blue-striped suit said. "Go hang your coat up and join me."

The host, who was standing nearby, took Dan's coat, and suddenly the detective had the distinct feeling he was in the presence of Don Corleone. The lawyer even began to look like Marlon Brando. "Have some wine." Biaggio said.

Dan sat opposite him. "Thanks, but I'm not allowed to drink on the job."

"Bread? And how about being off the clock for a while? I am. You should rethink the wine. Vitese Cabernet Sauvignon, two thousand twelve, a superb vintage."

"Thanks, but I'm not much of a drinker," Dan said as he placed his fob on the table and took a piece of rustic crusty bread from the basket that was sitting between the two men.

"Take a look at the menu," Biaggio said as he eyed the fob. "Mangia. Order anything you want."

Dan read the menu. "Know what? I'll have what you're having."

"You're a wise man," Biaggio said as he ordered two house specials.

Dan buttered his bread as the waiter filled the water glasses. "So why the niceties and the free lunch?" Dan asked.

"Relax," Biaggio said. "You got hobbies?"

Dan sat back and wondered about this line of bullshit, but he had no choice and decided to play along with the lawyer. "Baseball, football." Dan paused. "Sometimes I like to go to the range and shoot my Smith and Wesson."

Biaggio drank his wine. "I detect some sarcasm. No need, my friend."

Now, Dan wondered how high the attorney would pile it on before he got to the real reason for the private lunch. "Sorry, let's enjoy a nice meal," Dan said as a plate of veal parmesan was placed in front of each man. "Looks good," Dan said.

"The best. Enjoy." So you and your wife and kids travel much?" Biaggio asked.

Dan pointed his fork at the attorney. "Let's leave family out of this conversation. I know you know where I live."

Biaggio sipped his wine. "Sure. Your wife is quite lovely, works for Doctor Englander if I'm not mistaken."

Dan held his hand up. "Stop right there."

"Wait," Biaggio said. "Your little ones are adorable and I hear your older boy is quite a baseball player."

Pointing a finger at the dastardly lawyer, Dan said, "If you want me to leave now, I will. This lunch is over. If you mention or go near my family again, you'll be pissing through your ass."

Not flinching, the calm Biaggio said. "Settle down, my friend. Continue eating while we chat." The attorney smiled at the detective, raised his wine glass, and then said, "Fair is fair. What you did with my wife wasn't exactly kosher." Biaggio sipped his wine. "So, which one of you was Luke Hanson? And nice play, Larry Bird."

"That doesn't matter now," Dan replied.

"Right. I know your comrade is Burgess's neighbor. That game is over, detective."

Dan said, "If you say so."

"Don't bother calling my wife again. Like you said, I know where your house is. Finish eating. We have something else to discuss. No more family stuff. Agreed?"

"Agreed," Dan uttered.

There was a brief truce as they each enjoyed their meals. Biaggio polished off his second glass of wine and had the waiter clear the empty plates from the table. "Coffee, and dessert?" the gracious host asked his guest.

"It's your money. Like I said, I'm having what you're having."

"The waiter returned. Biaggio said, Cappuccino, and cannoli for both of us."

The drinks and deserts arrived. Biaggio took a bite of his cannoli. "Great," he said. "You agree?"

Dan took a big bite. "Fabulous, but this meal might be the only thing we see eye to eye on."

"We'll see," Biaggio said after finishing his ricotta-filled pastry. Wiping his face with a cloth napkin, he stared into Dan's eyes. "So how much does a good, smart detective like you pull down? Fifty, sixty, seventy grand?"

"I make enough. What about you?"

"You ever owned a Jag, Ferrari, or Lambo?"

"No, I'm a little less flashy. Honda."

It was time to cut to the chase, so Biaggio leaned across the table and stared directly into Dan's eyes. "Okay, detective. I can put a hundred grand into your bank account fifteen minutes after you leave here."

Dan glared at him. "Is that what this is about? A bribe?"

"Whoa. This is a business offer. How's two hundred?"

Dan bristled at that remark. "Really? So if I said yes, would you admit the Jag wasn't stolen and you'll tell me who you're protecting? Who was it? Paying off the Ibanez's was pretty slick, but I'm not that easy."

Biaggio furrowed his brows. "Okay, smart ass. You want to continue playing chess? I guarantee I'll mate you before you can admit defeat."

Dan stood, picked up his fob and said, "I wouldn't be too sure of that, my friend. Besides, I'm a card player, and I may have one or two aces up my sleeve. Game on, pal, and thanks for lunch."

Biaggio remained seated and pointed his finger at Dan as the detective stood. "You're a fool," the brassy lawyer said. "One last chance to accept my offer."

Dan never looked back, retrieved his coat, and exited the restaurant.

Chapter 49

Returning to the squad room, Dan threw his coat on his chair. "Come on, you gotta hear this shit," he said to his partner. "Captain is going to love this."

Dan stormed down to Syms's office, leaned on the desk and placed his fob on it. "This. This is it. Biaggio is dust. He tried to bribe me."

Syms kicked his chair back. "He what?"

"It's right there. That little gadget that looks like a fob, I got from the undercover unit before I left here. It's a pocket recorder." Dan paused. "I knew he was up to something. Great lunch by the way. Should have seen the arrogant son of a bitch. He sat at the table as if he were the Godfather, as if he was talking to someone he knew wouldn't dare refuse his deal. Bullshit. It's all here. He offered me a hundred grand to go away, then two hundred."

The stunned Syms leaned forward. "I want to hear it."

Scotty looked in awe at his resourceful partner, as Dan started the recording. Listening to the entire meal conversation, Syms said, "This is incredible. I want to hear it again."

Dan played it again, looked at Syms and said, "I want someone else to hear this to make sure we have enough to arrest him on a bribery charge." Dan paused and sat. "Sasser, let him hear this." The detective pulled out his cell called him. Syms and Scotty listened as Dan gave a thumbs-up. "He's coming," said the rogue detective while tucking the phone back into his pocket.

Syms rocked in his chair and looked at Dan. "Hardison called me upstairs after you left. He's not happy about hearing from Bainbridge and Biaggio, especially after being back only a few days. I had to explain everything to him. Dan, you're lucky the chief likes you, but he's begging you to keep everything above board."

"Thanks," Dan said. "I'll try my best."

Syms leaned forward. "Perhaps you didn't hear me good enough. There was nothing about trying your best. It was stay clean."

"That's what I meant, sir," Dan replied.

"On the other hand, the chief is in good spirits. He heard from Jalen, who settled the debt in Chicago, and then went to Puerto Rico with Shelaine. That's where her family is, and the two are staying there for a while before going to California."

Dan paced the floor. "Sasser said he'd be right over."

"Sit. You're going to wear out the new hardwood," Syms said.

It seemed to Dan like hours had passed. In reality it was only forty minutes before he heard footsteps and turned to see his friend coming toward them. Sasser strolled into Syms's office. "I might have to start charging you guys for my services," he said.

"Nice coat," Dan said.

"Thanks. It's my best bud, Calvin Klein. So what have you got?"

Dan pointed to the recorder on Syms's desk. "It's a recording. Listen to it. It's Biaggio offering me a bribe."

"Really? How the hell did you get him to do that?"

"He asked me to have lunch with him alone. I recorded this a few hours ago at Cefalu."

"Let's hear it," Sasser said. "You got a hanger in here?"

Syms pointed to the back of the door. "Make yourself at home."

Sasser hung his coat on the hook, and Dan started the recording. As they listened, the lawyer rubbed his chin. "Let me hear it again."

They all heard it one more time. Sasser was silent as he paced a few steps in front of Dan and Scotty. "You gonna press charges on a bribe?" the lawyer asked.

Dan saw the look of uncertainty on Sasser's face. "What's wrong?"

Sasser sighed. "It's a nice recording, but there's one problem I can see. He definitely offered you money, not once, but twice." The lawyer looked at Dan. "You said bribe, he didn't. He simply called it a business transaction." Sasser turned to Syms. "I think a good defense attorney could argue the supposed bribe was simply a job offer with a significant raise."

Dan stomped his foot. "Damn it. You think it's worth pursuing?"

Sasser shook his head. "I wouldn't. His attorney will make mincemeat out of the tape. I'd try again."

"Shit," Dan said. "This sucks. What about the innuendos about my family? He was more than hinting something bad could happen to Phyllis or my kids."

"Sounded that way to me, but again there was nothing direct, no stated threats. It's you reading through the lines, and some of those lines were your own ambiguities. I don't see anything criminal in those words."

"Damn," Dan said. "It's like he knew he was being taped."

Sasser looked at the recording device. "Was this in plain view while you were talking with him?"

"I had it on the table."

Sasser grabbed his coat. "Nice move. You think Biaggio hasn't seen one of those before? He certainly chose his words carefully."

Dan thought about that statement. "Holy shit. I don't believe it. He's smarter than I thought."

"Where should I send my bill?" Sasser said. "On second thought, maybe you should consider putting me on a retainer. Yeah, I'll have to take that up with Hardison."

"Thanks for coming," Syms replied.

Sasser exited, leaving Dan, Scotty, and Syms speechless.

Dan picked up the fob. "Biaggio knows what he's doing, but he hasn't won yet. I'll get him."

Syms pointed at Scotty while eying Dan. "Make sure he does it legally."

Dan was angry his taping effort went for naught, but what dug at him the most was Biaggio's references to the detective's family. Definitely out of bounds and it weighed heavily on Dan. He knew he couldn't tell Phyllis that she and the kids might be in danger.

As soon as he got home, Dan made it a point to hug and kiss his wife, Josh, and Kate. He even gave Connie a big hug. "What are you so happy about?" Connie asked. "You get a raise, or are you Captain now?"

Dan smiled at everyone, even though his insides were churning with hatred aimed at Biaggio. "Can't a man simply appreciate his family?"

The home phone rang. Dan was standing close to it and answered. "It's Mike. Hi, how's it going? How's your shoulder," he asked.

"Coming along. How's everything up there?"

"Great. School going okay."

"Yeah. Good baseball weather. It's hard sitting out."

"You'll be playing soon enough. Mom wants to talk with you. Let me put you on speaker."

"Hi, Mike."

"Hi, mom."

"Do you think you'll be coming home for Thanksgiving?" Phyllis asked.

"I don't think so. I'd rather come home Christmas break."

"I understand."

Josh shouted, "I'm getting braces."

Kate piped in, "Me too."

"Hey guys. I'll see you Christmas. Okay? I miss you." Mike paused. "Dad. I need to use your credit card again."

"For books or beer?"

"Not quite. I was looking at a Beemer."

"Right."

"I need to get a few things for the dorm and some clothes."

"Okay. Keep it reasonable."

"I gotta go. Will touch base next week. Love you."

The call ended and Connie said, "He sounds good. He'll be home for Christmas."

Dan smiled. "I wonder if a certain someone will be around for Christmas. Mike would like her."

Phyllis stared at Dan. "You really do have a thing for that dispatcher."

"Dispatcher?" Connie said.

Phyllis said, "Seems there's a cute dispatcher whom Dan already has as his daughter-in-law."

"What's her name?" Connie asked.

Blushing with embarrassment, Dan uttered, "Ashley. She's twenty-two. Mike's almost twenty. Okay, enough. Let's eat."

Connie stayed for dinner and left shortly afterward.

Dan relaxed in the den, but he gazed blankly at the TV. Phyllis picked up a book and she said, "What's going on up there in your head?"

Dan clicked the remote. "Nothing dear," he answered while picturing Biaggio's Jaguar."

CHAPTER 50

Dan was positive his strategy would nail Biaggio as an ambulance chasing scammer. The detective decided to check in with Matthew Greene to see if Biaggio or anyone else had contacted him. Greene answered his phone. "Detective Shield's, he said. "I was about to call you. You were right. Last night an attorney named Angelo Biaggio called me. He said he could get me ten thousand dollars."

"What did you tell him?"

"I said I'd think about it and let him know. He said not to wait too long."

"Great," Dan said. "I'd like you to contact Attorney Biaggio and tell him you indeed would like to have an easy ten grand in your pocket. In fact, feel him out for more, but do go along with him and follow his instructions. Ask to meet him in his office. Then call me back after your conversation."

"I'll do that later. I have to get back to Foreman's. They can't start on my car because they forgot to have me sign the work order."

Dan had an idea and said, "Can I meet you there? I have one small detail to talk to you about?"

"Sure. I'll be there around nine-thirty."

"Great. I'll see you then."

Dan hung up and walked to Scotty's cube. "I just talked to Greene. Biaggio did it. He called him and offered to get him ten thousand bucks if he faked an injury. I'm meeting Greene at the body shop. It seems he forgot to sign the repair authorization. I need to tell him exactly what to do when he meets with Biaggio."

"What time are we going?"

"You stay here. I'll take care of this."

One hour later, Dan waited in the body shop parking lot for Greene to show. He saw a blue Ford Taurus pull in and park a few spots down. Greene got out and Dan yelled, "Matthew!"

Greene turned and Dan caught up to him before the man got to the office. "Let's talk here for a minute," the detective said. "Then you can finish your business inside."

After their short discussion, Dan shook Greene's hand, and he knew his informer understood what the detective had told him to do.

As he drove back to headquarters, Dan thought about Biaggio's unsettling remarks about Phyllis and the kids. The rat-bastard had somehow seen her and their small children, and somehow he knew about Mike.

Upon entering the squad room, Dan stopped at Scotty's desk. "Our informant is on board. He should be meeting with Biaggio soon. Dan looked toward the captain's office and saw an empty chair. "Seen Syms?"

"He's upstairs with Hardison."

"Listen, I have an idea. That bastard Biaggio. I want to send him a hard message. He loves his fucking Jag. I want it stolen for real this time."

Scotty winced. "Oh no. Syms and Hardison will have our asses."

"I'll take that chance. Hampton was downstairs a couple of days ago, and we know where he hangs out. He'll love the Jag."

Scotty sighed. "Mind if I sit this one out? I never heard anything about this caper. Right? I don't want that shit-ass lawyer getting any ideas about Sally and the kids."

"I get it. You get a pass. I'm going to see Hampton after I get the tag number of the Jaguar."

Scotty stood and grabbed Dan's arm. "Wait. I don't want to miss out on the fun."

The detectives headed to the familiar hangout, and as soon as they entered, Dan saw Hampton who was sitting in a booth with the car thief's trusted buddy.

"Hi guys," Dan said. He eyed Rollin. "I need to have another little chat with your pal?"

Rollin got up. "I'll be outside having a smoke."

"I'm gonna grab a coffee," Scotty said.

Hampton chugged the remaining coffee from his cup. "I smell something, and it isn't a doughnut?" he said.

Dan slid in beside him and said, "How's it going?"

"Come on, you didn't come here to small talk me. What am I stealing this time?"

Dan grinned. "You know me too well, partner."

Hampton raised his brows. "Now I'm your partner? Seems to me I'm the one always in the holding tank."

"Not so. I'm down there a lot too."

Hampton sneered. "Yeah, but I'm in the side that's locked and can't get out."

"Look. I want you to do me a big favor and steal a Jag, only a few months old."

"What's the deal?"

"Last one. I promise. This one belongs to Angelo Biaggio."

"Another frickin' lawyer? What is it with you and lawyers?"

"How much do you think the Jag will get you?"

"Maybe a grand or two, depends on the model, maybe more. Where is it?"

"In the small lot in back of his office. A silver Jag."

"When?"

"Tomorrow morning."

Dan took out his notepad and handed Hampton the address and plate number.

"Know something?" Hampton said. "You'd make a hell of a felon. You sure you don't want to trade your badge for self-employment?"

Dan opened his wallet. "Here's my card again. Call me when it's done. Let me double check your number."

"Okay, I'll have Rollin drop me off."

Scotty held his hot cup of coffee and put a lid on it. Once the detectives got outside, Scotty said, "Hampton could get caught you know."

"I know, but I don't think he thinks about that. He knows what he's doing."

Scotty grinned. "Really? Then how come he's been in the tank so many times?"

Dan gave a wry smile. "I don't think he thinks about that either."

Chapter 51

Rollin had dropped Hampton off a block away from Biaggio's office. The large sign on the lawn left the car thief no doubt as to where he was headed. He approached the lawyer's driveway intending to sneak his way to the rear where the Jaguar was supposed to be. He stood a few feet from the driveway and jumped back as the Jaguar pulled into the street. He turned back toward where he'd been dropped off and called Dan. "Hey," he said. "I got bad news. I can't steal the car."

"You mean it's not there?"

"Kind of."

"What the hell does that mean?"

"I just saw a woman drive it down the street."

"What? You sure it's the right car?"

"If the license plate number you gave me is correct. That was the car."

"What did she look like?"

"Dark hair, maybe Hispanic."

"Stay put. I'll be right down to pick you up."

"Okay, but it's a little chilly so make it quick."

"We'll be down in a flash." Dan turned to Scotty and said, "We gotta go pick up Hampton."

"He got the Jaguar?"

"No. Come on. I'll explain on the way."

▲

Dan had heard Hampton's description of the woman who was driving Biaggio's Jaguar. The detective now knew who was behind the wheel when the vehicle struck Javier Ibanez.

Hampton was standing near a bus stop, and Dan pulled over to let him into the car. He got in and Dan was about to drive away. "Hey, there it is," Hampton said. "The Jaguar."

Dan stopped and they watched the car enter Biaggio's driveway. Dan saw Rozalie. "It all makes sense now." He thought for a second. "I'm parking in front of his office. You two stay put. I need to wait until she gets inside."

Five minutes later, the detective entered the lawyer's office. Rozalie wasn't at her work station. One of the paralegals came to the window. "Is Rozalie here," Dan asked.

"I just saw her. She's in with Mr. Biaggio. I can't interrupt them."

"Is she in his office often?"

"All the time."

"I see a few CD's behind you. Last time I was here Sinatra was playing. Any Reggae back there? Bob Marley perhaps."

"Rozalie's favorite. Sometimes she puts them in when Mr. Biaggio isn't here."

A few seconds later, she came out of Biaggio's office and sent the paralegal back to work. She was wearing a sexy, tight-fitting dress. Her long dark hair flowed down below the shoulders. *It was her. She drove the Jaguar that day too.* Standing at the window, Dan said, "Hi Rozalie. I came to see Mr. Biaggio, but I just realized I'll have to stop back later. We had discussed a business deal, and I wanted to finalize it. Tell him I reconsidered his offer."

"I will. He's got a client coming in a few minutes, so he wouldn't be able to see you now anyway."

Dan got back into his car. "No doubt about it. Biaggio is protecting Rozalie. She killed Javier Ibanez. She's prettier than I thought, and a hell of a bod. She'd had her hair in a bun before, and her wearing loose fitting clothes really fooled me. Bet your ass he's paying for hers, and wouldn't Cassandra love to know that juicy tidbit."

"Hey," Hampton said from the back seat. "You gonna drop me at the doughnut shop, or what?"

"Sure thing, buddy," Dan replied.

As Dan drove down the street, he spotted Greene's loaner as it entered Biaggio's driveway. "Good timing," he said to Scotty. "Looks like he's meeting with Biaggio now."

Having dropped Hampton at his hangout, the detectives returned to headquarters. "I can't wait for Greene to call me after his chat with Biaggio," Dan said. "We may have enough for a warrant. Hope the guy remembers what I told him."

"What exactly did you tell him?" Scotty asked.

"I told him to listen to everything Biaggio says and to follow the attorney's instructions."

Syms appeared. "How about a chat?" Dan said.

"Follow me."

The detectives entered the captain's office and Syms took his usual position behind his desk. "What have you got?" he asked?"

"The driver of the Jaguar," Dan said. "It was Biaggio's secretary Rozalie, and I'd bet my badge that scumbag lawyer is paying her well for services other than secretarial. I think his wife would love to hear about that."

Syms rocked back. "Maybe you can spring that news on her, but you have no hard evidence Rozalie was driving the car, and unless you can put her in the Jaguar, it's fodder for your file."

"Maybe so," Dan said. "But I may have another kind of evidence soon."

"What are you talking about?"

"Evidence of insurance fraud," Dan said. "We found a willing informant at Foreman Auto Body. His name is Matthew Greene."

"What?" How did you do that?"

After telling Syms about the chance meeting at Foreman, the captain nodded and said, "Go for it."

When they got back to the squad room, Dan headed to the water cooler and Scotty said, "What are you thinking?"

"It's time to see Cassandra Biaggio." Dan chugged a cup of water.

"You really want to go there?" Scotty asked. "Didn't she say not to call her again? And didn't Biaggio tell you that as well?"

"Right, but we have nothing to lose. We have to do it. I think she can nail her husband for us." Dan pulled out her business card and called Cassandra. She reluctantly answered. "I thought I told you not to call me."

"You did, and I apologize, but this will be the last time. It's important. We need to see you again."

"For what?"

"I think there's something you don't know about your husband and it's important that you know what he's been doing."

"What does that mean? You don't scare me."

"Hold on Cassandra, this isn't about scaring you, this is about enlightening you as to who your husband really is?"

Dan heard silence, and then she uttered, "What are you saying?"

"I'm saying meet me and my partner somewhere, and we'll make peace with you."

Dan heard a sigh. "How about meeting me back at the house I showed you a few days ago? I can be there in an hour."

"Okay," Dan replied. He turned to Scotty. "We're on. Stay here, I'll be right back."

"Where are you going?"

"Where do you think I'm going?"

"Got it."

Dan returned to the squad room. "Okay. Let's go."

Sixty minutes later, Dan's car was in the driveway as he and Scotty waited, hoping Cassandra would show. Dan was getting antsy, tapping his knees.

"Think she'll be here? Scotty asked.

"Let's hope she didn't call her husband. Damn it, she's late. Maybe she hit traffic. Then again maybe she didn't. If she doesn't show, we're shit out of luck."

Scotty spotted a car coming up the street. "She's here," he said as her car pulled into the driveway.

The detectives exited Dan's car as Cassandra got out of hers. "Thanks for coming," Dan said.

Without a smile, and sunglasses hiding her worried face, Cassandra walked to the front door with the detective's right behind her and she opened the lock-box. They entered the living room where she, Dan, and Scotty sat on a set of matching upholstered chairs. Cassandra placed her purse in her lap, removed her shades, and crossed her legs.

"Please listen," Dan said, holding his keys in his hand. "We have a couple of things to tell you." He paused. "We know who was driving the Jaguar."

She stared at Dan as her face grew taut.

"I know you know who was driving," Dan said. "I could tell the last time we met."

She sighed. "You don't understand."

Dan said, "Maybe I do. Your husband is having an affair with his office secretary, Rozalie. She was driving the car, wasn't she?"

Cassandra's eyes began to well up, and she removed a few sheets of Kleenex from her purse. Wiping her eyes before looking at Dan, she uttered. "You have it all wrong." She paused. "Rozalie did drive his car, and she did hit that poor boy. She was scared and fled." A long pause followed. "Rozalie Alcides isn't his mistress … She's his daughter."

Dan was stunned. "What?"

"Before we even knew each other, Angelo was in the Navy and he was on leave in Haiti where he met a woman and got her pregnant, but Angelo kept in touch. She died seven years ago, and he sent for Rozalie. He'd never abandoned her, sent her to school, gave her a job, an apartment, and she's starting law school soon."

Dan flashed to the photos in the lawyer's office and remembered seeing one of Biaggio in uniform with a Hispanic woman. *Oh my God. Rozalie's mother.* Dan was silent for a few seconds and then said, "I can see why he protected her, but it doesn't change things. She committed vehicular homicide, and he aided and abetted her."

Now in tears, Cassandra said, "I know." Dan and Scotty got up as she wiped her eyes with tissues. "You're going to arrest them aren't you?"

Dan extended his hand to her as she rose from her chair. "Yes, that's our job. I wish it was different." The detective had one more thing to show Cassandra and he took out his phone showing her a photo. "Do you recognize this bicycle?"

"That's Bryce's. Where'd you get that?"

Cassandra began to shake, and Dan never answered the question while he comforted her. "You knew it would end this way, didn't you?"

She wiped her tears and put her tinted glasses back on. "Yes."

They slowly walked toward the door, Dan's arm around her. "I'm sorry," he said. Dan pulled his arm back and she locked up before they headed to their cars.

Cassandra backed out and the detectives followed suit. "Never expected that," Dan said.

"A shocker for sure," Scotty replied.

Halfway back to headquarters, Dan's cell rang. It was Greene. He told the detective he'd met with Biaggio and did what he'd been asked to do. "Great. Where are you now?" Dan asked.

"At work."

"Where's that?" Dan asked.

"The Umbrella Insurance Company."

"I'm coming down there. Can you meet me in the lobby? Should be there in about twenty minutes. I need to pick it up."

"Okay."

Scotty asked. "Where we going."

"To the Umbrella Insurance Company. I have to meet Matthew Greene in the lobby. You can stay in the car."

Dan was on time and he met Greene in the lobby. After a brief conversation, Dan left the building and got back into his Accord. He said to Scotty. "Time to nail Biaggio."

CHAPTER 52

Armed with incriminating information, Dan and Scotty marched into the captain's office. "We got it. We have enough concrete evidence to arrest Biaggio," Dan said. He filled Syms in on the details. "We need warrants. One for Rozalie Alcides and one for Angelo Biaggio. Hers is for vehicular homicide and leaving the scene of an accident. His is aiding and abetting and insurance fraud. One other thing. I want a search warrant for Rozalie's cell phone."

Syms stood. "Let's go see Hardison."

They hurried upstairs to the chief's office. "Nice to see you in your favorite chair," Dan said.

"Beginning to feel like old home again. You got something?"

"Angelo Biaggio," Dan said. "We have him and we need warrants for his arrest and for the arrest of the driver of his Jaguar. I need a search warrant for a cell phone too."

"Let me have the details and I'll get Alcott to issue them pronto."

"Thanks," Dan said as he gave Hardison the info. "We'll have Biaggio in the jungle before midnight."

Dan noticed a chess set on Hardison's back table. "You play chess now?"

"Just learning, reading up on the rules."

Dan walked to the set. "Mind if I borrow one of these pieces?"

"You lose it and you lose your badge."

"I'll take my chances, sir."

The detectives returned to the squad room where Scotty sat patiently, while Dan paced back and forth waiting for the warrants. Dan envisioned barging in on Biaggio and hauling the lawyer off to jail, but the detective had mixed emotions, knowing Biaggio wasn't all bad. He had taken care of his daughter, something any father would have done. Even so, the truth was, they had both committed crimes punishable with jail time.

Syms appeared with the warrants in hand. "All yours. Go see Dixon and get a couple of black and whites."

Dan said, "Exactly what I was thinking."

The detectives hopped into a squad car with Ramirez and another officer, while two more uniforms followed in another black and white. The vehicles pulled into the law firm's driveway and stopped. As Dan exited Ramirez's car, he took a deep breath knowing he was about to arrest both suspects. He led the way with Scotty, Ramirez, and another uniform as they entered Biaggio's empty waiting room. Rozalie opened the glass window. "What is this?" she asked.

"I have a search warrant for your cell phone. Hand it over," Dan replied.

Biaggio and Sturgis came running from their offices as two paralegals stood and watched. "What's going on?" Biaggio yelled.

"Quiet," Dan said as Rozalie handed the detective her phone. "I'm searching her phone."

"You can't do that!" Biaggio screamed.

Scotty held the warrant in front of Biaggio's face. "I think this says we can, sir."

Dan paged through texts, finally coming to the day of the hit-and-run. "I knew it," he said as he turned to Scotty. "Serve the arrest warrants."

"Warrants?" Biaggio shouted.

"You and Rozalie are under arrest. She's being charged with vehicular homicide and leaving the scene of an accident."

"You can't prove that?" Biaggio said.

"I think I can," Dan said as he removed a fob from his pocket.

Biaggio's eyes lit up. "That's what you got? Bullshit. There's nothing on that thing that proves anything."

"You mean the recording from the restaurant?" Dan smugly asked. "I'm talking about this one. I think you need to talk to your wife. You see, we had an interesting conversation with her a little while ago. Wanna hear what she had to say? I know Rozalie is your daughter."

"You bastard."

"And this cell phone," Dan said. "Rozalie texted you right after she struck Javier Ibanez. That's all right here, so you're being charged with aiding and abetting and insurance fraud."

"Insurance fraud?" Biaggio angrily said.

"You had a meeting with a man named Matthew Greene. Dan pulled another fob from his pocket. Is there any need for me to tell you that conversation was recorded too?"

Rozalie was sobbing uncontrollably. "It was an accident. I was scared."

Dan turned to Ramirez. "Cuff them and read them their rights."

Biaggio shot a gaze at the stunned Sturgis. "Get us out as soon as you can," the arrested attorney ordered.

"I wouldn't be so sure of bail. Judge Alcott is on the bench," Dan quipped. "I hear Bainbridge is under investigation. Seems he allegedly accepts payments from legal professionals."

"You son of a bitch," Biaggio said to Dan. "You haven't heard the last of this. I promise you. You could have been a rich man."

"Maybe so, but I told you I'm a card player, and I told you I might have an ace up my sleeve. These fobs are my trump cards."

Dan reached into his coat pocket and looked the enraged attorney in the eye. The cagey detective held up the chess piece he'd taken from Hardison and said to the handcuffed lawyer, "Mr. Biaggio. With all due respect, in terms I know you understand quite well … I say CHECKMATE!"

EPILOGUE

Six months later

Dan knew the system, so he wasn't surprised Biaggio and Rozalie were out on bail. Biaggio had hired a high-profiled, powerful team of criminal defense attorneys to represent himself as well as Rozalie. The detective realized it could be a long time before Biaggio and Rozalie were prosecuted. Dan had a bad feeling that somehow neither would fully pay for their wrongdoings.

The seasoned detective also knew innocent people lose too. The Ibanez's were childless and without recourse against Biaggio since they'd signed legal documents and accepted the lawyer's hush money.

On the upside, Skeeter had left Charisa and her baby in a better place. The young mother and child were taken to a safe house where they stayed until they were reunited with an aunt in Trenton, New Jersey.

Pastor Jonathan had victimized seventeen teenagers. More than filling a void, the Uccello Community Center director, Taylon Baylor volunteered himself and his staff to mentor all but one of the Pastor's scarred boys. That victim, the oldest of the teenagers, had tried to commit suicide and was in hospital psychiatric care.

In addition to Taylon Baylor's mentoring, Phyllis had gotten approval from Doctor Englander to help Devon McRay.

Hernan Benedict never recovered from that frightening night, and suffered a stroke that took his life four months ago.

Moses Sterling was still running his convenience store, but his best customer, Bessie died.

Casey Wallace had gone back to his hometown in Alabama and was working as a security guard at a mall.

Chief Earl Hardison, was a happy man. Jalen, now drug free, and Shelaine had moved to California to be close to Terell. The chief proudly showed everyone pictures of his beautiful baby granddaughter, Earlene.

▲

Hancock Sasser sat in Syms's office along with Dan and Scotty. The lawyer smiled broadly. "I saw Dee McCray last week when she moved into her new ranch-style house. No stairs to contend with," Sasser said.

"You pick it up yet?" Scotty asked the attorney.

"It's in my car. Let's take a ride."

Syms stood. "Sasser. I'm really beginning to like you."

"What about us?" Dan wryly asked the captain.

"Get out of here," Syms barked.

Twenty minutes later, Sasser's recently purchased black Lincoln pulled into Dee McCray's driveway. He and the detectives got out and Sasser popped the vehicle's huge trunk. The house's front door opened and Devon waited for the trio to enter. Dee, using her walker, struggled to reach the door. She stepped aside as Sasser rolled a motorized wheelchair into the living room. "It's yours Dee," he said as they watched her sit … And while she cried in appreciation, Devon hugged his mother.

67492141R00159

Made in the USA
Columbia, SC
27 July 2019